THE
WRECKED SERIES

Reckless Memories

CATHERINE COWLES

Editor: Susan Barnes

Copy Editor: Chelle Olson

Proofreading: Julie Deaton, Janice Owen, and Stephanie Marshall Ward

Paperback Formatting: Stacey Blake, Champagne Book Design

This book is for all of my amazing sisters. They don't share my blood, but they share my soul. Thank you for your support, encouragement, and love. I am eternally grateful to be surrounded by so many amazing women.

Reckless Memories

Prologue

Isabelle
PAST

"I WOULD RATHER SIT ON A HILL OF FIRE ANTS IN MY underwear while eating ghost peppers." I leaned against the counter and popped a cracker into my mouth. My nose wrinkled. It was one of those multigrain ones that tasted more like cardboard than actual food.

"Isabelle Marie Kipton, I have had just about enough of your snarkiness, young lady."

But I wasn't a young lady, at least not in my mother's estimation. Young ladies were poised and put-together and never questioned the dictates their parents set for them. I questioned *everything*, never went along easily, and was far too disheveled to gain any sort of approval from my parents.

I stared unblinkingly at my mother, not giving an inch.

"You will sit at that dinner table, and you will be composed and polite to our company."

I let out a snort. "Like their daughter is composed and polite to me?" Lacey was more like the Devil incarnate, but she wore her pretty, polite mask perfectly. So, my mother might as well have thought she was the Second Coming.

Violet looked up from where she was arranging a platter of hors d'oeuvres. "Lacey snaps back because you bait her. Maybe you two are just more similar than you'd like to admit, and you ruffle each other's feathers."

I glanced up at my older sister. The perfect image of the young lady my parents wished I would be, with her impeccably styled hair and future-doctor composure. She might as well have been a stranger. When had that happened? I searched my mind for the date the switch had been flipped, when Violet had gone from friend and confidante, the sister who'd always had my back, to someone I couldn't even begin to understand most of the time.

"You can be friends with her all you want, Vi. I'll take a pass on having vicious snakes in my circle." I glanced at my mother. "Or sharing a dinner table with them."

Red crept up my mother's neck and seeped into her face. "What is wrong with you?" I stayed silent. The list of what my mother found wrong with me would take us all night to get through. "That's it. Hand over your phone."

My fingers tightened around the edge of the counter. "Are you seriously taking my cell because I don't want to have dinner with someone who's awful to me? Who bullies my friends, and is cruel to everyone who isn't in her little gang of followers? I've tried to tell you time and again that she's not who you think she is."

My mother held out her hand. "Perhaps if you kept better company, these things wouldn't be an issue. You are who you spend time with, Isabelle. And those girls you run around with are not what I want for your future."

My back teeth ground together as I slipped my hand into my back pocket, pulling out the device she'd requested and placing it in her palm. No phone meant no emergency line to my best friends, to Ford, to the people who kept me sane amidst the insanity that my mother brought about. I kept my face carefully blank. I wouldn't give her the satisfaction of knowing that she'd impacted me in any way. She didn't deserve to know she had that power.

"Since you insist on acting childish, you'll be treated as one. Your curfew is now nine p.m."

I gave her nothing. I was already a prisoner in this home full of people who'd rather judge me than try and understand where I was coming from. God forbid they actually listen to what I had to say.

My mother let out an exasperated sigh. "Why can't you be more like Violet? She's polite and helpful, yet you insist on creating trouble and strife."

It cut more than it should have. If I'd had a dollar for every time she'd said something similar to me, I'd be able to go to college anywhere I dreamed. "But I'm not like her, am I? So, it's probably safer that I'm gone when your friends are here. You wouldn't want them to know just what a disappointment I am, now would you?"

"Iz…" Violet started towards me—to comfort or placate, I wasn't sure—but I ducked out of her hold. I didn't want her reassurance. I wanted out of this space that felt too tight, as if the walls were closing in on me.

My dad strode into the kitchen, drawn by the raised voices. "Just let her go, Heather. She's sixteen, she can choose to skip out on one dinner."

Mom's glare cut to my dad, a clear threat of the price he'd pay later for defending me. But he was used to her vindictive streak by now and didn't waver. She turned back to me. "Fine. Be selfish and immature. It's not like I should expect anything different from you."

I didn't say a word, just snatched a granola bar from the

pantry and ran out the back door, out of that suffocating house, and towards freedom.

～⊙

I hunkered down, burrowing into the scattering of pillows I kept in the old tree house at the back of our property, and turned up the music pumping into my headphones. If the songs were loud enough, I could drown everything out: the frustration, the disappointment, the hurt. But some days, there wasn't a decibel high enough or a playlist long enough. And nothing could erase my mother's wrath that I'd be dealing with for weeks to come.

I gazed up at the ceiling of the tree house, to the wild mural I'd been slowly adding to over time. My own secret garden. I'd painstakingly doodled and painted hundreds of flowers, interwoven with gnarled vines, as if I could build my own little world here.

I turned the music up another couple of clicks, softly singing along. Music and art. I could lose myself there. I could feel free for a handful of moments before the world came crashing in again.

I felt a tug on one of my earbuds, and it popped free. I stifled a scream as I took in the dark blond head of hair that appeared in the opening of the floor. My hand flew to my chest as my heart rattled. "Geez, give me a heart attack, why don't you?"

Ford hoisted himself into the tree house, tanned muscles bunching and flexing with his graceful movements. I swallowed against the dryness in my throat. "My ears are bleeding, Trouble. I thought a cat was being killed up here, but nope"—he shot me a grin—"it's just you butchering Bob Dylan's greatest hits."

I threw one of the pillows beside me at Ford's head. "Bite your tongue. I have the voice of an angel."

He scoffed but scooted closer to me, leaning against the wall. "So…"

"Yes, Cupcake?"

Ford gave a strand of my hair a quick tug. "You know, the football team started calling me that because of you."

My eyes went wide. "Oh, man. That makes me ridiculously happy."

"One of the guys from another team asked me out after a game, assuming they called me that because I was gay."

Laughter rolled through me, taking over and causing tears to pool in my eyes. "What did you say?"

"I told him I was flattered, but I had a girlfriend." I arched a brow at him. Ford grinned. "I *was* flattered, he's a hell of a cornerback."

I shook my head. "You're my favorite."

Ford tilted his head so that he could meet my gaze. "But you abandoned me to face the firing squad without you?"

I winced. "How bad?"

"Trouble, there is smoke coming out of your mom's ears. And Lacey, she's just…" He gave an exaggerated shiver. I covered my face with my hands, shaking my head. Ford knocked his foot against mine, and I peeked out between two fingers. His lips twitched as his blue eyes seemed to sparkle. "Making a stand, or just avoiding?"

Ford's words made warmth spread through my chest. He understood me better than almost anyone. I let my hands fall away from my face. "I can't handle Lacey for three solid hours. It's bad enough I have to deal with her at school nine months out of the year."

Ford chuckled. "So, you left me to deal with them alone."

"I'm sure Violet protected you."

He shook his head, a gentle smile on his face, the one he wore only for my sister. "Vi's too nice to stand up to either of them."

A pang of jealousy pierced low in my belly, followed quickly by a flood of guilt. These feelings that had built over the past couple of years made me feel like a horrible human being. I cleared my throat. "Probably better that way, wouldn't want her to lose a hand. Lacey's liable to bite it off."

Instead of laughing like I thought he would, Ford studied me carefully. "Things getting worse?"

I pushed myself up against the pillows, letting out a sound of frustration. "Mom is making it worse by trying to force some weird friendship when she knows we don't get along." Not getting along was the understatement of the year. No, of a lifetime. Because that's precisely how long Lacey Hotchkiss had seemed to despise my two best friends and me. And in typical mean-girl fashion, she had made sure that the rest of our classmates knew all the ways she found us lacking.

"But she's never made you run before." Of course, Ford knew there was more. "Talk to me, Trouble."

I hated the tears that gathered at the corners of my eyes. I bit the inside of my cheek to fight them off until the metallic taste of blood filled my mouth. "She stole my clothes."

Ford's brows drew together. "What are you talking about?"

I toyed with a tassel on one of my pillows, braiding and unbraiding the strands, unable to meet his gaze. "At the beach last week. I was changing in one of the stalls. I hung my bathing suit over the door, and when I bent down to get my bag, she pulled it out from under the stall while one of her minions grabbed my suit."

A muscle in Ford's cheek seemed to flicker. "What did you do?"

I'd been freezing and terrified. All I could think about was if I'd have to walk out there stark-naked to try and find my friends. I stood there for thirty minutes before they found me. "Caelyn and Kenna finally came looking for me. Luckily, between the two of them, they had an extra shirt and shorts." But I'd had to walk home with no bra or underwear. I'd felt oddly vulnerable.

A memory of the tears I'd fought the whole way home had anger simmering in my belly.

"This isn't okay. Why didn't you tell me? Or your parents? Or Vi?"

I released my hold on the tassel. "I didn't want to put you in the middle again. And my bag was sitting on the front steps when I got home. They'd never have believed me." They never had before. And Violet had her head stuck in the sand about Lacey.

Ford knocked his knee against mine. "I'm sorry, Trouble. I hate that Vi and I are leaving you here to deal with this on your own."

I forced a bit of brightness into my tone that I didn't feel. "You guys have to go and get educated. I don't want a bunch of idiots for a sister and brother-in-law."

Ford chuckled and tousled my hair. He and my sister weren't engaged yet, but it was a running joke that I called him my brother-in-law because it was only a matter of time. But that wasn't the truth of it. I used the nickname to remind myself of how Ford saw me—as a little sister. To remind myself of what he would always be to me. A brother. The only problem was, he didn't feel like any sort of brother. He felt like something else entirely. *Stupid freaking hormones.* I was blaming it all on puberty. It had ruined everything.

I glanced up at Ford, a lock of his hair sweeping over his forehead in that perfect way it did. "Are you getting excited?"

He gave a little shrug. "Mostly. Sometimes, I wish we were going farther than just Seattle."

"Why don't you? You guys can always transfer next year."

"Vi doesn't want to stray too far from home."

I rolled my eyes. My sister always played it safe, did everything by the rules. And Seattle University was the closest college she could find to our tiny island off the coast of Washington. "Is it because my parents want her to stay close?" She almost always did what they asked of her. Ford was her one big rebellion. They had never been crazy about him, had thought she could do better, but he'd worn them down over time. How could he not? Even people as blind as my parents had to see how much he adored my sister.

Ford cleared his throat. "I think it's partly that, partly that she doesn't want to be so far away from everything she knows, everything that's comfortable."

I groaned. "I'm sorry, Cupcake. You deserve to have some adventures." I'd give anything to get off this tiny island and experience more of the world, to feel...free.

"I bet I'll be able to bring her around. Not in time for this semester, but maybe the next."

"If anyone can, it's you."

Ford toyed with the edge of a pillow. "What about you? Any ideas where you'll apply?"

I had two years left at Anchor High, but I'd started sending away for college brochures when I was a freshman. "Anywhere that's not here."

Ford chuckled as a blond head poked through the door in the floor. My sister eyed us both for a moment and then let out an exasperated sigh. "I should've known the duo of destruction would be in their secret hideout."

I gave a shrug and did my best to curve my mouth into a smile. "Hey, I offered to make it the trio of terror, but you always refuse to go on our missions."

Violet shook her head as she crawled into the tree house and settled on my other side. "I just didn't want a rap sheet at the tender age of ten."

I let out a laugh. "Toilet-papering Lacey's bike with Ford was worth a month of grounding."

Violet looked towards our house. "You'd think they'd have

learned by now that it's not smart to try and force you two together."

"She stole my prized Polly Pocket and wouldn't give it back. The toilet-papering was justified."

Vi let out a light laugh, dainty and beautiful, just like she was. "Maybe it's better to play along and let Mom and Dad think you're toeing the line. Would that be so bad?"

I bit down on my bottom lip. "Yes, it would be." I looked up to meet my sister's gaze. She just didn't get it. "They want me to have *acceptable* friends. To them, the daughter of a lawyer is appropriate, no matter how much of a raving bitch she is." Because as awful as Lacey was to me, she was even worse to Kenna for some reason, and I would never let someone into my life who hurt my best friend, even if it was only for show.

A hint of annoyance flashed across Violet's expression. "Please don't call her that. I know you two don't get along, but she's my friend."

Ford shifted in his seat. "Vi, I don't know if you have the whole picture."

Her gaze snapped to him. "I don't think you do either. Iz eggs Lacey on, and Lacey isn't as tough as she seems. It hurts her feelings."

"Guys, stop. I can handle Lacey. And I can handle Mom and Dad."

Violet looked back at me. "By hiding away and making Mom so mad, it looks like she's going to explode?"

I let my head fall against the wall of the tree house. "Okay, that might not have been my best plan."

"You think?"

Annoyance made pinpricks dance across my skin. "I can't just go along with whatever they want like you do. I'm not built that way. They should be happy they have one perfect daughter and let me go my own way."

Violet's eyes widened as if I had struck her. She even fought perfectly. Never raised her voice, simply let her hurt shine through, making me feel as if I'd kicked a defenseless puppy. "I'm not perfect," she whispered.

"Damn near. Close enough," I grumbled.

Ford sat up, shifting towards Violet, and I immediately felt the loss of his presence. His warmth, his comfort, his strength. "All right, ladies, you're both perfect in my eyes, but let's focus on what's truly important right now...food."

His statement startled a laugh out of me. "Food?"

"Yup." He patted his stomach. "I just had to sit through a meal of ridiculously fancy rabbit food that maybe filled an eighth of my stomach, and Trouble hasn't had any dinner at all. What do you say I take my ladies to The Catch for some greasy goodness?"

"I don't know, Ford, my parents—" Violet stopped speaking at Ford's look and then started again. "I'll talk to them."

I bumped my sister's shoulder. "Thank you."

Vi shook her head but gave a small smile and then scooted towards the opening. "You guys meet me at the car. It'll probably go over smoother if I talk to them alone."

This was the sister I missed, the one who was always on my side even if she didn't understand where I was coming from. "Hey, sissy?" She looked back at me. "I love you the mostest."

"Love you the mosterest." She winked as she disappeared down the ladder.

Ford stood, and I followed, carefully making our way down the side of the tree. When we reached the bottom, I saw that it was starting to rain, one of those perfect summer storms. We dashed to Ford's SUV and jumped in. He glanced over at me. "She just wants the best for you. You know that, right?"

I dug my fingernails into my palms. "I know. It's just exhausting sometimes."

"What is?"

"Living in someone else's shadow."

Ford reached over and squeezed my knee. "It's impossible for you to live in someone's shadow, Iz. You shine way too damn bright. You're both your own unique brand of perfect."

That familiar warmth lit in me again. When the world made you feel dull, it was such a gift to have someone who thought you shined.

The back door opened, and the spell was broken. Ford released his hold on me and turned to face Violet, who slid into the backseat. "I face the parentals for you, and you steal shotgun?"

I let out a laugh. "Hey. You snooze, you lose." I pressed my lips together. "They're letting us go?"

"After some convincing. You're on dish duty for a month."

I sighed. "Could be worse."

Ford turned the key in the ignition, flipping on the windshield wipers and then backing out of the driveway. "Hopefully, this rain means people will stay home, and we won't have to wait long for a table."

There weren't a lot of restaurant options on an island of fifteen hundred people, and The Catch Bar & Restaurant was a local favorite. "Ford, your family owns the place, I really don't think we'll have to wait."

He chuckled. "If my dad's working, he'll make sure every paying customer gets seated before us."

"I think it's nice how committed your dad is to giving everyone great service," Violet said.

Ford snorted. "Nice, except when I'm starving. Remind me to eat before I come to one of your parents' shindigs again."

"I'll make sure to pack you a snack next time."

Ford grinned into the rearview mirror. "I love you, babe."

Their banter and the pet names had my stomach churning. I tried to tune them out, to get lost in the rain streaking down my window and the forest zooming past as we skirted the island. A flash of something appeared in the corner of my vision. "Ford!"

The deer launched itself into the road as Ford slammed on the brakes. Everything slowed. Moments marked by heartbeats between breaths. The SUV spun towards the cliff. I lost all sense of direction. Another vehicle's horn blared. Headlights flashed. Someone screamed. It might've been me, but I couldn't be sure.

There was a deafening crunch, and then blinding pain. Fire seemed to lick my skin, but there were no flames, only shattered glass and twisted metal. I tried to keep my breaths shallow, it seemed to help the burning. "Sissy? Ford?" There was no answer.

I twisted in my seat, the panic fighting off the pain. "Ford?"

His head was slumped at an unnatural angle, and my heart seemed to ricochet around in my chest. "No, please no." I reached out a shaky hand, pressing two fingers to his neck. The steady thump against the pads of my fingertips was the best feeling I'd ever experienced.

"Isabelle?" I turned at the hoarse sound of Violet's voice. My breath caught in my throat as I took in the blood coating the side of her face.

"I'm here." I reached back to grab her hand, the action causing fire to blaze along my ribs. I cried out.

"I feel funny."

"It's going to be okay." Sirens sounded in the distance. That was good. That meant help. "Vi, what hurts?" There was no answer, and my gaze shot back to my sister. "Vi!" Her eyes fluttered. "You have to stay awake, Violet." That's what they always said in those medical dramas.

Her eyes opened, but her body seemed to go rigid, as if she were having a small seizure. And then…nothing. Silence but for the far-off sirens and the pounding of the rain. Silence as my sister stared back at me, eyes unnaturally wide and unblinking. Silence as I watched my sister slip from this Earth.

Chapter One

Bell

"DON'T YOU FEEL SO MUCH BETTER STARTING YOUR day like this?" Caelyn beamed as she rolled up her yoga mat.

Kenna scowled down at her own mat. "I'm not sure how twisting yourself into a pretzel is supposed to help you find inner peace."

I stifled a laugh. "It makes her happy to give us these classes, so just roll with it." I liked yoga just fine, but I loved how happy these mornings made Caelyn. It didn't hurt that we held the sessions in a park overlooking one of Anchor Island's most gorgeous beaches. The expanse of grass where we placed our mats dipped and rolled until it met up with a rocky shoreline, the coast ebbing and flowing from gray beaches to craggy cliffsides. The salty sea air that drifted in was a balm to any wound.

"I don't even work up a sweat," Kenna groused.

Caelyn wrapped an arm around Kenna, making her bristle.

"Not everything is about pushing your body to its breaking point. But, trust me, your muscles are getting stronger because of this practice, and so is your spirit."

"Sure, sure, oh Zen one." Kenna shrugged off Caelyn's arm and went back to rolling up her mat, making sure the edges were perfectly even before placing it in her bag.

I pinched her butt, and she squealed, whirling on me. I shrugged with a grin. "Serves you right for being so grumpy."

"I'm not grumpy. I'm just stressed."

I eased myself down onto the grass to roll up my own mat. "What's going on?" I gave her hand a little tug when she didn't answer.

Kenna sighed but sat, Caelyn doing the same. "One of the accountants from the Shelter Island office is out on medical leave, and I agreed to take on a handful of her clients. It's more work than I thought it would be."

Caelyn and I shared a look, but Kenna held up a hand before we could say anything. "I don't want to hear it."

I gave her my most angelic smile. "What? That you work too hard? That you're going to give yourself an ulcer? That you have no life?"

She stuck her tongue out at me. "Some friend you are."

"Real friends speak the truth."

"Yeah, yeah. I'll be fine. It's only for another month or two."

Caelyn reached over and squeezed Kenna's knee. "Just let me know what I can do to help. I can do the grocery shopping for you and Harriet when I go for myself and the tiny terrors."

Kenna's expression gentled, and she shook her head. "You've got enough on your plate. I can handle this."

Both my friends had more than their fair share on their respective plates because while they appeared as different as night and day—Kenna with her sleek brown hair and perfectly styled athleisure outfit, and Caelyn with her wrists full of mismatched bracelets and hair in a wild pile atop her head—they were more similar than anyone would've guessed. They gave and gave and gave some more. Kenna caring for the woman who'd raised her from the age of eleven when Kenna's own mother couldn't be bothered with the responsibility. And Caelyn giving up college and her dreams to come back to the island to raise her siblings when they had been removed from their parents' custody.

I slapped my hands down on my knees. "Ladies, divide and conquer. I've got grocery shopping for both of you this month. Email me your lists on Tuesdays." I turned to Kenna. "If Harriet has any doctors' appointments, just make sure they're in the morning, and I can take her."

Caelyn ran her hands over the lush grass beneath us. "And I can cook dinner for you and Harriet. Just swing by my place on your way home from work, and I'll have some containers ready to go for you."

Kenna's lips pressed into a thin line. "You guys are making me feel like a slacker."

"Oh, please." Caelyn waved a hand in front of her face. "Says the girl who's done my taxes for free every year since you graduated."

"That's nothing—"

"It's not nothing." Caelyn cut her off. "It's friends helping however they can." She looked from Kenna to me, her eyes misting. "It's what we do, right?"

"Damn straight." I pushed to my feet and reached out a hand to each of the women who were more like sisters than friends. Women who had seen me through my darkest days and walked alongside me through it all. "Now that we've got everything settled, I need to get home so I can shower before I get started on inventory at the bar." The scar tissue along my ribs pulled as I dragged the girls to their feet. I ignored it and the reminder the twinge brought.

I gave them both quick hugs and headed for my car. The ocean breeze caught my hair, the blond strands blowing in my face. I pulled them back, capturing them in a quick topknot before climbing behind the wheel.

Pulling out, I rolled my window down as I guided my car through the winding island roads, needing another hit of the sea air. Anchor Island was a small place, with less than two thousand people in the off-season. If you'd lived here for longer than a year, you knew just about everyone. It was both a blessing and a curse.

When I'd left for college with Caelyn and Kenna, I'd sworn never to return. Now, I knew never to make vows like that because the Universe was a fickle creature, and she liked to make you eat those kinds of promises. With three kids under her care, Caelyn had needed all the help she could get, so as soon as Kenna and I graduated, we'd headed straight back to Anchor.

The Hardys, looking out for me like always, had offered me a job at The Catch, as well as the apartment over the bar. I'd been there ever since. Having them made me feel like I hadn't lost it all that summer night over a decade ago. And I liked helping them as much as I could, even if it meant setting aside my own dreams for the moment.

I'd been pulling double shifts since Frank's stroke last year. Trying to cover as much ground as I could so that Hunter, the brother who hadn't abandoned his family in their time of need, was still able to run his construction business, and Kara wasn't worried to death about both her husband and the bar.

Hunter had told me that he was working on getting me some help, but I had no idea where he would find it. We simply didn't have the budget to hire someone to work enough hours to make a real difference. I turned onto Main Street and grinned. Shopkeepers were out in full force today doing spring prep: filling planters, touching up paint, anything to attract those tourist dollars.

The mixture of craftsman, Victorian, and old-timey brick buildings was only one of the many things visiting folks loved about Anchor. However, the charm of downtown wasn't lost on me either. The island might be a reminder of my most painful memories, but it also housed all my very best ones, too. And unlike other people in my life, I wasn't willing to lose the good memories just to keep out reminders of the bad.

I pulled into a reserved parking place at the back of the two-story brick building with *The Catch* painted in a large, artful white font on the side that was a stone's throw from the rocky beach. I grabbed my bag from the passenger's seat and headed for the staircase that climbed the stone facade. I really needed some twinkle lights or something fun for the stairs. I'd decorated my balcony with lights and plants, but the steps had no personality. I put it on my mental list to remedy that soon.

I unlocked the door and pushed it open. Glancing at the large clock on the wall, I winced. I hurried through my shower but took time to blow-dry my hair, so I didn't end up with pneumonia. That was the last thing I needed.

I switched off the hair dryer, running my fingers through the soft waves that fell just past my shoulders, dusting along my collarbone and meeting up with the blossom-filled vines that curved around one shoulder. I pressed my palm against one of the violet blossoms that arose from an especially vicious scar. I squeezed my eyes closed. "Miss you, sissy."

I thought of her almost every day, but it was especially strong around birthdays and anniversaries. And tomorrow was the day we should've been celebrating with her favorite ice cream cake from Two Scoops.

I took a deep breath, opening my eyes, making myself take in my appearance, forcing myself to look at the scars. They were beautiful in their own way. I'd made them that way, designing tattoos that didn't cover the scars but wove around them. Images that honored my sister and me. Magical vines that sprouted violets and bluebells.

The process had taken weeks. Painful hours on a bed in a tattoo shop in Seattle. But it had been worth it. Because when I looked at my body now, I didn't just see pain. I remembered my sister and how much we had loved each other, even if we had been as different as night and day. I pressed my palm harder against the violet that lay just above my heart. I wished we would've had a chance to rediscover the closeness we'd had when we were younger.

I broke my stare with the mirror and headed for my bedroom. I pulled clothes from a dresser I'd picked up at a garage sale for ten bucks and refurbished. There was almost nothing in my space that didn't hold meaning. I'd spent too many years in a house that held so little of it. I wanted my home to be an extension of me. That typically came from pouring sweat equity into each piece of furniture and decorating my space with photos, personal art, and plants.

I pulled on a pair of jeans and a worn tee that hugged my curves. Slipping on a pair of boots, I was ready to go. I reached for my phone to check the time, but it wasn't in its usual spot on the dresser. *Shit.* I must've left it in the car.

I grabbed my keys and headed for the back door. As I pulled it open, my steps faltered, the sight in front of me a sucker punch in the same way it was every year. I bent down to pick up the bouquet of violets and the envelope. I inhaled deeply, the sweet scent of the blooms wrapping around me, both painful and a comfort.

I slipped a finger under the seal and carefully ripped it open, wondering what memory I'd get this year. There was never a note, only a bouquet of violets and a copy of an old photo of my sister. I had no idea who brought them, but I'd gotten them every year since Violet's death, always sometime the week of her birthday. For a couple of years, I'd thought it was Ford, his way of comforting me from afar, but I'd given up on that silly hope and started to just appreciate the gesture for what it was. Marking a life that had meant so much to me. Honoring all the memories she'd left behind.

I pulled out the glossy paper and let out a strangled laugh. The photo was one of my favorites from the memorial website my parents had created for Vi. It had been taken after Violet and I had worked on an art project in the back yard. My mother had given us each an old shirt of my father's to wear as a smock. Violet's had two or three small smears of paint. Mine, on the other hand? It was covered in every color of the rainbow. There was even paint on my face and in my hair. It was so perfectly... us.

A pang hit my heart, a crack of energy that was both agony and gratitude. That potent mixture almost brought me to my knees. I clutched the photo to my chest and took a deep breath. I had to trust that Vi knew the truth, that I desperately missed her, even though we hadn't been in the best place as sisters when she died. I needed to trust that wherever Violet was, she knew that I loved her.

Chapter Two

Ford

"HEY, FORD!" THE GIRL WHO CALLED OUT OVER THE pounding bass looked vaguely familiar. A model maybe? Or an up-and-coming actress?

"Hey, babe." She batted her eyes, but I kept moving through the bar towards my office. I wound my way through the sea of bodies, careful to avoid tipsy partygoers with precariously balanced drinks.

I pushed open the door to my office, and when it shut behind me, I leaned against it, a whoosh of air expelling from my lungs. Silence. Blessed silence. The choice to soundproof this room had been so worth it.

I pushed off the door and cracked my neck. I was getting too old for this shit. It might be time to move from hands-on management of my bars and clubs to simply startup. Let someone else deal with the headaches of the day-to-day. Maybe I'd take off and travel for a bit. Go visit all my friends, who seemed to have fled Los Angeles over the past couple of years.

I crossed to my desk and eased into the chair. Papers littered the surface in front of me. I rubbed my temples. A vacation. I just needed a vacation. A breather from the everyday monotony of it all. Then I'd find the fun in all of this again. The thought sounded like a lie, even to me.

My phone buzzed in my pocket, and I stood to pull it out. My brother's name flashed on the screen, and I winced. My finger hovered for a count of three before I hit accept. "Hey, Hunter. What's up?"

"You need to come home."

My blood turned to ice. "Dad?" My voice grew hoarse on the single word. Memories of the call I'd gotten from my hysterical mother, telling me that my father had suffered a stroke, flooded me.

"He's okay. The same. But I need you to help out at the bar."

I eased back in the chair, my gut souring. "I can float the bar some money to hire more permanent help."

"What the fuck is wrong with you, Ford? This is your family's legacy. The Catch has been run by a Hardy for generations. We don't need your fancy Hollywood money, we need *you*. Or are you too good for your family now, too?"

I gripped the arm of my chair, the sleek metal frame biting into my palm. "You know that's not why I left."

Hunter blew out a long breath. "You were never going to be able to avoid this place forever. Mom and Dad miss you, and I can't keep covering for your ass."

"I see Mom and Dad plenty." It was true. I regularly flew them out to LA or some other place they'd been dying to visit, but I hadn't set foot on the island in years. Shit, it had been over a decade now, eleven years. At first, my parents hadn't minded. They'd understood. And they'd gotten a kick out of seeing new and exciting places. But over the years, I'd seen the sadness, the disappointment.

"They need their sons. Both of us. I've been trying to run the bar and my construction business at the same time, and I just can't do it anymore. They're both suffering. It's time for you to step up."

A vise tightened around my rib cage. "I can't."

Hunter was silent for a few moments. "If you don't come home, we're going to have to sell."

His words seemed to slice at my chest. I hadn't seen the bar in what felt like forever, but somehow, the idea of losing it, letting go of something else that felt like it was a part of me, was more than I could take. "Okay."

"Okay?" There was shock in my brother's voice. Maybe he'd expected me to tell them to sell, but I couldn't. Because he was right. The Catch was our family's legacy. I wasn't going to let them down because I couldn't deal with the ghosts of my past.

"Yeah, okay. I need a couple of days to close up shop here and get a manager in place at my LA bars. But I'll be there soon."

Hunter cleared his throat. "Thanks, man."

The words seemed to be dragged out of him. And didn't that make me feel like an asshole? When had things gotten so strained with my brother that thanking me was akin to pulling teeth? "Thank you for all you've been doing. I'm sorry I haven't been pulling my weight."

"You covered all the medical bills, that helped a lot."

I heard the unspoken words, "*but you haven't been here.*" God, I was a selfish prick. Sure, I'd spent a month in Seattle with my parents when my dad was in the hospital and then a rehab clinic, but as soon as they'd returned to the island, I'd run straight back to LA like the coward I was. I couldn't pull that this time. I'd just have to hope that I could get the bar back on its feet quickly.

"I won't leave the hands-on stuff to you anymore, Hunt." I'd get the pieces we needed in place before I came back to LA so there wasn't such a heavy load on my brother's shoulders.

"It'd be a nice change," he grumbled.

Shit. I had a lot to make up for with my brother. "I'll see you in a few days."

"In a few days."

Hunter hung up without a goodbye, and I let my phone clatter to my desk. A few days. Seventy-two hours to wrap up my life in LA. Four thousand, three hundred, and twenty minutes before I had to face a daily reminder of the cruelest truth. I'd killed the one person I should've protected above all others.

Chapter Three

Bell

"BELL, YOU HERE?"

I glanced up at the clock on the wall. "Shit," I mumbled to myself. It was already past eleven. I'd gotten lost in inventory hell and had made painfully little progress. Between running the orders, managing staff schedules, payroll, and working double shifts more often than I wanted to admit, I needed help. "Back here, Caelyn." I made my way out of the stockroom and into the bar.

Caelyn grinned at me as she wound her hair into a topknot. "You have the angry-eyes thing going on. Inventory?"

I blew out a breath that sent my hair fluttering around my face. "Yes."

"You know I would've come in early to help."

I tossed her a rag and scooted a spray bottle across the counter. "I know, but we just can't swing paying anyone for extra hours right now."

Caelyn got to work wiping down tables in the central area of the restaurant while I started on the bar top. "Things still tight?"

I bit my bottom lip and nodded. "Hunter says he's working on getting us some help. Hopefully, that'll come sooner rather than later."

"I hope so, too, but you know you don't have to pay me. I'll help off the clock. I'm worried about you, Bell. You're going to run yourself ragged trying to keep this place afloat."

The concern in her eyes had warmth spreading through me. "Thanks, but I've got it handled."

"Those dark circles under your eyes say otherwise."

"Says the girl working two jobs and taking her siblings to every extracurricular activity known to man." Caelyn stuck out her tongue and tossed her rag at me, but I caught it before it could get any nasty cleaning goop on me. "You're lucky I have catlike reflexes."

Caelyn smirked. "Maybe I'll start calling you kitty cat instead of Bell."

"Only if you want to be on bathroom duty all summer."

Her mouth fell open. "You wouldn't."

I arched a brow at her. "Try me."

Caelyn shook her head. "You are vicious, woman."

"And don't you forget it."

We worked in a choreographed routine that spoke of all the hours, days, and years we'd been at this. Soon, the lunch rush was upon us. Hank was cooking up orders in the back, and Darlene had joined Caelyn on the floor. There were few restaurants that stayed open year-round, and The Catch had been a staple on Anchor forever. But things had picked up even more since Frank's stroke. It was the island folks' way of supporting one of their own when they knew we were struggling to keep our heads above water. But the tourist rush was around the corner, and that should take the pressure off for a while—as long as we could keep up with the demand.

"Bell."

I turned at the familiar voice and grinned, rounding the bar and throwing my arms around the tall, muscled man. "Hunt, I missed your ugly mug. You've been working too hard lately." If the man spent any more time on his construction sites, he was going to start breathing sawdust.

He leaned back. "You wound me. How will I ever go on when you insult me so?"

I let out a laugh and released him, slapping his chest. The action stung my palm, and I scowled at Hunter. "You've got too many muscles." I swore he got more of them every time I saw him, and he was certainly never hurting for female company. But to me, he'd always be like the brother I'd never had. One who'd stepped in when the other male in my life had tucked tail and run.

He laughed. "Sorry?" The word was a question as he shook his head at me. "Do you have a minute? I need to talk to you about something."

I assessed the bar situation. I had drinks that needed refilling, and at least two groups that looked ready to place their orders. "Give me a few to get this under control, and then I'll find you. Are you grabbing lunch?"

Hunter nodded, his brown hair that was slightly shaggy on top, falling into his eyes with the motion. He inclined his head towards a booth along the wall. "The boys and I are all here."

I glanced over to see his core construction crew flirting shamelessly with Caelyn as she took their drink orders. I grinned. "Okay, I'll be over as soon as I've got this handled."

"Sounds good."

Hunter headed off to his table, and I refilled beers and sodas as I memorized an order from a couple visiting from Seattle. Apparently, tourist season was starting early this year. Praise the vacation gods. I poured a Guinness with practiced ease as a shadow fell over me.

"What can I get ya?" I asked as I pulled down the tap for another beer and glanced up. The air vanished from my lungs as though one of those vacuum seals had sucked it right out. There was zero oxygen left for my organs, and I couldn't seem to get my lungs to reinflate so I could take in more.

Blue eyes I could never seem to forget seared me, nailing me to the spot. That same rogue piece of hair fell over his forehead. But the hair itself was darker, no longer quite as blond. And the man was darker, too. I could see it in his eyes, in the way he held himself. The sympathy that flared to life in my chest had fury following close behind. Anger at myself. At him. At the world.

Cool liquid ran over my hand, and the boy I used to know scowled. "Watch what you're doing."

I flipped up the tap, and that rage in my chest lit up, spreading throughout my body. "Watch what I'm doing?"

His scowl deepened. "Yeah, you're wasting beer. Jesus, who has my brother been hiring, idiots?"

I reacted before I could think better of it. I took the dark beer in my hand and upended it right over Ford Hardy's head.

Chapter Four

Ford

"**W**HAT THE FUCK?" I WIPED THE FOAMING LIQUID out of my eyes. Had my brother hired some chick with rage issues? What was he thinking? No wonder the bar was struggling.

The woman in front of me was fuming. Her cheeks had turned a pretty shade of pink, eyes blazing. She looked gorgeous. A little bit crazy, but stunning, nonetheless. I needed my head examined. It was the little crinkling of her nose that had me sucking in a sharp breath.

Those little wrinkles that appeared on the bridge and between her brows as green eyes filled with tears had memories slamming into me with the force of a freight train. She always used to cry when she got mad. She might be yelling her head off at the same time, but if she was truly furious, her eyes would fill as she struggled to get her words out. This wasn't a stranger. This was the girl who'd been like a little sister to me for most of my life. "Trouble?"

I might as well have jammed a knife into her chest from the look on her face, the pain in her eyes. She said nothing, just turned on her heel and fled.

"Oh, shit." A familiar voice cut through the noise of the crowd, but I couldn't drag my gaze away from the open doorway Isabelle had disappeared through. She was here. Working for my family. And she was drop-dead gorgeous. *Fuck.*

A hand clapped me on my shoulder. "Let me get you a towel."

I shrugged off the grip. "Seriously, Hunter? You couldn't have warned me?"

My not-so-little brother ground his teeth together. "The last thing you needed was another excuse to bail."

His shot hit true. Right in the gut. "Get me a damn towel."

He rounded the bar and tossed me a rag from the pile of clean ones on a shelf. "Here. Give me a minute. I'll be right back."

Within sixty seconds, the towel was soaked. I made my way around the bar, careful to avoid dripping on paying customers, and grabbed two more bar rags, doing my best to get as much of the beer off me as possible.

"What'd you do to piss that firecracker off?"

I looked up, my gaze meeting a face barely containing its laughter. The guy appeared as if he'd be more at home in LA, surfing in Venice before grabbing his acai bowl from some organic juice bar. But he had a burger and an empty beer in front of him. "Was that your beer that ended up on my head?"

His lips twitched. "I think it's a pretty safe guess."

"Guinness?"

"Yup."

I grabbed a glass and poured him a beer. "On the house."

"Thanks, man. I'm Crosby. You new?"

"More like old." I glanced over my shoulder and caught sight of Isabelle wrapped in my brother's arms as he rubbed a hand up and down her back. The couple of steps I took towards the open doorway were instinctive, some damn invisible pull. I could just catch their muted words.

"I'm sorry, Bell. That's what I wanted to talk to you about. Ford's gonna be back for a while to help out." Hunter leaned forward and pressed his lips to her hair. *When the hell did that happen?* "I should've told you sooner, but I honestly wasn't sure he'd show. He just texted and said he'd made it to the island, I didn't think he'd come straight here."

Isabelle shoved at his chest, creating just a bit of distance between them. "I deserved better than this. Especially from you. You know better than anyone what he put me through." Her green eyes, sparking with anger, caught mine over Hunter's shoulder. She didn't look away. She opened herself to me. Let me see the true depth of her pain. It was raw and ragged, and it wrecked me in a heartbeat. Just like I knew it would.

It was why I'd stayed away for so long. Sure, it was all the memories this place held, but more than anything, it was her. I'd missed her like a lost limb, ghost pains and longing for something that no longer existed plaguing me daily. But I'd been behind the wheel that night, and there was no way she didn't hate me for what happened. I'd known the second I came to in the emergency room and they'd told me that Violet was gone. I'd known Isabelle would hate me forever. But knowing and seeing it were two very different things. Seeing it might strike me down where I stood.

Isabelle slipped out of my brother's hold. "I'm taking a break. You or your lap dog can cover for me."

"Fuck." Hunter pinched the bridge of his nose and let out a long breath as he headed in my direction.

"What part of you thought it was a good plan to not warn *either* of us?"

He glared at me. "Don't turn this around on me. There's only one person who's at fault here." I felt the color drain from my face. "Jesus, Ford, not because of the accident. Because of how you acted *after* it. You don't think it damn near killed that girl to lose her sister *and* you in one fell swoop?"

I ran a hand through my hair, and it came away sticky. "I didn't have a choice. You know what her parents threatened."

"I know between that and losing Vi, we just about lost you. But I also know that you could've contacted Bell later. You know I would've gotten a message to her in a heartbeat. But you just walked straight out of her life."

"Bell?"

Hunter's expression grew shuttered, a little pain of his own shining through. "Don't call her Isabelle. And sure as hell don't call her Trouble. She goes by Bell now. Everything else…it just brings back memories, I think."

I rubbed a hand along my stubbled jaw. "How long has she been working here?"

"Since she graduated from college."

"Why didn't you say anything?"

Hunter pushed off the counter he leaned against. "You're a real piece of work, you know that? You don't get to have it both ways. You can't refuse any mention of the island or the people you left behind and then act all wounded that you weren't kept up-to-date. We were following your orders."

My back teeth ground together. He was right, of course. Less than two hours on the island, and I was already losing it. It felt as if my skin were too tight for my body, every movement stiff and a little bit painful. And it was only going to get worse.

Hunter shook his head, moving on from my silence. "Are you staying with Mom and Dad?"

"No. I got a rental on the bluff."

He let out a low whistle. "Mr. Bigshot is back in town." The statement could've been simply a brotherly jibe, but it held just a touch too much venom. "How long's your lease?"

It was the same as asking the one question I didn't want to answer. *How long are you staying?* "I'm confirmed through summer, but there's an option to extend if I need to." I wouldn't need it. I would work my ass off to get the bar on its feet again so that I could leave this place behind and never look back. I'd return to LA and figure out what was next for me. There was one thing I was sure of, it wasn't Anchor.

Chapter Five

Bell

I PUSHED OPEN THE BACK DOOR OF THE CATCH, THE SLAM OF it against the brick wall a satisfying sound. I strode across the patio, scattered with tables but thankfully empty of customers, and headed straight for the beach. I had to keep moving. It was the only thing I knew for certain. I had to keep my body in motion, or the energy crackling through my veins would explode out of my skin, and I would lose it.

Lose it on a level that would mean I would frighten everyone around me. I pushed my legs to walk faster, my boots kicking up stones along the rocky shore. The ocean had always given me a sense of peace, but even the crashing of the waves and the smell of the salty sea air couldn't calm me now.

I pressed on, picking up my pace even more. I kicked at a piece of driftwood in my path, sending it flying back to the sea. If only I could drop-kick Ford back to Los Angeles as easily. A trickle of guilt slid through me at the thought, quickly morphing back to anger. I didn't have anything to feel guilty about. He was the one who ran away. The person who knew better than anyone the pain of losing Violet. I'd never understand why he'd made the decision to leave instead of letting us lean on each other. But the why no longer mattered. Only his actions did.

Actions that had left me alone and grieving while my family fell apart around me. Alone to deal with surgeries and the hours upon hours of painful physical therapy. Alone to face the blame and pressure of my parents. Alone when they tried to twist me into some sort of Violet 2.0.

Sweat trickled down my back, and I ripped open the snaps on my flannel shirt, tearing it off. I balled it up, fingers digging into the fabric. I kept pressing on, feet moving even faster until I was almost running, memories assaulting me in a way they hadn't in years. Crying in my hospital bed, my body shuddering with sobs and pain. My sister. Ford. I'd lost them both. Violet had no choice, her life had been ripped away from her in a single second. But Ford…he had *chosen* to leave. And that might've left the deepest wound of all.

My steps slowed and I pressed the balled-up flannel to my mouth, letting out a guttural scream. Pouring out every ounce of pain and grief, every last bit of dashed hopes and dreams left in ruins, every memory tainted by betrayal. I expelled it all and then collapsed to the ground.

Rocks bit into my backside, but it barely registered as sobs wracked my body. I'd made peace with Violet's death, with the turn my life had taken, even with losing Ford. I'd worked so damn hard to find peace, and all it had taken was Ford striding through the door to smash it all to smithereens.

I hugged my knees tighter to my chest, rocking myself back and forth, not stopping until my tears had slowed and my sobs had quieted. I let my head fall to my knees, pressing my eyes against them, trying to relieve some of the pressure gathering there. I pressed harder. I wasn't going to give in. Wasn't going to let this man's presence take me out. I'd overcome so much worse than him. I'd get through this, too.

I lifted my head, resting my chin on my knees as I stared out at the ocean. I wasn't alone anymore. I'd built a family of my own choosing. They weren't my blood, but they were mine. I had people at my back, who would see me through this season of storms.

A fissure of pain lanced my chest. Did Kara and Frank know that their son was back in town? Hunter had kept it from me, but I was shocked that Kara had done the same. She and Frank had become second parents to me in the years following the accident. People who understood me far better than my own family ever did. It was Frank who taught me how to refurbish furniture pieces, and Kara who helped me learn how to pick and choose which ones were worth salvaging. They never pushed, but always supported.

But Ford was a topic never raised when I was present in the Hardy household. I picked up snatches of updates here and there. I'd even given in to Googling him in college, coming across an article in the *LA Times* titled "The Nightlife King Spreads His Kingdom Across LA". There'd been a photo of him with one of those ultimate fighters and a famous musician, with a bevy of beautiful women behind them. He didn't seem to be suffering one bit. Meanwhile, I was reminded of that night every time my scar tissue pulled, or I was forced into an awkward encounter with my parents.

I pressed my hand against my ribs. I could feel the raised flesh through my tank top. The pain was gone now. My body had healed, as had my soul. So, why did it feel as if both were being ripped wide-open?

The wind whipped up, swirling my hair around me, the cold ocean breeze a balm to my overheated skin. The sound disguised the approaching footsteps. I didn't hear a thing until two forms began to lower themselves, one on either side of me. I couldn't tear my eyes away from the surf, its pounding rhythm the only thing I was certain could keep me calm.

Caelyn wrapped an arm around me, while Kenna pressed her shoulder into us. A huddle against the storm. My safe harbor.

They said nothing for a long time as I stared out at the ocean, knowing their presence was what I needed most. As much as they wanted to fix everything for me, they didn't have the magical powers to bring my sister back or prevent Ford from turning into a giant asshole. I glanced up at Kenna. "Caelyn call you?"

"Of course, she did."

Caelyn squeezed my shoulder. "Hunter said to tell you he's covering the bar for the rest of the day."

I scoffed. "Like that makes up for this." He should be thanking his lucky stars I loved his parents so much. If I didn't, I would've quit on the spot.

"He didn't give you any warning?" Kenna asked.

"Not a damn word other than to tell me he was working on finding us some help."

Kenna let out a low whistle. "Some help."

"I have no idea how I'm going to work with him."

Caelyn released my shoulder and began running a hand up and down my back. "I overheard them talking. Ford's only staying through the summer. Maybe it'll be good. You've been saying Frank and Kara could use more help, and I know you and the bar need it."

I winced. I'd bitched on more than one occasion about how Ford had left his family high and dry. I knew he'd sent them money; I'd overheard Frank and Hunter talking about it. But money wasn't the same as support. I knew that better than anyone. I'd take love and support any day. "God, I'm such a hypocrite."

Kenna straightened, turning to face me. "You're a hypocrite because you don't want to work with a man who smashed your heart to pieces? Who abandoned you in the worst moments of your life? When he had to know that you needed him? We were crazy close growing up, Bell, but Caelyn and I both knew it was Ford who was your best friend. You guys just had this weird bond, and he shat all over that."

Caelyn's mouth pulled into a hard line. "That's not helping, Kenna."

"What? It's the truth. It's not going to help Bell to pretend this is going to be all sunshine and roses. It's going to suck big time."

"Thanks," I said with a startled laugh. The laughter grew until tears were streaming down my face, and my friends were looking at me as if they were slightly concerned for my mental state. "This is going to be a disaster." More bubbled laughter escaped. "But I have to do it because Frank and Kara need both their sons around. And Ford can't run the bar alone. He hasn't been here in years." My gaze jumped from Kenna to Caelyn and back again. "Did Caelyn tell you I dumped a beer on Ford's head? There's a chance I could cause him real bodily harm before this is all over."

Caelyn stifled a laugh, but Kenna raised her hand for a high five. "That's my girl." I didn't take the offered hand. She shrugged and lowered it.

I let out a long breath. "It's going to kill every time I have to see him. It just—it brings everything back. I thought I'd done such a great job of dealing with it all. Of making peace. I've been happy. But when I looked up and saw his face…every shored-up wall I'd built seemed to crumble around me."

"Oh, Bell." Caelyn wrapped me in a hard hug. "You have done a great job of dealing with everything, and you *are* happy. Ford being around isn't going to steal all that away. It was just a shock, that's all."

Simply the mention of his name made me wince, and Kenna caught the action. "Maybe you can schedule him to work opposite your hours so you don't have to see him."

I nibbled on my bottom lip. "I don't even know if I'll still be in charge of the schedule. He runs all those fancy bars back in LA. I'll bet Hunter wants him to run the show here, too. It is his family's place, after all." My heart clenched. Over the years, I'd started to think of The Catch as my place, the Hardys as my family. Somehow, I'd slipped into the vacancy Ford had left. But now he was back, and that spot didn't feel like mine anymore.

Kenna grumbled a colorful insult under her breath. "If Hunter hands everything over to Ford, he's more of an idiot than I thought. That man may be God's gift in Hollywood, but these are the islands. It's different up here, and he's been gone a long time. You know this community better than anyone, and you've seen that damn bar through more ups and downs than I can count. *You're* the one who's kept it afloat."

I flipped a stone over and over between my fingers. "But we've been struggling."

"Everyone has," Caelyn interjected.

"She's right, Bell. Small businesses everywhere are hurting, and Anchor is no different. Once tourist season picks up, The Catch will be just fine. You'll see."

I glanced between my two friends. "We should do some sort of rain dance, but for tourists. That way, if the season's good enough, Ford will escape back to LA, and life can go back to normal."

Caelyn straightened. "I bet we can find something on the internet."

Kenna groaned. "I am not dancing naked around some firepit." She turned in my direction. "I'm sorry, Bell. I love you, but not that much."

I laughed, but Caelyn's eyes narrowed. "I'm not talking about naked dancing, though it might do you some good to loosen up like that. It might open up that sexual block you've got going on."

"Sexual block?"

Caelyn threw up her hands. "You need to get laid, girl. Your crankiness is bringing us all down."

Kenna's cheeks reddened. "I'm doing just fine in that department."

"Mm-hmm," Caelyn muttered.

I held up my hands, forming a T with them. "All right, all right. Time out. No naked dancing unless with a partner of your choosing. That's the rule."

Neither Caelyn nor Kenna could hold in her laughter. Caelyn reached out and grabbed my hand, squeezing it. "You going to be okay?"

I licked my suddenly dry lips, the thought of facing Ford every day for the next few months making my stomach cramp. "I have no other choice." I closed my eyes briefly before opening them again. "It's just a few months. I can handle anything for a few months."

At least, I hoped I could.

Chapter Six

Ford

I PULLED MY SUV INTO AN EMPTY SPACE IN THE CATCH'S small parking lot. Switching off the engine, I simply sat there, staring out at the beach. I'd slept like crap last night, tossing and turning. The second I'd descended into sleep, dreams had haunted me, my subconscious taking me through my own little horror show. But it was the happy memories my mind played while I slept that were the worst. The ones where Violet's blue eyes sparkled when she smiled, or the times when the two of us chased Isabelle around their back yard, Trouble's laughter floating on the air. They were the worst because for the first few seconds after I woke, I'd forget everything I'd lost. Then reality would come crashing down around me once again.

It was Isabelle who haunted me most now, though. And the reminders were everywhere. Not just in my dreams, but around every corner at the bar. Hell…this beach held an endless supply. I'd spent countless afternoons exploring this stretch of coast-line with her while Vi was at cheer practice or one of her other myriad activities. Afternoons that had knitted our friendship into the very core of who I was.

"What's got you so moody, Cupcake?"

I threw a mock scowl in Isabelle's direction. "I'm not moody."

She picked up a piece of driftwood, studying it for a moment. I could never tell what it was she looked for in these pieces, something invisible to most that told her it could be transformed into some work of art. "You're worse than a PMSing girl watching The Notebook."

I let out a bark of laughter. "Way to hit me where it hurts."

Isabelle peered up from the wood. "Something's wrong. You've been quieter than usual. And you didn't even laugh when Hunter tripped over his shoelaces for the eightieth time yesterday."

I studied her for a moment, the girl who was so wise beyond her years and seemed to see things no one else could. I eased down on a log, staring out at the water. "I got into a fight with my dad."

"About?" Isabelle took the open spot next to me.

"I don't want to come back and take over the business right away. I mean, I love Anchor, The Catch, that's my future. But I want to do and see other things first."

Isabelle turned the piece of driftwood over and over in her hands. "You're allowed to want more from your life than what others think you should have." I glanced over to see her studying the nicks and grooves in the stick. "You don't have to fit into their mold."

"Neither do you."

I gave my head a swift shake, trying to clear the memory that still had a hold of me. The images that reminded me just how much I had lost when I crashed that SUV. My hands fisted around the steering wheel, the leather creaking. I released my hold, letting my arms fall to my sides.

Sitting here was only making things worse. Before long, my mind would come up with every worst-case scenario possible.

Every brutal accusation Isabelle could possibly sling at me. I moved before I could think of all the reasons not to, pushing open my door and sliding out. I beeped the locks as I strode towards the worn back entrance.

Fishing the keys my brother had given me out of my pocket, I unlocked the door and stepped through. The bar was silent, but the lights were on. Knowing the Isabelle from a decade ago, I'd been expecting loud, thumping music as she danced around the space, getting it ready for the day's customers, not the pristine quiet that greeted me.

"Isabelle?" I couldn't bring myself to call her "*Bell*," it felt weird, like a foreign name on my tongue, for someone I'd once known almost better than myself. But I sure as hell wasn't going to call her "*Trouble*" and see that stark pain in her eyes again.

There was no answer. I moved through the space, fully taking it in for the first time now that it was empty of customers, and I wasn't covered in beer. It looked surprisingly good. Whoever had remodeled the interior had done an incredible job. The floors were cement with an artfully distressed finish. The bar itself a perfect juxtaposition of gleaming redwood on the top and what looked to be roughed-up reclaimed barnwood on the front. Above it hung Edison lights that brought out the warmth of the wood and the red in the brick walls.

Maybe my brother had sunk the bar's whole budget into redoing the interior, thinking it would fix all our problems. I needed to go over the books. A stylish setting was important, but a successful bar and restaurant was so much more than that.

I rounded the bar and headed down a hallway covered in photos from generations of Hardys and our employees, both celebrations and everyday snapshots. Memories of running down this hall to visit my dad danced in my head. Hunter and I would race each other, yelling our heads off as we went, my father consumed by laughter by the time we reached his office.

My hand hovered over the familiar red door. I gave two quick knocks.

"Come in."

I pushed open the door. Isabelle sat behind the same desk my father had for my entire childhood, her hair piled on top of her head, held up by what looked like two pens. She was surrounded by papers and a computer that looked to be a decade past its prime. I couldn't help but drink her in. She was unrecognizable yet undeniably familiar. The multiple piercings lining her ears were new, and a glimpse of a tattoo peeked out from the scooped neck of her tee. Those curves that filled out the shirt definitely hadn't been there eleven years ago. *Shit.* I could not be seeing Trouble in this way.

And I shouldn't be calling her that, even in my head. Not anymore.

As if she could read my mind, Isabelle's green eyes flashed, a hint of anger and defiance dancing in their depths. She quickly covered it. I hated the action. The girl who used to tell me everything was now a woman hiding it all away and out of my reach. I got that, but it didn't mean it didn't hurt.

"Hey, Isabelle." My voice came out rusty, as though it hadn't been used in weeks.

She flinched. "Call me Bell, everyone else does."

"Okay…Bell." I forced the name to curve around my tongue. It didn't feel quite as weird to say it as I'd thought it would. But I found myself wondering if the name fit the woman before me and if I'd ever have the opportunity to find out.

She cleared her throat. "I wasn't sure if you'd be in today."

I slid into one of the chairs opposite the ancient desk. "I'm here." Our gazes locked. A silent standoff. "Look, I'm sorry this got dropped on you—"

Bell held up a hand to cut me off, her eyes boring into mine. "Your parents, Hunter, they're everything to me. If they want you home, great. They want you to run the bar for a few months? Fine. You and I? We can pretend we've never met before today. Fresh start for both of us."

I stared at her, not blinking, eyes going dry. It was what I'd always wanted, wasn't it? To pretend like the past hadn't happened. To bury it so deep that it couldn't rear up unexpectedly and sucker punch me. So why did it twist something deep in my gut to have Bell want to erase every memory we'd shared?

I'd gotten so damn good at wiping the slate clean, at building an imaginary past so intricate that I almost believed it was real. My life in LA had been full, happy. I had a job I loved. A great house in the Hollywood Hills. Amazing friends who had become family. But that family had no idea what had brought me there. They had no idea what I'd lost, and everything I'd thrown away. To them, I was the life of the party, the one always ready with a joke or a helping hand, but I never opened up my past for discussion.

I cleared my throat. "Whatever you want."

She gave me a quick nod. "I've been managing the place, so I just need to know what you want to tackle, and what you want me to keep running."

My eyes widened. I'd thought she'd simply been bartending here, maybe placing orders. I had no idea she was running the whole show. "Why don't you walk me through what you think is working and what isn't? We can figure out the best ways to divide and conquer after that."

Surprise and a healthy dose of skepticism flashed in those moss-green eyes. "You don't just want to implement whatever it is you do at your fancy Hollywood clubs?"

I couldn't fight the twitch of my lips. "I don't have a one-size-fits-all approach for my bars. And even if I did, it would be incredibly short-sighted of me not to listen to the person who's been running this place for the past few years, the woman who knows the community way better than I do."

Bell straightened in her chair, a lock of hair falling out of her haphazard bun. "Well, that's good to hear."

"I'm not here to take over and make your life miserable. I'm just here to help."

Bell's gaze hardened. She opened her mouth to say something and then snapped it shut, closing her eyes and taking a deep breath.

I had the urge to reach out, to round the desk, and pull her into my arms the way I had countless times before. To comfort her. Except I couldn't do that because I was the one causing her pain. That familiar knife carved into my chest just a little bit deeper. I wanted to apologize, to beg for forgiveness, but I didn't have the words. "*I'm sorry*" felt like the biggest cop-out imaginable. A pathetic Band-Aid for a lethal wound.

In that moment, I would've given anything to take Bell's pain away. I would've traded places with Vi in a heartbeat. I'd wished it countless times. Gone over the moments leading up to the crash so often that they were forever burned in my brain. I thought of all the things I could've done differently, all the things that might have meant that Vi was still here and Isabelle didn't hate me.

But I couldn't rewrite history, and I didn't have the words to make any of this better. I didn't think any words had that power. But maybe I could help with the bar. Set Bell and my family up so that at least they weren't drowning in worry anymore. It was such a pathetically small thing. But it was something. And something was better than nothing.

Chapter Seven

Ford

I PUSHED OPEN MY SUV'S DOOR AND STEPPED OUT ONTO THE grass in front of the house that hadn't changed at all in the eleven years I'd been gone. Even the shutters were painted the same color. My chest tightened as I moved onto the brick path and strode towards the house.

The front door opened before I reached the steps. "Hunter told me you were here, but I didn't believe it. Not until now, when I saw you with my own two eyes. Get in here, baby boy!"

Heat crept up my neck as I jogged up the steps. "Maybe we could cool it with the 'baby boy'?"

She chuckled and wrapped me in a hard hug. "I've told you a thousand times. You're my first—"

"You'll always be my baby boy," I finished along with her.

I pulled back but kept a hold of her shoulders. "You look great." And she did. The dark circles that had lined her eyes the last time I saw her were gone. She had color back in her cheeks, and the worry lines that had pinched her brows were fainter now.

She swatted my shoulder. "Your flattery will work every time. I've got some cookies cooling in the kitchen. Why don't you head into the living room and say hi to your dad while I get them plated up?"

I nodded, swallowing hard. The last time I'd seen my dad, he'd still had trouble with his speech and needed help walking to make sure he didn't lose his balance and fall. There was something about seeing a parent, a person you'd always seen as invincible, struggle so much. It killed a little something inside you. I walked through the small foyer, heading for the living room, but stopped dead in my tracks. A familiar photo hung on the wall. Me, Violet, and Isabelle, arms wrapped around each other, smiling so widely you could see that Isabelle was missing a front tooth.

The pain that shot through my chest was what I imagined it felt like to be hit by lightning. The blast was instantaneous, gone in a matter of seconds, but the aftereffects could stay with you for weeks. I squeezed my eyes closed, stepping away from the pull the photo had on me and into the living room.

"Ford." My eyes flew open at the sound of my father's voice. He stood from his recliner, and I started forward, not wanting him to fall. He chuckled. "Don't worry, I'm not going to take a tumble. I'm doing much better."

"Dad." My voice was hoarse as he wrapped me in a warm embrace, one arm thumping me on the back. When he released me, I studied him carefully. "You do seem a lot better." There was a clarity in his gaze that I hadn't seen since before the stroke.

Dad eased back into his chair, gesturing for me to take a seat on the couch. That was new, but the recliner was the same one he'd had since my childhood. "I'm doing great. Just some weakness in my right arm. And I get tired a bit quicker than normal."

My mom scoffed from the doorway as she carried in a tray

with cookies and three glasses of milk. "Don't let him convince you he's ready to run a marathon, he still needs plenty of rest."

He snorted in response. "The woman would have me napping every hour on the hour if she could."

"Heaven forbid I try to keep you healthy. You know if you die on me, I'm going to get one of those hard-bodied young fellas who like older women."

My dad straightened in his chair. "You will do no such thing, Kara."

She grinned, bending down to give him a quick kiss. "Take care of yourself, and I won't have to."

I rubbed at my eyes but couldn't help the laughter that escaped me. "I think I'm going to need to bleach my ears *and* my eyes."

"Oh hush, you." Mom swatted my shoulder as she set the cookies on the coffee table. She eased down next to me on the couch. "So, where are you staying? We've got plenty of room here, you know."

Spending months at my parents' house with my mother hovering would be more than I could take. I needed space and solitude if I was going to make it through this summer. The modern craftsman I'd found was perfect. Spacious, with a killer view. If it had been anywhere else in the world, I would've loved staying there, but it felt more like a beautiful prison. "I got a place up on the bluff."

My mother's brows pulled together. "Does it have everything you need? What about food? You're so used to being able to get takeout in the city. Maybe you should stay here instead."

"Now, Kara, the boy needs his space. He's a grown man now."

I reached out and squeezed my mom's hand. "I'll be fine. I can cook for myself, you know. But I'll be at the bar most days, so I can always grab a meal there or somewhere else in town." I hadn't done much exploring yet, so I had no idea how much everything had changed and what my options might be.

My parents shared a look, and I straightened. "What?"

Dad cleared his throat. "Have you seen Isabelle yet?"

My jaw worked. "You mean *Bell*?"

"I'm taking that as a yes, you've seen her."

"She poured a beer over my head."

My mom gasped. "What did you do to that girl to make her do that?"

I bristled. Bell and my mom had always been close. Mom gave her the warmth and affection she'd never received from her own mother. Apparently, not much had changed. "I didn't do anything," I muttered.

Dad scoffed. "She has one of the kindest spirits I've ever seen, you must've done something to get her so riled."

I twisted in my seat. I should've kept my damn mouth shut. "I think I just surprised her, is all. Hunter didn't tell her I was coming."

"I am going to thump that boy upside the head the next time I see him. What was he thinking, not telling her you were coming back?" My mom stood, placing cookies on napkins and handing them to Dad and me. She was always one to busy herself whenever she got agitated.

"Bonehead move if I ever heard one."

"Frank, don't call your son a bonehead."

"You said you were going to thump him upside the head."

"I'm his mother, it's my right."

"Well, it's my right to call him a bonehead."

I couldn't hold in my laughter.

My mom's head snapped in my direction, and her face softened. "I missed hearing that sound around here."

There was a longing in her voice, even though I was sitting right in front of her. The tone had my chest twisting, the guilt tying up my insides just a little tighter. "I'm sorry I stayed away for so long. I'll come back more often now." The words were out of my mouth before I could think about them. Anything to ease the pain my mom carried. I'd figure out a way to deal with it. To be the son she deserved.

"Oh, baby." She sat down next to me, gripping my hand tightly. "I know this is hard for you. But I can't say I'm not happy to have you home."

I swallowed hard. "It is. But I don't want to hurt you because I'm weak."

"You are not weak." My dad's voice cracked through the room like a whip. "You went through a trauma, a loss. It's understandable you wanted to avoid reminders of it. And all the damn small-town gossip."

I winced. I knew that had been incredibly hard on my parents. And the Kiptons hadn't made it any easier, refusing to let me or my parents see Bell in the hospital. Threatening a wrongful death suit if I contacted any of them. It had just been easier to stay in Seattle, to slip away into the night and never look back. But it was also cowardly, and it was what let those vines of self-hatred take root. And they dug their claws in deep.

I looked up at my mom. "How's Bell doing?" The nickname still felt foreign on my tongue, but I was getting used to it.

"You didn't ask her yourself?"

I set the cookie my mom had handed me on the side table, my stomach not ready for food—even one of my old favorites. "She wants to pretend we have no history. Said it's best if we start from scratch." Mom's brow furrowed. "I get it, I really do. I can't imagine how hard it must be to work with the person who was behind the wheel that night. I'm sure there's at least a part of her that blames me."

My mom's eyes bored into mine, gentle but searching. "Ford, if there's one thing I know for certain, it's that Bell doesn't blame you for what happened that night."

"You didn't see the pain in her eyes."

Mom sighed, her eyes misting. "That girl has been through way too much. Losing her sister. Losing *you*. Recovering from her injuries. It was weeks before the Kiptons would let us even visit her. And Bell didn't understand what was going on behind the scenes. Didn't know what her parents were putting *you* through."

"Wait, you told me Bell was fine. After the accident, you said she was okay." It was one of the things that had allowed me to stay in Seattle, to not look back. Now, all I could see was Bell in a hospital bed, alone and scared.

My parents shared another of their looks, but it was my father who spoke. "She was, and she is, but she had some injuries that required surgery, and her body was banged up. Her recovery took time."

Nausea swept through me. "You should've told me."

Dad's face hardened. "Why? So you could blame yourself for one more thing? You were drowning, and I wasn't going to throw one more weight your way. Bell is fine, she made a one-hundred-per-cent recovery, and she did it quickly."

I swallowed against the dryness in my throat. "I get it." I'd more than worried my parents that first year of college, merely going through the motions of life. It was my mom who had suggested looking at other schools, ones that didn't hold the reminder of Violet and all the plans we had made. I'd ended up at UCLA the next year, and that had jumpstarted my life. Sunshine, classmates who had no idea of my grief...I'd reinvented myself, and it had worked.

Mom squeezed my knee. "I hope you two will find your way back to that friendship you shared. You're different people now, but your hearts are the same."

We were different people. And I was surprised by how much I hated that Bell was a stranger to me now. It felt wrong on every level. But I was the one who had turned her into an unknown entity. "I'll try."

"Good. She really only has our family, Caelyn, and Kenna. Those parents of hers are worthless." My mom's tone turned fierce, a mother bear protecting her cub.

"Are they still around?" They were two people I could definitely do without seeing.

Mom's lips pressed together in a firm line. "They are. And after everything they put Bell through, I'd like to drop-kick them every time I run into them."

My body tensed, muscles straining. "What did they put her through?"

She shook her head. "More of the same, but worse. Trying to turn her into a mirror image of Violet. The pressure they put on her to be perfect…it just makes me so mad."

My body eased. I knew the Isabelle of yesterday, and the Bell of today could handle any pressure her parents put on her. She was strong, so fiercely and unapologetically unique. She'd never bow down and become what someone wanted her to be. But I knew that came at a cost, and the price was a close relationship with her parents. "I'm glad she had you through it all."

My mom rose, picking up cookie remnants and glasses. "And now, she has you, too. You'll find your way back."

I wasn't so sure about that. Some wounds were too deep. Some history too painful. You could forgive, but you'd never forget.

Chapter Eight

Bell

"**B**ELL!"

I turned at the familiar voice, a huge grin on my face. "Mi, what are you doing here?"

Mia's strawberry-blond hair flew behind her as she launched herself at me. I caught her with a stifled laugh. "Cae-Cae said we could have dinner here tonight. And Kenna's here, too!"

I glanced over her head to see Kenna, Caelyn, and Caelyn's other two siblings, Will and Ava. I blew a raspberry on Mia's neck. "Well, isn't that lucky for me? My favorite people all in one place."

Kenna sidled up next to us. "We thought you could use a little backup."

Mia looked at Kenna and then back to me. "Whatcha need backup for? Are you playing cops and robbers?"

I laughed. "No, but maybe we should." I balanced Mia on my hip and reached out to squeeze Kenna's arm. "Thanks."

"You got room for all five of us?" Caelyn asked as she helped Ava out of her coat.

"Always." I pointed to a booth against the wall. "How about that one?"

"Perfect." Caelyn turned to Will. "Can you take the girls over and get them settled? Help them decide what to order?"

"Sure." He reached out to Mia, and she flung herself from my arms to his. She loved her big brother. My lips pursed as I watched Will guide them over to the booth and help them in. He was mature beyond his years. He and Caelyn hadn't had a choice. But it hurt my heart to know that he'd lost his chance at a real, carefree childhood. Caelyn had tried to urge him to hang out with his friends, join sports teams, anything she could think of, but he spent most of his time at home with her and the girls, helping as much as he could.

Caelyn arranged the coats piled in her arms. "So...?"

I grimaced, glancing over my shoulder to the bar, where Ford was pouring drinks and chatting with customers. If he was unhappy to be here, he hid it well. "I've mostly avoided him."

Kenna snorted. "And how long are you going to be able to keep that up?"

I bit my bottom lip. "Not long. He's going over the books and the day-to-day details this week, but at some point, we'll have to make a plan for the future."

Caelyn wrapped an arm around me and squeezed. "How's your heart doing?"

Cracking like a glass in sub-zero temperatures. "It's better today."

"Good. I'm going to make sure the girls aren't planning to order ice cream sundaes for dinner, and then I'll come and check on you."

"I'm fine. I promise." I had to be. There was no other choice. I'd get through this just like I'd gotten through everything else in my life to date.

Caelyn headed for her siblings, and I turned to face Kenna.

Her arms were crossed under her chest, and her brow had a slight arch to it. "Don't bullshit me, Bell. How are you doing?"

I sighed, flicking a brief glance at the bar. Ford was grinning at a woman, and his forearm flexed as he handed her some sort of fruity concoction. I forced my gaze away. "I honestly don't know. I'm all over the place. I feel like a bundle of exposed nerves."

"Bell..." Kenna lowered her voice so that no passersby could overhear us. "If this is too much, you can quit. We need a secretary at the accounting firm. Come work with me."

The idea of sitting behind a desk all day made me cringe. And the thought of leaving the Hardys in the lurch made me physically nauseous. "I can't. I'll get through this. Promise."

Kenna scowled in Ford's direction. "Fine. Come on, I need a drink."

I smiled at the floor as we headed to the bar. Kenna made her way to an empty stool as I rounded the counter. "What'll it be?"

"Vodka soda with a lime, please."

"Coming right up." I reached for the Grey Goose, my pour automatic and precise, the gift of having done this for so many years.

"Come on, Brown Eyes. You can be a little more exciting than that."

I stifled a giggle as I watched Crosby scoot over a stool, beer in hand. Kenna's eyes narrowed on him. "Kenna. My name is Kenna. One word, five letters. Is it really that hard to remember?"

He grinned at her, and I had to admit, it was devastating. "Everyone calls you Kenna. I need something a little more original."

She rolled her eyes as she took the vodka soda I handed her. "I'd hardly call *Brown Eyes* original."

"Fair enough. I'll keep working on it."

"Please don't."

I couldn't hold my laughter in anymore. "You two are worse than an old married couple."

Kenna turned her glare on me. "Like I'd ever stoop that low."

"You wound me."

I felt his energy before I heard his voice. It was heat and a faint buzzing. I kept my gaze focused straight ahead.

"Hey, Kenna." Ford rested a hand on the bar. It was at least six inches from where mine was placed, but I still had to fight the urge to pull away, to step back, to flee and never look back.

"Ford." Her voice was cold, the tone generally reserved for those who had hurt someone Kenna loved. *Oh, shit.* "I'm surprised to see you here. I thought for sure you'd have bailed again by now."

Ford's forearms flexed as he gripped the bar. "I'm here for the next few months. I just want to help."

Kenna scoffed. "Day late and a dollar short."

"Brown Eyes…"

Her head snapped in Crosby's direction. "Stay out of this, surfer boy, you don't know a damn thing about what's going on."

He held up his hands in defeat.

Ford pushed away from the bar, straightening to his full height. "You don't know a damn thing either, Kenna."

She rose from her stool. "I know more than you. You know why? I was here. I went to the hospital every day. To those god-awful physical therapy appointments when she got out. To the *funeral*. And where were you?"

"Kenna…" I didn't know how to finish that sentence. All I knew was that she had to stop. I didn't want her to bare my scars for all to see.

Kenna shook her head and picked up her drink. "Sorry, Bell. I'm gonna go sit with the kids."

I nodded and watched her move through the crowd. When she scooted into the booth, I looked back to Crosby, and then my eyes traveled to Ford as if they couldn't stay away any longer. There was so much pain in his eyes. "I'm sorry. She's protective."

Ford's jaw worked. "Understandable."

"She shouldn't have said anything."

Ford opened his mouth to speak, but Crosby spoke up first. "God, I love when her fire sneaks out."

His statement startled a laugh out of me. "You know, one of these days, you're going to push her too far, and I'm not going to do a damn thing to save you."

Crosby glanced over at Kenna. "Someone's gotta startle a little life into her."

I turned back to Ford, and he looked so damn lost it had my heart cracking a little bit more. But I didn't want my heart to crack for him. He was the one who had left without a word. He hadn't earned this emotion, my heart breaking for his pain. I straightened my spine. "I'm going to work the floor for a bit. You got back of bar?"

He started at my voice but nodded roughly. I took off without another word, striding between tables, looking for any excuse for escape.

A hand snaked out and gripped my wrist. I whipped around and ready to elbow whoever it was in the gut. "Whoa, there! It's just me."

I grimaced at Hunter. He'd been calling nonstop for the past two days. I hadn't called him back. I wasn't ready for the conversation we needed to have. We'd become close in the years since the accident, and he was one of the people I trusted most, but he'd fractured that bond in a way that wasn't easy to repair. "What are you doing here?"

He winced and rubbed his jaw. "The boys and I thought we'd get a few beers and some grub."

I glanced around at the two other men at the table. I knew them both to varying degrees. Pete was a transplant from Seattle, having moved to Anchor for a quiet place to raise his family. But Ethan had grown up with us and had been in the same grade as Hunter and me.

I forced a smile. "Hi, boys. What can I get ya?"

Pete grinned down at the table. "Still pissed at Hunt?"

I scowled at him. "Wouldn't you be?"

"Lay off, Pete." Ethan gave me a gentle smile. "You hanging in there, Bell?"

I tried to push the smile wider. "Right as rain. Now, let's get you your drinks. What'll it be?" I let myself zone out to the rhythm of waitressing, the sea of familiar faces, and did everything I could to avoid the blue eyes behind the bar.

I trudged up the stairs at the back of the bar, my legs feeling like they were carrying an extra fifty or sixty pounds. Everything hurt. I'd been on my feet since ten that morning, and it was now after one a.m. My bed was calling my name, but I desperately needed a shower to clean off the day—both the physical labor and the emotional pain. Showers always seemed to help. The pounding of the water against my skull dulled the painful memories.

I reached into my back pocket and pulled out my keys. Unlocking the door, I stepped inside and kicked off my boots. "Shower. A shower will make everything better." And it did. I turned the water as hot as I could stand it and let everything melt away. When I got out, everything was clearer, a little less ominous.

I twisted my hair up into a towel wrap and secured it in place. It would just have to do because I wasn't standing here for another thirty minutes blow-drying my hair. Crossing to my dresser, I went straight for my comfiest PJs, the flannel ones covered in bright ice cream cones. As I pulled them out, my hand stilled on the top drawer. I opened it and carefully lifted out the scrapbook.

Its clothbound cover was fraying slightly at the edges, and slips of paper and ribbon stuck out from the pages. I set it on my bed and quickly put on my PJs. Sliding under the covers, I pulled the scrapbook onto my lap. A therapist my parents had forced me to see after the accident had suggested the project. An artistic outlet and way to remember my sister.

It had taken me over a year to complete the thing. It was part photo album, part mixed-media art piece. As sentimental as I was, I had always kept a memory box full of mementos from my childhood. It had been stuffed full of photos, ribbons from various contests, ticket stubs, paintings, and so on. I pulled from that, photos I got from family and friends, and multiple trips to craft stores.

Each page of the scrapbook told a story. And those together, showed a life. The pages weren't in chronological order. It would've been too depressing to flip through it, knowing when I was getting close to the end. Instead, I jumped around in a pattern that was my own. Violet's ninth birthday, the day I was born, a family vacation to Disneyland.

Each page layered a varied array of photos, paint, memorabilia, stickers, doodles, and more. I grinned down at a picture of the two of us outside The Tower of Terror at Disneyland. I had a massive smile on my face, while Violet looked a little green. My parents had refused to accompany me on the ride, so Violet had gone, even though heights made her sick to her stomach. I'd made it up to her by using all my saved-up allowance to buy her a porcelain statue of Sleeping Beauty she'd been eyeing in one of the gift shops. It was one of Violet's belongings I'd insisted on keeping after her passing.

I flipped a page, and my hand stilled. The photo I'd glued to the paper was gone. I'd decorated the area surrounding it with drawings of trees, marsh grass, and the pond where the picture had been taken. It should've been three smiling faces looking back at me. Violet, me, and Ford. My fingers skimmed across the page where the snapshot had been, the paper torn away just slightly. Had the glue dried out and the photo come loose?

I went to the drawer where I kept the book. Searching inside, I came up empty. I tried to think back to the last time I'd taken it out. Maybe a couple of months ago? My stomach twisted. It must have fallen out, and I'd thrown it out when cleaning up and not paying attention.

"It's just a picture." I knew I had a copy of it on my computer. I could always print it out and replace it. But something about it sent a chill skittering down my spine.

Chapter
Nine

Ford

I TOOK A PULL FROM MY BEER AS I FLIPPED OVER ANOTHER page of spreadsheets.

"Drinking on the job already?"

Even Bell's voice was different, huskier somehow, yet hauntingly familiar at the same time—just like everything else about her. God, I'd missed her giving me shit. There had been so many times I'd almost picked up the phone. So many times I'd almost come back to see her. But the fear of what I'd find when I got here had always kept me away.

I took another sip of the beer. At least she was talking to me today. "Hank's making me an early lunch. I think I can handle one pale ale."

Bell's nose scrunched as she took in my beverage. "Girlie beer."

I barked out a laugh. "Don't pull any punches."

She started at the sound of my laugh, her eyes widening, and then her expression closed down, shutting me out. I hated every wall she put between us, that *I* had put between us. Bell turned towards the back hallway, clearly ready to retreat to the office until the doors opened to patrons. But I didn't want her to go. "Wait."

She froze, then slowly turned towards me, her expression guarded. "Yeah?"

I inclined my head to the stools next to me. "Grab a seat. I wanted to go over some things with you." I raised a brow when she didn't move either way.

Bell straightened her spine and headed back in my direction. I bit back a grin. Trouble never could back down from a challenge. The flicker of my lips faded away when she left a stool in between us. A barrier. "What's up?"

I gave my head a little shake and gathered up the papers in front of me. "You've done a good job of keeping this place afloat." I looked over at Bell, but she said nothing, a passive mask covering her features. My hold on the papers tightened. "What? You don't believe me?"

"I'm waiting for the *but.*"

"There is no but. You're the reason this place didn't go under." I met her gaze and held it, willing her to really hear me. "Thank you"—I cleared my throat—"for being here when I wasn't. When I couldn't."

Bell's jaw hardened. "I'd do anything for Frank and Kara."

It cut. Not her dedication to my parents, but the fact that she had to make it clear that her contribution to The Catch's future had nothing to do with me. "I imagine we owe you some back pay."

Her eyes hardened, the green glittering like gemstones. "I didn't do it for the money."

She said "*money*" like it was a dirty word. *Shit.* I was making a mess of this whole thing. "I didn't mean that you did. But I can tell you've been putting in extra hours."

"They were my hours to give."

I ran my hand through my hair. This was getting us nowhere. "Well, thank you. I mean it. And the place looks amazing." I'd expected to find a large payout for a bar remodel somewhere in the books, but I'd only found expenses for paint, secondhand light fixtures, and other inexpensive items.

Bell straightened one of the bar menus in the holder in front of her. "We did what we could with what we had."

"Well, let's see if we can get you a little more to work with."

Her brow arched. "You don't want to be in charge of the budget?"

I took another pull of my beer. "No. You're making sound decisions with the bar. You've been more clever than I might've been. I just want to get you a little more breathing room."

The set of Bell's shoulders eased, and there was a mirroring sensation in my chest. "Okay. What are you thinking?"

"The lunch and dinner rushes are holding steady. That will always be our bread and butter, but I think we can get the after-hours crowd to pick up a little more."

Bell traced an invisible design on the bar top. "Maverick's has become more of the late-night spot. It's rowdier. Loud music. Where people go to blow off steam."

"I don't want to attract a rough crowd. I don't think that's wise. But what would you think about live music on the weekends?"

She was silent for a minute, and I was surprised by how much I wanted her to like my idea, how much I craved her approval. Years ago, the roles had been reversed. It was always Bell coming to ask me what I thought about this or that, if I liked a drawing she was working on or whatnot. And now, I was holding my breath to hear what she thought about a business move.

"I think it could work..." She started drumming her fingers on the bar. Now that was familiar. If Bell didn't have something to doodle on, she always pounded out a beat while she was thinking something through. "We could attract more tourists that way, some of the locals looking for date night options. We should consider offering a late-night menu—limited, of course. Things that Hank could prep, but a line cook could make."

"That's a great idea. Finding the right music is going to be key to attracting the crowd we want."

"You're right." Her fingers picked up their pace along the bar. "I know a few guys who have a country/folk sort of feel. That might be a good fit. Something people could dance to or just sit by and listen."

"That sounds perfect. Maybe we could do themed nights. Mix it up so people don't get bored?"

"That's a great idea. The only problem will be finding a variety of musicians."

I grinned, a million memories sliding through me. "Just as long as we aren't desperate enough to throw you up on stage."

Bell laughed, and it was the sweetest sound I'd heard in a long damn time. "My musical genius is above your pay grade."

The front door swung open, and I glanced at my watch. It wasn't quite time to open our doors. "Sorry, we're not open—"

My words were cut off as Hunter strode in with Ethan in tow. "Come on, big brother, I think I've earned early access." His gaze flicked to Bell, concern filling his expression, but he kept that false smile on his face.

She hopped off the stool. "I gotta go check the tables out back. If you ask nicely, I bet Hank will fix you boys something before he's officially on the clock."

Hunter's shoulders sagged as he watched Bell head out the door to the back patio. "Fuck."

"She still not talking to you?"

Hunter shook his head and scrubbed a hand over his jaw. "Nope. I screwed things up good this time."

Ethan slapped him on the back. "It's Bell. She'll forgive you. You just gotta give her a few days to stew."

My gut burned at the guys' familiarity with Bell. The feeling crawling around inside me felt a whole lot like jealousy, thick and insidious. It had always been the three of us growing up: me, Violet, and Trouble. I'd had a crush on Vi since the moment I met her in preschool, with her shiny blond hair and pale blue eyes. I'd been sunk. Her baby sister had just been a part of the package, and before long, we were an inseparable trio. Hunter had never been crazy about Vi and Bell, had always opted to hang out with Ethan instead, but it looked like that was one of the many things that had changed over the years.

I wanted Bell to have good people in her life, and my brother was the best. But I guess, when it came down to it, I wanted a space there, too. I'd missed her. More than I wanted to admit. Hearing her laugh earlier had been the best kind of pain, full of the sweetest memories and the deepest longing for a time that was gone forever. Because I would never be that person again, the boy who thought he was a man. One who had never experienced true devastation. The man I would've been if the accident had never happened was a stranger to me. All I knew was who I was now, but I wasn't sure how much I even knew him anymore.

"Earth to Ford. What the hell, man?"

I was jolted back to the present by Hunter's voice. "Sorry. What?"

A muscle in Hunt's cheek ticked. "How's she been?"

I glanced towards the back door, my hand tightening around my beer. "I'm honestly not sure. She seemed to be letting her guard down a bit today...until you walked in."

Hunter's gaze hardened, and I knew I'd crossed a line. *Shit.* I was supposed to be making amends with my brother, not making things worse. "I fucked up. I admit it. I should've told

Bell I was calling you from the beginning. But she's acting more pissed at me than she is at you, and *I* stayed."

I swallowed back the retort on my tongue. I'd bought that anger and more. "Ethan's right. You know how Trouble's temper is. Just give her a few days to cool down."

Ethan slapped his hands down on the bar. "All right, this family tension is making me feel super uncomfortable. So, how about we eat instead?"

I let out a chuckle. "Fair enough. What do you guys want?"

Caelyn appeared from the hallway with a tub of ice. "Holy hot guys." She let out a low whistle. "What're you doing here so early? Not that I'm complaining about the eye candy."

Ethan grinned. "Early lunch. The boss is buying."

Hunter scowled and knocked the ball cap off Ethan's head. "I said we could break for lunch early, not that I'd buy you food. You eat too much. You'll bankrupt me."

Ethan patted his stomach. "I'm a growing boy."

"Growing a beer gut, maybe," Hunter chided.

"Here, I can take your orders and give them to Hank." Caelyn pulled out a pad and pen from under the bar and started scrawling.

I turned to face my brother. "Did you have the guys help you fix up the bar? I've been meaning to tell you how great everything looks." Hunter just stared at me, and everyone else grew quiet. "What?"

It was Caelyn who spoke up. "It wasn't Hunter. I mean, he helped with some of the heavy lifting, but it was all Bell."

My brows rose. "Bell?" When I knew her, she'd had zero interest in renovation or anything of the sort.

Hunt cleared his throat. "Yeah. She's been taking online classes for interior design." He glanced around the space, a small smile tipping his lips. "She's got a real knack for it."

I looked around the bar with new eyes. Taking in everything from the big changes, like the poured cement floors, to the small details, like the distressed metal menu holders. Everything fit together in an effortless balance of rustic chic. And I knew after looking at the books that she'd made things look a lot more expensive than they were. "Why isn't she taking classes in Seattle?"

"I'm just going to get this order in with Hank." Caelyn hustled towards the kitchen as if the bar were on fire.

Hunter and Ethan shared a look, but Ethan spoke. "Caelyn has custody of her siblings. Got it when she was just twenty-one. She was drowning, trying to make it work those first couple of years. Bell and Kenna came back as soon as they graduated. Hell, they practically lived with them for a year."

I swallowed hard. I'd missed so damn much. "Why does Caelyn have custody?"

Hunter stiffened on his stool. "The state took the kids."

"Those parents always were a waste of space," I muttered.

Ethan's expression hardened. "Understatement of the century."

My gaze traveled to the back door. That now-familiar pull had returned. Why the hell hadn't Bell told me that she'd been the one to renovate the bar when we'd gone over the expenses from the past few years? My gut twisted. The better question was why *would* she? She didn't trust me. Wanted me out of her life as fast as humanly possible. I could leave her the bar at the end of summer. I could give her the island then, too. But I wanted to earn her forgiveness first. Her forgiveness and, hopefully, even her friendship.

I pushed to my feet. "I'll be back in a few."

Hunter's brows drew together. "Where are you going?"

"I need to talk to Bell about something." The look on my brother's face was not a happy one. I bristled. I still hadn't figured out what was going on between the two of them. If they were friends or more. But it didn't matter. I had atoning to do, and he wasn't going to stand in my way.

Chapter Ten

Bell

I COLLAPSED INTO ONE OF THE WROUGHT IRON CHAIRS ON the back patio, rubbing the spot between my breasts. Tears burned the backs of my eyes. Everything was a swirling mess of emotions. Life turned on its head by one single action. One person returning.

Not only was I in a fight with Hunter, but there was a longing within me that I hadn't felt in years. A grief that had dulled, suddenly flaring to life again in vivid technicolor. It wasn't grief for my sister, but for my friend. A yearning for the man that was now right in front of me. I'd put the loss of him to rest long ago, but it was as if seeing him again had brought it all back. He was right there, close enough for me to reach out and grab. But I'd never be able to keep him there.

Ford had made it clear that he wasn't on Anchor to stay. He was just another tourist passing through. But one who had the power to leave wreckage in his wake. And those ruins would be me. He wouldn't even mean to do it, but I'd be destroyed all the same. It was happening already. Just those little glimpses of the banter we used to share, the comradery, the support. He'd give me those glimpses, maybe even a long, hard look, but then he'd take them with him when he left. And I would have to live with that hole in my chest all over again.

The hinges on the back door squeaked as it opened. I didn't look to see who it was, just kept staring out at the ocean. There was no one in the bar that I particularly wanted to talk to at the moment. If I didn't make eye contact, maybe they'd get the picture and leave me the hell alone.

"Why didn't you tell me it was you who renovated the bar?"

Ford's voice was rough, his tone a little bit pissed, a touch hurt. I could still read him like we hadn't been apart for over a decade. I lifted a single shoulder and then let it fall. "What does it matter?"

He yanked out the chair next to me, the metal grating against the stone patio. "It matters to me."

I kept my gaze trained on the water, saying nothing. Silence was my only armor. Each word I gave him would make it harder when he walked away, went back to his fancy LA life, and left my memories to dim.

Ford reached out his hand, snaking it under the table and resting it on mine, squeezing. The move took me by surprise, and I didn't have a chance to sidestep it. Honestly, though, I wasn't sure I would've tried. It was the first time he had touched me. The first physical comfort I'd gotten from him in eleven years. His palm seemed to burn my skin, searing itself there. I stared down at our hands. His looked different than I remembered, a little more weathered, tanner than before.

He squeezed again. "Bell...I want to fix things between us. I know it won't be easy, but I'll do whatever I can." His jaw worked. "I miss my friend."

I swallowed, a jumble of emotions gathering at the back of

my throat. "Some things aren't fixable." It was physically painful to say that, as if each word were made of a ball of barbed wire. But it was the truth. A reality I'd learned the hardest way. There were just some things that couldn't be fixed by any amount of apologies or superglue.

Ford's hand spasmed around mine. "Please. You have to let me try."

I didn't have to let him do shit. But as I stared into his blue eyes, ones that hadn't changed a bit, I found that I was still a sucker for his pain. Would do whatever I could to ease it. Even if that made me stupid. Even if it meant that I'd be hurting even more in three months' time. I swallowed that ball of emotion again. "I can't give you what we had before—" My voice hitched. "It's too hard, and I…I'm not the same person I used to be."

"Neither am I, Bell. It would be impossible for us to be those people."

"All I can give you is a fresh start. We can get to know each other as the people we are now." My gaze hardened. "I don't want to dig up the past, Ford. It's a no-go zone. You go there, and we're done." It was too hard. I couldn't go there with him when all I'd wanted for so many years was his comfort and support. To talk about Violet with the one person who'd loved her as much as I did, but who also understood us both better than anyone.

Ford gave my hand one more squeeze and then released me. Suddenly, there was air back in my lungs, as if I could finally take a breath after holding it for far too long. Still, I missed the touch just the same. "I can do that, Bell." He eased back against his chair. "Hunter and Caelyn said you're taking interior design classes."

"Those two are worse gossips than the Anchor knitting circle."

Ford chuckled. "Those ladies still at it?"

I grinned. "Worse than ever."

"So, you thinking of starting your own business?"

I rolled my lips together and looked down at my hands. "I'm not sure. I love reinventing a space, bringing old pieces of furniture back to life. I've done a few projects here and there for friends…the bar is the biggest by far, though."

What I didn't say was that the bar was meant to be my business card. Something that could show what I was capable of. But my daydreams of restoring furniture and spaces as a career had gone by the wayside when I stepped in to make sure The Catch stayed afloat.

"You did a great job."

I arched a brow at Ford. "Really? Mister fancy city, who probably pays someone hundreds of thousands of dollars to decorate his clubs, thinks my two-thousand-dollar reno of The Catch is great?"

Ford shook his head but did it while grinning. "I should've known you'd never let me live down creating swanky bars for a living."

I chuckled. "They're just so *pretty*." I said "*pretty*" as if it were a dirty word. The photos I'd seen of Ford's clubs were beautiful, but they were too perfect, everything sleek and matching. I needed something with a little more soul.

Ford's grin turned into a smirk. "You looked me up."

I shrugged. "I might've given you a Google."

He barked out a laugh. "That sounds like something dirty."

"Trust me, if Googling was dirty, I wouldn't be doing it to you."

There was a quick flare of heat in Ford's eyes before he hid it. A flame that had my stomach dipping like I was on a rollercoaster. Not once in all the time we'd spent together had I ever seen any hint of attraction, any sign that he saw me as anything but an honorary kid sister. The briefest flicker of hope tried to take root in my belly, and I immediately locked it down. I was not going there. Couldn't for many reasons. I forced my gaze away from Ford's broad shoulders and stubbled jaw.

His throat cleared. "I really did mean it. You did an amazing job with the bar. I might have to hire you away. Bring you to LA for my next project."

"You couldn't afford me, and I can't say I'm dying to visit a city where half the residents have plastic in their faces." Okay, so I was a little bitter. But it almost felt like Los Angeles was the city that had stolen Ford away. I wasn't eager to stroll its streets.

Ford laughed. "It's not that bad. There're lots of little hidden gems only longtime locals know about, and you can't beat the view from my house."

"And the access to swimsuit models."

"I won't lie and say that's a hardship."

I threw up my hands with a sound of disgust. "Men."

"What can I say, we're visual creatures. We like looking at pretty things."

I just shook my head and turned back to the ocean.

"So, how are your parents?"

The question had the bit of ease that had slipped into my muscles fleeing again. "They're the same." Nothing and no one would ever change Bruce and Heather Kipton. Not even the death of one daughter, and the fleeing of the other. Everything would always be someone else's fault. They would never consider looking around to see if they might be the cause of anything.

"They still on the island?"

"Yeah. Dad still has his practice, and Mom's still organizing events for whatever charity she's into this month."

"You see them much?"

I didn't. I barely saw them at all. I'd tried when I got back from college. Did a couple of family dinners. But each one included a pitch from Dad on taking the MCAT so I could apply to medical school and join his practice, and Mom's subtle digs at my clothes and hair. The final straw had been when my mother had wailed, "Why can't you just be more like your sister was?" when I refused to be set up with one of her friend's sons. I saw them only in passing now. And it was always awkward.

I didn't want to go there with Ford. It would feel too much like the way things used to be. I pushed to my feet. "I'd better get back to it. We're about to open."

A muscle in Ford's cheek flickered. "Of course. I'll be right in."

I headed for the bar, leaving Ford to sit and stare at the ocean—just like he'd leave me one day soon.

Chapter Eleven

Ford

THE BELL OVER THE DOOR OF THE MAD BAKER JINGLED as I pushed inside. My palms dampened as I took in the familiar sights and smells. I'd mostly been avoiding my old haunts. Hell, I'd been avoiding the shops in town entirely. They all held reminders of Violet. Of Bell. But my conversations with Bell and the guys the other day had been a wake-up call. I didn't want to lose her.

Lose her wasn't exactly the right phrase. She'd been lost to me for over a decade, but seeing her again…I knew I didn't want that to turn into forever. She might not be able to forgive me for the accident, for not facing her afterward, but maybe I could worm my way back into her life. And if there were any remnants of the girl I used to know, her stomach was a great place to start.

"Lordy be, is that you, Ford Hardy?" Jules Bloomington, the owner of The Mad Baker, stepped out from the kitchen. Her hair was all white now instead of the salt-and-pepper I remembered, her face a little more lined, but her smile was just as warm as it had always been. She rounded the counter and held out her arms. "Get over here and give me a hug, boy."

Something in my chest loosened a fraction as the older woman wrapped her arms around me. "Hey, Jules."

She squeezed me hard and then released me, smacking me upside the head as she did so. "What were you thinking, staying gone so long? We missed you around here." Her eyes narrowed ever so slightly. "That shadow of yours missed you especially."

Heat crept up the back of my neck. "I haven't been ready to come back."

"You ready now?"

"I'm not sure, to be honest. But I'm here."

She gave me a quick nod of approval. "Actions are more important than words anyway. What can I get you?"

I took in the bakery cases full to the brim with pastries, cakes, and pies. The store was aptly named, with cakes decorated in outrageous designs and baked goods in all sorts of combinations you thought would be odd but were actually delicious. "Are the snickerdoodle muffins still Bell's favorite?"

A huge smile spread over Jules' face. "They sure are, and I just pulled some out of the oven." She turned to the kitchen. "Carissa, will you grab me two snickerdoodle muffins?" I pulled my wallet out, but Jules held up a hand. "Don't even think about it. This is a welcome back gift. It does my heart good to see you coming to your senses."

I cleared my throat. "Thanks, Jules. I missed you, too."

"That girl missed you more." A wistful look filled her features. "She still comes in every Saturday like the three of you used to. Still gets an ice cream from Two Scoops every year on the day school lets out. Vi might be gone, but there are still people here who love you."

"Jules..." Her name came out as a hoarse plea. I couldn't take it. Couldn't handle her words. Just being in the bakery was almost too much to bear. The treats I used to pick up to leave in Vi's locker as a surprise. All the times we'd brought Bell here to escape the girls' parents. But when you added the pain I knew Bell had experienced because my reflexes hadn't been fast enough… It was all too much. That familiar, insidious black tar of self-hatred inched through my body in a slow wave.

"I'm sorry. I shouldn't have brought it up. I'm just glad you're back." Jules smiled at me, but it was forced now.

"It's okay." I looked out to the street. The sidewalk the three of us had walked down countless times. It felt like another life. But it was one I had to make peace with. Because if I didn't, I'd lose everything I had left: my family, the bar, Bell. I'd pushed them all to the side for so long, I'd forgotten how important they were to me. But less than a week back, and I knew I didn't want to put them on the back burner ever again. They were too important. Too vital. So, I was just going to have to deal with the past.

"Ford, do you remember my granddaughter, Carissa? She was quite a bit younger than you, but she grew up here, too."

The brown-haired girl, who looked to be in her early twenties, blushed as she handed Jules a bakery bag, and I was hit with the memory of a little girl helping Jules frost cupcakes on the weekends. "Yeah, nice to see you again, Carissa."

She ducked her head but smiled. "You were Violet's boyfriend, right?" As soon as the last word was out of her mouth, her eyes widened. "Sorry, I shouldn't have said that. I just meant that I remember you two. You guys were such a cute couple."

I fought the wince that twitched through my muscles. "It's all right."

"Well, uh, I better get back to it." Carissa turned on her heel and fled back to the kitchen.

Jules let out a little laugh, handing me the bag. "That girl is as flighty as a feral cat, but she's a damn good baker."

I forced a smile. "Must've learned from the best."

"Now don't you go kissing up to me, Ford Hardy. Those muffins are your only freebies."

"I'll pay my way next time. I promise."

"Sounds good. Don't be a stranger. And tell Bell I said hi."

"I will," I called over my shoulder as I opened the door and stepped out into the cool spring air. I headed back towards The Catch, paper sack in hand. Each storefront I passed held another memory, a mixture of joy and pain. The restaurant I'd taken Violet to on our first official date. The florist where I'd gotten her homecoming corsages. The paint-your-own-pottery shop we'd taken Bell to every year for her birthday. My chest got tighter with each step, but I didn't fight it the way I usually did. Instead, I let the memories come, passing through me from one shop to the next.

My gaze caught on a figure across the street. One all too familiar and not exactly welcome. Heather Kipton froze mid-step, her gaze narrowing into a glare. I thought that maybe there'd been a flicker of pain in her eyes, but now I only saw hatred. It wasn't the first disdainful gaze that had been sent my way since I'd returned, but it was the fiercest.

That familiar vise tightened around my ribs, making it hard to take a full breath. This was what I would have to live with, day in and day out, for as long as I stayed on Anchor. The looks that accused without saying a single word. I forced my eyes closed for a brief moment. It was worth it. For my family. For Bell. It wasn't forever, it was just one summer. I could endure anything for that long if it meant earning their forgiveness.

I blinked, my vision coming into focus again, but Mrs. Kipton was gone, almost as if she'd never been there at all. I looked around as I crossed the street, no sign of her anywhere. God, I was losing it. Or maybe my mind was simply looking for excuses to leave Anchor already. But that wasn't going to happen.

I rolled my shoulders back as I reached the door to The

Catch, pulling out my keys and unbolting the lock. I shut the door behind me, flipping the lock back into place. The lights were on, and music was playing low in the background. My gaze caught on Bell behind the bar. Her hair was piled high on her head as she stretched up on her tiptoes to count bottles of liquor on a shelf. She wore a t-shirt that hugged her curves in a way that meant torture for every guy that walked through the doors of this place today. *The Catch* was printed in distressed red lettering across her chest. I swallowed hard, forcing my gaze away. I didn't remember that anywhere in the uniform.

I cleared my throat, and Bell startled, a hand flying to that chest my eyes hadn't been able to look away from. "Geez, Ford. Give a girl a heart attack, why don't you?"

I held up the bag. "I come bearing gifts."

Bell's eyes lit up in a way that made the green seem to sparkle as she took in the bag. "Jules?" I nodded. "Snickerdoodle?"

"Yup. But one's for me."

"I'll get the coffee." She paused, her smile faltering slightly. "How do you take yours?"

It was one of those moments where we both realized that the people we were now were strangers to each other. We hadn't drunk coffee when we were in each other's lives. God, we'd been babies. Babies who'd had to grow up way too damn fast. "Black. I take mine black. How do you take yours?" I couldn't resist asking. There was so much about this Bell I didn't know, and I wanted to change that.

Her lips tipped up. "With enough sugar and cream, it might as well be a milkshake."

I chuckled. "Always did like those sweets."

"Some things never change." She headed back to the kitchen.

I grabbed napkins from behind the bar and pulled the muffins out of the sack as she reemerged. "You working on inventory?"

"Yes." She groaned as she hopped up on a stool and set down our mugs. "It's the bane of my existence."

"Well, good thing I'm here. It goes a heck of a lot smoother with help."

Bell bit into her muffin and moaned. I averted my eyes. "These are too good. I have a mental deal with myself. I'm only allowed to go into The Mad Baker twice a week. I always fail."

I laughed and took a bite of my muffin. It was even better than I remembered. "God, I missed these."

Bell shifted in her seat and said nothing. What could she say? That it was my own damn fault I missed them? That it served me right? I changed the subject. "What do you think about having auditions for bands next week? I can put an ad in the paper, maybe online somewhere?"

Bell took a sip of her coffee. "Sounds good. We should put some flyers up around town, too."

"Great idea." Silence filled the space around us. I broke off a piece of my muffin. "What's your favorite movie?"

Bell cocked her head to the side, her lips fluttering as if she were holding in a laugh. "Random much?"

I shrugged. "We're starting fresh, gotta ask you questions if I'm going to get to know this Bell person." I raised an eyebrow. "She seems like kind of a shady character, but her movie preferences might change that."

Bell chuckled. "*The Princess Bride*." Same as it had always been. There was something comforting about that. We might be different people, but there were parts of us that were the same, that recognized each other. "What about you?"

"*Die Hard*."

"The best Christmas movie ever."

I twisted in my seat to face her. "Yes! Why do people argue that it's not a Christmas movie?"

She grinned. "I watch it every year."

My mind filled with an image of Bell curled up on the couch, surrounded by pillows and blankets, eating Christmas cookies and watching Bruce Willis kick some serious ass. In that moment, I realized I didn't know what her Christmases looked like at all. I knew every detail of what their celebrations had looked like before, from the Kipton family Christmas party, to Violet and Bell's gingerbread house decorating, to how their parents used to hang Vi's and Bell's stockings on the ends of their beds. But it seemed like Bell had little to no relationship with her parents these days.

I hated the thought of her being lonely on a day that she'd always loved. Guilt crept back into me at the idea that it might be my fault. I cleared my throat. "What are your other Christmas traditions?"

There was no hint of sadness in her expression. Instead, her smile grew wider, twisting something in the cavity of my chest. "The Christmas Eve parade through town, of course. Kenna and I have a sleepover at Caelyn's. We all bring sleeping bags out into the living room and camp out by the tree. The kids love it. In the morning, we exchange gifts, and Caelyn makes a feast that would make the White House jealous."

"That sounds like a perfect Christmas."

Bell's smile turned gentle. "It is." She took another sip of her coffee. "What about you? Your family goes to LA, right?"

It had never bothered me before, asking my family to come to LA or some other destination for the holidays. But now, being back on Anchor, seeing all that I'd taken my parents and brother away from on Christmas, I felt like a selfish ass. "Yeah. I usually fly them down there, or sometimes we do Hawaii or Mexico."

Bell's face screwed up in an adorable scrunch. "It just seems wrong to be in a bathing suit on Christmas."

I laughed. "The poolside margaritas make it worth it."

"Give me my hot cocoa and freezing cold beach walks any day."

A sharp pang lanced through my chest. I missed those. Especially when I went with Trouble. She was always on the hunt for some sort of treasure: sea glass, a unique shell, a piece of driftwood in a cool shape. We'd lose ourselves on the beach for hours. Vi never wanted to go on those treks once the weather had turned. She'd always been delicate and, it seemed, too fragile for this world.

I blinked back to the present. Bell stared at me with a look of concern. "Are you okay?"

"Yeah. Just…lost in memories, I guess."

Bell laid a hand gently over mine. It was the first time she had voluntarily touched me, the first time she had reached out. The warmth that filled her flowed into my hand. She opened her mouth to say something, but then stopped herself. She squeezed my hand and stood. "Thank you for the muffin."

"Anytime." I watched as she walked away, feeling the divide between us expand with each step she took. I hated every inch of distance.

Chapter Twelve

Bell

I CROUCHED DOWN, RUNNING MY HANDS OVER THE WORN wood of the credenza. It needed some serious TLC, but I could give it that. As I stared at the piece, I could imagine it coming back to life before my eyes. Sanding it, replacing broken cabinet pulls. Maybe I'd paint it teal. That was the perfect color for this piece.

"Isabelle?"

I jerked at the sound of the name that no longer felt like mine. I stood up, wincing. "Hey, Mom. What are you doing here?" Garage sales weren't exactly my mother's typical haunts. They were one of my safe zones. I'd become a master at determining those areas on my tiny island over the past few years. Become skilled at avoiding any potential run-ins with my parents.

She smoothed invisible wrinkles in her windbreaker. "I'm just out for my morning walk." She glanced over at the array of goods on the Perkins' lawn. "What are you doing here? Does your job pay so little that you have to purchase other people's castoffs?"

My back teeth ground together. "You never know what treasures you can find at a garage sale."

My mom scrunched up her nose as if she smelled something especially rancid. "I hope you're not thinking of putting that piece in your little apartment."

"Don't worry about it, Mom. It's not your concern."

Her spine straightened. "You'll always be my concern, Isabelle."

"Please don't call me that."

"Why? It's your name."

"I've told you repeatedly, I prefer Bell." But she'd never acquiesced to my requests, just kept right on calling me *Isabelle*. My father had stopped saying my name altogether, as if by doing so, he wouldn't have to anger my mother or me. But it just made me painfully sad.

"I named you. And I didn't name you after something you find in a church steeple or on a bike's handlebars. I named you Isabelle, which is a beautiful name. I don't understand why you don't want to use it."

"I've explained it to you many times, you just don't want to hear it." I kept my voice gentle, even though I was feeling anything but. I'd told my parents that I felt like I needed a fresh start. Asked them to call me Bell instead of Isabelle. Even broke down in tears when I explained why. It had gotten me nowhere with her.

My mother huffed. "It's just childish."

"Fine, Mom. I've got to get going. I'll see you around. Tell Dad I said hi."

"Wait."

"Yes?"

She tugged on the tie of her windbreaker. "Have you heard that Ford Hardy has returned?"

I kept my face a carefully blank mask, not giving away a single hint that her question sent me back more than a decade. To a time when she'd told me that Ford had left and wanted nothing to do with me. I hadn't believed her, but my unanswered calls and unreturned text messages had proven me wrong. I met my mother's stare. "Yes."

"You will not see that boy, Isabelle."

I let out a strangled laugh, but the sound was ugly and twisted. "Whatever you want, Mother." I turned and made a beeline for Laney Perkins, ignoring the sound of outrage my mother made as I went. She had no control over me any longer.

"Hey, Bell. How are you?"

"Good, Laney. How much are you asking for the credenza over there?"

Laney winced. "That thing has been sitting in our garage for almost ten years. I should be paying you to take it off my hands."

I grinned, but it wobbled a bit, still not quite able to shake off my mother's words. "How about ten bucks, and I'll come back in an hour or two with a truck?"

"You've got yourself a deal. Can't wait to see what you turn it into."

"Hopefully, I can make it beautiful. See you a little later."

I took off down the street, abandoning my car and choosing to go on foot. The Hardys were just a couple of blocks away, and I hoped I could sweet-talk Frank into letting me borrow his truck to get the credenza back to the workshop behind The Catch. There was a slight pang in my chest at the thought. I used to bribe Frank to help me load and unload whatever furniture piece I'd purchased, but since his stroke, he just wasn't stable enough. But he was getting stronger every day, and I had to hold on to that fact.

I jogged up the familiar brick path and rang the doorbell. The door swung open, and Kara beamed at me. "Bell! Get in here. You have been far too absent from this home lately."

I stepped inside and into Kara's warm embrace. "Sorry, Kara, things have just been crazy."

"I can only imagine." She kept a hold of me, whispering into my ear. "I didn't know he was coming home. I wouldn't have stopped it, because Lord knows I want my boy as close as I can have him, but I would've given you a heads-up so you could prepare."

Her surprise confession had me sucking in a pained breath. This woman knew me so well. Understood that I'd be hurting, might have even felt betrayed. But, of course, she hadn't known. She was too kind, too empathetic, to let something like that come to pass without talking to me. "Thanks, Mama K." I hadn't called her that in years, but it seemed fitting now. "I'm glad you have him back."

I was happy for her. She'd been without Ford close for too many years. There was a fluttering in my chest, a hint of longing. The knowledge that I wanted Ford back in my life, as well. But I was too damn scared to reach for it.

Kara released her hug but held on to my shoulders. "Love you as if you were my own, Bell."

My voice hitched. "Love you, too."

"What's all this blubbering and fussing going on out here?" Frank asked as he emerged from the living room.

Kara waved a hand in front of her face. "Oh, hush, you. We're just telling each other how much we love each other."

Frank rolled his eyes heavenward but wisely said nothing about our teary expressions. He turned back to me. "You here for me to whip you in gin rummy for the millionth time?"

I laughed and cracked my knuckles. "I wouldn't mind a round or two, but I really came to see if I could bribe you out of your truck for about an hour."

Frank's expression brightened. "You find a new piece?"

"I did. A credenza at a garage sale a few blocks over. Gonna need a lot of work. Maybe you can come by the shop next week and hear my plan of attack."

Frank rubbed his hands together. "I'd love to. I'm going batty cooped up over here."

Kara cleared her throat. "Excuse me?" I couldn't hold in my laughter. Frank was going to get it for that comment.

"Love you more than life, sweetheart. But I'm gonna go crazy if you keep me locked up much longer."

Kara huffed, but her expression gentled, and she gave him a quick kiss. "You're lucky I love you, *and* that I'm willing to drive you over to The Catch next week."

"You're the light of my life." Kara scoffed, and Frank chuckled. "Come on, Bell. School me in a couple of hands of gin rummy, and then I'll toss you the keys to the truck."

I followed Frank into the living room. He settled in his recliner, and I sat on the couch. I slid out one of those tv trays that hid beside the sofa and set it up. We'd played countless hands of rummy on this tray as soon as Frank had been well enough to spend his days in the recliner instead of in bed.

"So…" Frank started as he shuffled the deck of cards.

"Yes?"

"How are things going at The Catch?"

A stiffness I couldn't seem to fight invaded my muscles. "It's going well. Ford has some good ideas."

Frank began dealing out cards. "That's good. He treating you okay?"

"He's the perfect gentleman." He had been. I had been the one trying my best to keep him at arm's length. It wasn't fair, I knew it, but it was the only defense I had.

"Good. Now, I'm not going to be the perfect gentleman." Frank grinned, a wicked one so similar to his son's. "Prepare to be trounced!"

We lost ourselves in round after round of gin rummy, laughing until my stomach hurt and just enjoying the trash talk and reminiscing. The time flew by. I glanced up from my cards and peeked at the clock on the wall. "Okay, old man, this has to be my last hand."

"She's calling me old, that means she doesn't have squat."

I laughed as I lifted a card from the draw pile. My mouth formed a smirk as I slowly stood.

Frank's face fell. "Oh, don't you dare."

With a dramatic flourish, I flipped the cards over to reveal three queens. "Gin."

"You card shark," he accused. I began my very elaborate victory dance that included my version of the running man and some lassoing moves above my head. "You know, it's not polite to shove your victory in the loser's face."

As I started to laugh, a throat cleared from the entryway, and I whirled around. Ford leaned against the wall, a smile that seemed to be holding back a laugh spread across his face. He wore a navy sweater that hugged those broad shoulders and defined chest, and dark-wash jeans that clung to muscular thighs. I swallowed hard. "Hi." The greeting came out as a squeak.

"That was some victory dance there."

My cheeks heated. "Gotta celebrate the wins in life."

"Sounds like a good plan to me."

I shuffled my feet. "Well, I better get going." I turned back to Frank. "Thanks again for letting me borrow your truck."

Frank stood and tossed his keys to Ford. "Why don't you drive Bell? You can help her get the credenza in and out of the pickup."

My eyes narrowed on Frank. "I was going to call Kenna to help me."

"But Ford's right here. So, why bother Kenna?"

Ford eyed me cautiously. "I'm happy to help."

My gaze jumped around the room, looking for some invisible excuse, a way of escape. There was nothing. "All right. Thank you."

Ford chuckled. "You sound like I just offered to give you a root canal with no Novocain."

I scowled at him. "I just don't want you to have to go out of your way on your morning off."

"Bell." Ford took a few steps towards me. "I want to help. Let me."

I swallowed the emotion gathering at the back of my throat. So many different things swimming around, and that damn longing strongest of all. I wanted nothing more than to hurl myself at Ford, to have him wrap me in his arms and tell me that everything would be okay. I straightened my spine. I didn't need that. I'd made everything okay without him. I didn't need him now.

"Let's go." My tone was clipped, cold, but it couldn't be helped.

Ford led the way out of his childhood home. I looked back to give Frank a wave and saw a look of worry etched along the lines of his face. *Crap.* I didn't want to put any added stress on the man's shoulders, that was the last thing he needed. I forced a smile and then turned to the driveway.

Ford beeped the locks on his dad's truck. "So, where's this furniture we're picking up?"

"Just a couple of blocks away. On Cedar." I climbed into the passenger seat and buckled myself in.

The trip to the Perkins' house was silent, the quiet making the drive seem twice as long. Each second made my skin itch a little bit more. I hated the way things were, it felt wrong and unnatural, but I had no way to fix it. I think that's why I loved bringing these old pieces back to life. There was so much in this world we had no control over, things, people, and relationships that were shattered beyond repair. But these forgotten tables, dressers, chairs…those I could fix, *those* I could give a second chance.

Ford pulled the truck to a stop in front of the Perkins' house. "Is that it?" He inclined his head to the credenza with a *Sold* sign on it.

"Yup." I unbuckled my seat belt and reached for the door handle.

His brows pulled together. "It, uh, looks a little worse for wear. What are you going to do with it?"

I felt too vulnerable telling Ford about the thing I loved to do most in this world. It was too personal, too intimate. Sharing my favorite movies and holiday traditions was fine, but I needed limits, boundaries. They would keep me safe when Ford bounced back to LA. "I'm just grabbing it for a friend."

Ford eyed me as if he didn't believe a word I'd said but shrugged. "All right, then. Let's get it loaded up."

Between the two of us, lifting it into the bed of the truck wasn't too bad. Frank had some rope in the cab that we used to secure the credenza, and then we were off. Five minutes later, we were pulling into the parking lot at The Catch.

I unbuckled my seat belt. "Let me grab a dolly from the shop, and I'll be right back." I jogged towards the large shed that sat on the edge of the parking lot. Just a handful of steps away from Ford, and I could breathe easier. It was as though the weights that had been sitting on my lungs had finally lifted.

I took a deep breath as I entered the shop, the scents of wood and metal filling my lungs. I let their comfort wash over me and tried desperately to fuse it to myself, to hold it close so that it could carry me through the next ten minutes. I grabbed the dolly from the corner and opened the large double doors. When I got back to the truck, Ford had already untied the credenza. "Thanks."

"No problem."

Slowly and carefully, we lifted the piece out of the truck and placed it on the dolly. Guiding it towards the shed wasn't too hard, we just had to avoid the potholes in the parking lot. Placing it in the center of the shop had me breathing a sigh of relief. We were done.

Ford looked around the space. "This place hasn't changed at all."

Memories of Ford and me watching his dad work on various projects filled my mind. We'd sit on the bench against the wall and hand Frank tools as he asked for them. I bent and picked up the dolly, placing it in the corner. "I've been keeping it tidy so it's ready for him when he's up to his projects again."

Ford was suddenly close, placing a hand on my shoulder. His touch froze me to the spot, searing my skin. I wanted so badly to lean into the touch, to silently ask for more. "Thank you, Bell. For everything." He let out a sound of frustration, his hand falling away, leaving me cold. "Thank you isn't even close to enough. I wish there were words that fit, but everything I come up with is so damn lacking."

My chest squeezed. "You don't have to thank me, Ford. I love them. I'll do whatever I can to help."

He nodded. "Come on, I'll drive you back to your car."

"Thanks." I shrugged out of the coat I'd been wearing. The sun was out in full force, and moving furniture had only made me warmer. "Let me just throw my jacket upstairs, and I'll be right back."

"I'll lock up while you do that."

I tossed Ford my keys. "The pink one is for the shed."

His brow arched. "Pink for a tool shed?"

I laughed as I jogged away. "Girls can build stuff, too, Ford."

I took the outside stairs two at a time until I reached the landing outside my apartment. I slowed and looked down. There was a package there, wrapped in brown paper and tied with twine, a slip of paper under the string. I lifted it up, pulling the note free. *Don't forget her.*

My overheated skin turned cold as I took in the sloppily scrawled words. *What the hell?* My hands trembled ever so slightly as I pulled off the twine and tore the paper. As the wrapping fell away, I sucked in a sharp breath. It was a scarf I hadn't seen in at least a dozen years. Pale pink and blue plaid. One of Violet's favorites.

My gaze darted from the scarf down to the parking lot and back again. I turned on my heel and jogged back down the stairs, forgetting all about putting my jacket in my apartment. I crossed the parking lot in long strides as Ford headed for his dad's truck.

"Were you at the bar today?" My question came out a bit harsher than intended, but I couldn't seem to hold back the anger that simmered under my skin.

Ford's brow furrowed. "Yeah for about ten minutes before I went to my parents'. Why?"

I held up the scarf. "Is this your sick idea of a gift? Like I would ever forget Vi!"

Ford's body seemed to lock as he zeroed in on the scarf. His Adam's apple bobbed as he swallowed, looking away from the fabric and back to me. "I didn't leave anything for you. That was on your doorstep?"

I took a minute to take him in, study his features for any sign of a lie. I saw nothing but the truth staring back at me. "Yeah. With a note that said, *'Don't forget her.'*"

Ford took a step closer, taking inventory of the items in my hands. "I think we should call the cops. That's not normal, Bell. For someone to come to your home and leave that? And how did they get it? It's Vi's, right?"

My stomach twisted in a painful squeeze. "Her favorite."

"That's sick. We need to call someone."

It was sick. Sick and cruel. My jaw hardened, flashing back to my run-in with my mother that morning. She wouldn't pull something like that, would she? I gave my head a little shake. "It's just someone who has zero common sense. Probably thought they were doing something nice and didn't realize how creepy it would come across."

"Bell…"

I held up a hand. "It's fine, Ford. Let's go get my car."

A muscle in his cheek ticked. "I don't like this. Promise me you'll at least tell the staff to keep an eye out for anyone lurking around."

"Sure. Now, let's go." I couldn't seem to help the shiver as I climbed into the truck, my gaze sweeping the street and the beach, looking for anything out of place. But everything was just as it should be.

Chapter Thirteen

Ford

I BIT BACK A CURSE AS BELL EMERGED FROM THE HALLWAY OF The Catch. The music and din of customers eating and drinking seemed to create a fuzzy, tunnel-like effect as my eyes zeroed in on her. The woman was trying to kill me, one outfit at a time.

Every day for the past week, there was something I wasn't able to take my eyes off of, but it was never what I expected. She didn't doll herself up in the typical bar gear or outfits that were screaming for attention. She was simply herself, a mishmash of styles with a hint of something that was uniquely Bell.

Tonight was the worst, though. And the best. The thoughts circling around in my brain were going to send me straight to hell. She wore a black knit dress that clung to her curves in a way that had my eyes tracing every dip and bend. Necklace after necklace looped around her neck, dipping in and out of her cleavage, and seeming to interweave with the tattoos peeking out from under the dress. But it was all balanced out with a pair of Chucks on her feet, as if she were saying she didn't care about what was expected, she was going to be comfortable.

I loved it. It was the Isabelle I remembered but come to life in a new way. It made me feel like the cavern between us wasn't so big, after all. But I also hated it because the desire that erupted every time I looked at Bell was quickly followed by guilt that ate away at every part of me. This was Vi's little sister. I couldn't be looking at her this way.

"Dude, you've got a little drool."

Crosby's voice jolted me out of my perusal. I cleared my throat. "You need another beer?"

He chuckled. "I'm good with this one. You should come to the bonfire after closing."

"Bonfire?" Those get-togethers used to be regular occurrences for us locals, but I hadn't seen evidence of one since returning.

"Yeah, Sunday nights are perfect because you guys close early, and the tourist crowd is already on their way back to the mainland."

I'd gone to so many over the years, almost always with Violet on my arm, loving the feel of her cuddled close as the fire burned against the backdrop of a dark ocean. I tried to touch that feeling, to grab hold of how it had felt to love her, but I couldn't. Hadn't been able to in years. It was like a photograph now, one that I could take out and look at, be so damned glad I had it, but I couldn't submerge myself in it.

Maybe time had dulled it all, the good *and* the bad. Perhaps it was that I wasn't the same boy who had loved her. One of the things that was hardest when I thought about it all was the what-if. If I would've swerved thirty seconds earlier, would Vi and I still be together? Or would college have eventually torn us apart? It was like looking at a choose-your-own-adventure book. I could see infinite possibilities for how it could've gone down, from married with five kids to broken up freshman year. But none of them felt real. They all felt like someone else's life.

"Ford, are you having a stroke, man? It's just a bonfire, I'm not asking you to build me a jet-propulsion engine."

I grinned at Crosby and rubbed a hand over my stubbled jaw. "Sorry. It's just been one of those weeks."

Crosby returned my smile. "Having the hots for your dead girlfriend's little sister will do that to a man." My body gave a small jolt at his words, and Crosby grimaced. "Sorry, that came out a little more honest than maybe it should've."

"It's not like that." It was totally like that. But I needed to bury that shit and do it fast, because the last thing I needed on the road to winning Bell's forgiveness was me drooling over her like a pathetic hound dog. She was beautiful, and I'd always loved her as a friend. It was understandable that my body and brain were going a little haywire getting to know this new and grown-up Isabelle. I just needed to put her firmly back in the little-sister category.

Crosby popped a French fry into his mouth. "She looks at you the same way."

My eyes narrowed on him. "Don't go stirring shit." Bell didn't look at me that way. She looked at me with a mix of longing and anger, as though she wanted what we used to have but knew it was impossible. And that broke my damn heart.

Crosby held up his hands. "Okay, okay. You guys figure out who left that shit on her doorstep?"

My jaw hardened. We hadn't. And Bell was taking it all too lightly. I'd put Caelyn, Darlene, and Hank on alert, and they were keeping an eye out for any customers lurking where they shouldn't be. So far, nothing. "Not a damn thing."

"Maybe Bell's right, and it was just someone who thought they were doing something nice and didn't realize how creepy it was." Crosby didn't sound like he believed a word that was coming out of his mouth.

I reached for a glass and poured two more beers, handing them to customers at the bar. "We're all keeping an extra eye out so, hopefully, whoever this is gets the picture that they can't keep that shit up."

"Then you better go to this bonfire."

"Why?" All my muscles seemed to get a bit tighter.

Crosby grinned and took the final swig of his beer. "Because Bell and her girls are going."

My jaw worked back and forth. "I'll be there as soon as we close up."

Rocks crunched under my feet as I made my way from the back patio towards the beach. The fire was blazing high, and about two dozen people milled around it. Kenna and Caelyn were laughing with Darlene. Ethan was shooting the shit with Crosby. And plenty of other familiar faces were crowded around the flames.

But my eyes searched for one figure in particular, and when they locked on her, my whole body tightened. She was standing away from the bonfire, arms wrapped around her middle, in what appeared to be an intense discussion with my brother.

Hunter reached out, his hands gripping her upper arms as he seemed to implore her to listen to him. I took two steps forward before stopping myself, the urge to rip his hands from her body so strong. But why? He wasn't hurting her. They obviously had shit they needed to work out, but seeing him touch her…it burned low in my gut.

They both seemed to freeze as Hunter said something I couldn't hear to Bell. After a moment, her head dropped to his chest, and he wrapped his arms around her. I wanted to look away, but I couldn't. I'd never been an overly jealous person. But there was no denying that's exactly what thrummed through my veins right now.

I forced myself to turn away, to head towards the fire. Crosby lifted a hand in a wave and beckoned me over. I gave a chin jerk to him and Ethan. "Hey, guys."

Ethan held up a beer. "You want one?"

I shook my head. "Naw, I'm good." A beer would only sour in my stomach at this point.

"Ford, you do any paddleboarding?" Crosby asked.

"It's been years, but I used to."

"You wanna go tomorrow morning? I'd ask this knucklehead, too, but he starts work too early for me."

Ethan chuckled. "Some of us have to work regular hours."

Crosby grinned. "Perks of running my own firm."

Ethan tipped his beer in Crosby's direction. "I don't think a cottage behind The General Store and one lawyer counts as a firm, buddy."

"Hey, now," Crosby groused, "I have an assistant, so technically, there are two employees. Therefore, firm."

I kicked at a rock by my feet. "Good to know I have someone who can bail me out if I get in trouble."

"Anytime."

My gaze caught a movement out of the corner of my eye. It was as if my brain was already trained to seek her out. Bell appeared by the fire again, Hunter at her side, not touching but close. Bell took a step towards the flames, holding her hands out to warm them. She needed a damn jacket. We were almost into summer now, but it was still freezing at night.

I started to move nearer, to give her my coat, when something in the way the firelight danced across her skin caught my eye. It was the tattoos, but it wasn't. Something under them, maybe? As though the skin almost had a silvery hue in places. It looked raised. My brain put the pieces together in fits and starts, both quickly and too slowly. "Scars." The word seemed to be pulled from my throat, raw and jagged. "She has scars."

I looked at Crosby and the guys for answers, as if they would know why, how.

"You didn't know?" Ethan asked.

"Know what?" I growled.

Ethan's jaw ticked as he looked at Bell and then back at me. "She has a bunch of scars from the accident. Got those tattoos to cover them."

"I—I have to go." The world seemed to close in around me as I rounded the fire, only one thought pounding through my mind on repeat. *I hurt her.* Not only had I stolen Bell's sister, I'd marked her for the rest of her life.

Blood roared in my ears as I reached Bell. I couldn't see anyone but her, couldn't see anything but those tattoos. Ethan was wrong, they didn't cover the scars, they seemed to wind around them as though the marred skin and ink combined to form a single image. I reached out and grabbed her shoulder. "Bell—" Her name was strangled by the emotion trying to escape my throat.

Bell's eyes flared. "What's wrong?"

"I need to talk to you."

"Okay—"

She couldn't get out another word before I was dragging her back towards the patio. The parking lot lights cast enough of a glow that I could see my way, and when I came to a stop, I saw the concern written all over Bell's face, too. She was too good. Too pure. After everything I'd put her through, she was still worried about me. "Bell…"

She gripped my hands, her skin so smooth and delicate against my own, flesh that I had torn and broken. "What's wrong?"

"I'm so sorry—"

Her eyebrows pulled together, clearly not following. "For what?"

"God, Bell. For so damn much. For driving too fast in the rain. For joking around with you and Vi instead of watching the road carefully enough. For not reacting quicker." My voice hitched. "I didn't know. I didn't know you got hurt." I reached up, unable to stop myself, laying my palm over her heart, right where her tattoos and scars peeked out from her dress. "Your scars. They're my fault. Of course you can't forgive me. You have to live with the reminder that I left you with every damn day."

Bell ripped herself away from me, eyes blinking rapidly before the green seemed to spark with fire. "You think I'm angry with you because of my scars?"

My mouth opened and closed, but I couldn't seem to find words. Of course she was angry with me because of the scars.

Bell leaned forward and placed a hand over her chest. "These scars don't make me ugly, Ford. They tell the world I'm a survivor."

Chapter Fourteen

Bell

I COULDN'T BREATHE. IT WAS AS IF THERE WERE SO MANY emotions thrumming through me, they were crowding my very muscle and sinew and overtaking my organs. I couldn't seem to suck in any air. I stormed towards the bar. I had to get away from Ford, needed distance so I could *breathe*.

I yanked open the back door and headed for the stairs. Just as I was about to reach the bottom step, a hand caught my elbow. "Bell, wait—"

I whirled on Ford, the anger and grief and every other messy, ugly, raw emotion flowing off me in waves of heat. "You left me!" Ford's hand dropped from my elbow as he staggered back a step. "You knew what my parents were like, how cold that house was. You knew I'd just lost my sister. No one would've understood my grief like you. Not a single person. Because you lost her, too. But instead of being there for me, letting me be there for you, you ran. And never once did you look back until Hunter forced your hand."

My chest heaved, and with each inhale, the air seemed to force my anger and hurt through my body in a staccato beat. "I needed you." The sentence came out as a whisper. It held all of my pain in its words. "I needed you, and you just left. Like it was the easiest thing in the world."

My gaze traveled over Ford's face. There was only one word to describe it. Ravaged. His chest rose and fell in a rhythm that matched my own. I hated his pain, wanted to reach out and pull him to me, but I couldn't. Because as much as I didn't want him to hurt, I couldn't let him close enough to cause me more pain.

"I never blamed you for the accident, Ford." It was crazy to me that he would ever think such a thing. "No one is to blame. For so long, I wished there was. Anyone or anything to focus my anger and hurt on. But it's not you. It's not the deer. It's not the rain."

Tears filled my eyes. "But you didn't give me a chance to tell you any of that." Just saying the words aloud had a hot poker piercing the cavity of my chest. Was that really the kind of person Ford thought I was? Growing up, I'd always thought he knew me better than anyone. I loved my sister, but Violet didn't understand me, my need to be my own person, to go against our parents' wishes. Kenna and Caelyn knew me, but I'd always shared a piece of myself with Ford that I'd held back from everyone else.

To have the one person you trusted with your whole self think so little of you, believe that you would blame him for an *accident* simply because he was the one behind the wheel… My muscles seized at the thought. I opened and closed my fists, trying to get the rest of myself to release. I couldn't take it anymore, it hurt too much.

"Bell—" Ford took a small step forward.

I jerked back, shaking my head. "I guess we didn't know each other as well as I thought we did." I ran up the stairs and into my apartment, slamming the door behind me. I paced the hardwood planks, back and forth. I couldn't stay here. It was as if I could feel Ford's presence through the walls.

I glanced out the window to the parking lot below. Ford's SUV was still here, but Caelyn's and Kenna's cars were both gone. I grabbed my purse and keys and headed down the outside stairs. I held my breath as I reached the bottom, as if that might make me invisible. I darted to my car and slipped behind the wheel.

I didn't let out my breath until I was a block away from The Catch. My body seemed to operate on autopilot, making each turn and stop just like I had countless times before. I parked in front of the small house on a quiet street. I closed my door as silently as possible, walking up the tidy pathway, barely taking notice of the new plants Caelyn had put in the ground for spring.

I jogged up the steps and pulled out my spare key. I ducked inside, locking the door behind me. I let my purse fall to the floor in the living room as I climbed the ladder to the loft above the space. Hoisting myself up, I slipped off my shoes and sat down on the bed.

Caelyn stirred. "Bell?" Her voice was thick with sleep. "What's wrong?"

"Can I stay here tonight?" My voice cracked, the tears flowing freely.

"Oh, Bells." Caelyn held up the covers, and I crawled in, my body shaking with silent sobs. Caelyn wrapped her arms around me in a hug. "What happened?"

It took a minute for me to even get a single word out. "Ford," I whispered between sniffles.

She nodded, understanding, not asking anything more. "I'm so sorry you're hurting." She took my hand, squeezing it. "I'm here for you, always."

"I know. Thank you." Caelyn always knew the right thing

to say—or not say. She never judged or criticized, simply supported wherever you were on your journey. I snuggled deeper under the covers. "Love you."

"Forever, sister."

I forced my eyes closed, trying to think of anything but the look of devastation on Ford's face, the feel of his betrayal across my skin. *I'm not alone.* I said it over and over again in my head until sleep finally claimed me.

⌒◎

"Bells! You're here, and it's not even the weekend!"

I grinned at Mia as I flipped a pancake on the stove. "I had an impromptu sleepover with Caelyn last night."

Her hands went to her small hips. "You had a sleepover and didn't tell me?"

I bit back a laugh. "How about we have our own this weekend?" Mia's lips pressed together as if she were considering whether that was enough to make amends. "I'll bring treats from The Mad Baker..."

She brightened. "Deal!"

Treats made everything better. I slid the final pancake out of the pan and onto the platter. "Go grab your seat, Mi, the pancakes are ready."

"Yes!" She shot her little fist into the air and ran for the table.

"Hey, Bell." Will sauntered into the kitchen. "You stay over last night?"

"I did, and my payment is pancakes."

Will's gaze traveled over my face, lingering on my eyes that I knew were still red and a little bit puffy. He didn't say a word about it, though. "I'll get everyone's drinks."

The whole crew gathered around the table. Caelyn smiled at me. "Thanks for making breakfast."

"Anytime."

The meal was filled with laughter and getting updates on what the kids had been up to at school and after this week. Ava was competing in a spelling bee. Mia was thinking about taking gymnastic classes this summer. And I even got Will to open up about what books in English class he was enjoying. It was just what I needed.

After breakfast, Caelyn and I sat on the front porch steps, keeping an eye on the kids as they waited for their buses. She knocked her shoulder into mine lightly. "How ya feeling this morning?"

I blew out a long breath. "I'm not really sure. Not as raw as last night."

"That's good." She stayed silent then, letting the quiet draw more out of me.

"He thought I blamed him for Vi's death."

Caelyn inhaled sharply. "Seriously?"

I nodded, still not quite able to wrap my head around the fact that he could think such a thing. "And he thought I was mad at him because of my scars. I don't think it ever crossed his mind that I was hurt and angry because he left. I just"—I sighed—"I thought he knew me better than that."

Caelyn rubbed a hand up and down my back. "Grief has a way of warping the way we see ourselves and the world around us. Him thinking those things, it doesn't have anything to do with you. It's because *he* blames himself."

Caelyn's words had my gut twisting, guilt swamping me. I didn't want to feel sympathy for Ford. I wanted to hold on to my anger. Because anger was a much more comfortable place for me to live than the messiness of the other emotions that swam around Ford and me. "I hate that he's been living with those thoughts in his head. But I just can't let go of my mad either."

"You're allowed to have both, Bell." Caelyn's hand stilled on my back. "You've always been all or nothing. But life is shades of gray. You can be upset and hurt and still love him."

My body tensed when she said "*love*." Of course I loved Ford. He'd been in my life since the day I was born. But the word had guilt bubbling up inside me. Guilt for the feelings I'd had for my sister's boyfriend, guilt for the strands of attraction I still felt today.

Guilt because I was here, and she wasn't.

I swallowed it all down, trying to lock it away. "For so long, I wanted nothing more than for him to come back. And now...I just wish he'd stayed in LA." Because while Ford had been gone, I'd put my broken life back together. I had been doing just fine. No, more than fine, I'd been doing great. And having him back... it was like having mostly healed stitches ripped open.

"You might not be glad now, but you will be one day."

I twisted to face Caelyn. "Why?"

She lifted a shoulder and gave me a small smile. "Because he's a part of you."

Chapter Fifteen

Ford

ASHARP BREEZE CUT IN FROM THE OCEAN AS I WALKED along the shore. I welcomed the slight sting against my cheeks. I hadn't slept a single minute last night. After Bell had stormed upstairs, I'd stood in stunned silence for...I didn't know how long.

I'd spent the night circling everything around and around in my brain, trying to figure out how I'd gotten things so wrong. I landed on one thought. Because I was selfish. I had been so wrapped up in my own grief and guilt that I'd assumed that Bell felt the same way I did. That it was my fault. That she wouldn't want the reminders my presence would bring. Sure, it hadn't helped that Heather Kipton had said that Bell didn't want to see me, but I had known to take everything that came out of that woman's mouth with a grain of salt.

It was that selfishness that had done the most damage. Not believing Heather's lies. Not my inability to avoid the deer. Not the scars that had been carved into Bell's skin. And I had no idea how to heal a wound that I'd inflicted by being so focused on myself. And it wasn't just Bell I'd hurt this way. It was my parents. Hunter. Friends from high school that I'd ignored and let fall away.

I scrubbed a hand over my stubbled jaw and turned to face the water. I wanted to fix it. To heal those relationships. But I had no idea where to even start. Wave after wave crashed into the shore. I could feel each hit. Each collision a reminder of the hurt I'd inflicted on those I loved because I couldn't deal with the past.

I inhaled deeply, the cold salt air stinging my nose. I had to face it. I might not be able to heal the past hurts, but I could keep myself from inflicting new damage. I glanced around, taking stock of where I was.

A small smile pulled at my mouth as I shook my head. I'd been walking for hours. Walking and thinking and torturing myself with all the mistakes I'd made. And I'd ended up at the base of a cliff that held the graveyard Violet rested in.

I was moving before I could think better of it. Making my way towards the beach stairs that climbed the cliffside. I hadn't set foot inside these grounds since I'd returned, hadn't even really considered it. But I knew in this moment, I needed to. I had to face it. I couldn't run anymore. It would eventually destroy me and everyone I loved.

By the time I reached the top of the steps, I was breathing heavily, part physical exertion and partly the anxiety whipping through my body. I took in the headstones dotting the well-manicured grass. There were new ones, and ones that looked to have been there for hundreds of years, battered and worn by the seaside weather.

The first step was the hardest, as if there were an invisible force field working against me. I moved forward anyway. Each step was a little easier. I wove my way through the maze of graves, scanning the names. I had no idea where Violet's was. I'd never asked my parents, and they wouldn't have dared to bring it up.

My steps faltered as I caught sight of the headstone, the rock that marked a life cut way too short. It was perfectly Violet, understated yet somehow elegant. It held her name, the dates she'd lived, and who she was. *Daughter. Sister. Child of God.* I think Violet would've liked it if she could've seen it. Who knows, maybe she could. There was nothing on the stone that represented who she was to me, though. Nothing that read *first love* or anything like that.

I wanted to be represented there somehow. I needed something that showed what she meant to me. She was my first everything. Date. Kiss. Fumbling sex. We'd grown up together. Built an innocent life, one that was full of hopes and dreams and grand plans. But it had fractured, exploded into a million pieces. Violet's pieces were irreparable. But mine, they'd come back together in a new image. One that wasn't as naïve as the old me. A reimagined person that knew the reality of loss and pain. That knew life didn't always work out as you planned.

"Hi, Vi." My voice came out ragged, as if I'd smoked an entire pack of cigarettes the night before. I licked my lips that suddenly felt as dry as the desert. "I'm sorry I haven't been by before. It was just too hard." I blew out a harsh breath. "God, that makes me sound like such a coward." I tipped my head back, shaking it and grinning up at the sky before looking back at the stone. "But if anyone would understand and be forgiving, it would be you. You always let me off the hook."

I studied the flowers around the headstone. They weren't bouquets like on the other graves. They were neatly potted plants, clearly carefully tended to. I eased myself onto the ground, leaning against the marker behind me. "Your sister doesn't brush stuff under the rug like you. Can't let it go quite so easily."

They were always as different as night and day, but those

differences seemed to stand out in even more stark contrast now. The things I'd loved so much about Violet—her gentleness, the comfort we had with each other—I didn't know if they'd be enough for me now. Just thinking about it had my gut churning. My relationship with her had always been easy. We knew each other backwards and forwards.

My mind caught on that last point. *But did we?* She knew my favorite pizza toppings and that I always sat in the middle seat of the middle row in a movie theater, but did she know the stuff that lay below? I hadn't shared with her how much I'd wanted to travel the globe. Had only hinted that I had doubted our plan of going to Seattle University and then moving back to the island to get married and start a family.

I'd loved Violet. But it was an innocent, naïve love. That didn't make it less, it simply made it part of my journey—just not the fire that would consume my entire path.

"I'm so sorry, Vi." My voice hitched as a tear escaped. "You deserved so much more. A life full of all your dreams coming true. God, I want that for you so badly. Even if I don't think I was the man to give it to you."

I leaned forward, pressing my palm to the smooth stone. "I'll always love you. But I have to let this guilt go." I would've given anything in that moment to hear Violet answer me, to hear her voice just one more time, telling me that everything was going to be okay. But all I got was the wind.

I sighed and leaned back, staring at the stone. "I hurt Bell. I hurt her, and I don't know how to fix it. If you were here, you'd help me. We'd wear her down together, no matter how stubborn she was being."

I plucked up a blade of grass and twisted it around my finger. "She's amazing, you know that? She single-handedly kept the bar afloat, helps Caelyn with her brother and sisters, and she's beautiful. God, Vi, she's heart-stopping."

I bit the inside of my cheek. "You'd be so damn proud of her. I love watching her shine." But it was more than that, words I couldn't say out loud. Places I couldn't allow myself to go, even in my head. There was this pull to Bell, low and steady but getting stronger every day. I didn't know what to do with it. I kept trying to fight against it, but I was beginning to doubt I was strong enough.

The sound of a twig snapping had my head jerking around. My eyes scanned the trees that lined the graveyard. There was a flash of movement, and then nothing. It had to be a deer. Tourists had started feeding them, and now they were as brazen as could be. But a little flicker of unease slid over my skin just the same.

Chapter Sixteen

Bell

THE SOUND OF THE BACK DOOR CLOSING HAD MY SPINE straightening and muscles tensing, but I didn't dare look up. I kept my eyes firmly focused on rearranging the bottles of liquor after I'd dusted the shelves. Footsteps echoed against the cement floors. I became singularly focused on making sure the labels were all facing out towards the bar. The scent of snickerdoodle muffins and a hint of woodsy cologne filled my senses, tempting me to turn. I refused.

A throat cleared. "I brought you the good stuff."

Slowly, so very slowly, I pivoted. I focused on the bag in Ford's hands. I couldn't seem to make myself take in his face, scared of what I might find there. "Thanks. There's coffee in the kitchen."

"Look at me, Bell." I couldn't. "Please." It was the rawness in his voice that forced my gaze to obey. There was so much pain in his eyes, agony that called to my own. I took a single step forward. "I've fucked up so many times. But nothing will ever hurt more than you thinking I didn't care. I thought about you every damn day, wanted to call, to come and see you—"

"Then why didn't you?" My tone wasn't accusing, it was matter-of-fact. I just needed the truth.

Ford set the bakery bag on the bar and scrubbed a hand over his jaw. "I've been thinking about that a lot over the past twelve hours. And there's not a simple answer."

My back teeth ground together. "I've got time." No more runaround. I needed to hear it all.

"Okay." Ford let out a long breath, steadying himself as if preparing for battle. "Did you know your parents threatened to sue me?"

My body jolted as if I'd just touched a live wire. "What?" *No.* I knew they had been angry after the accident, hurting. But threatening to sue Ford? There was no way.

He edged a little closer. "It's only part of the picture."

A sickening feeling took root in my stomach. "Can you give me the whole thing?" Violet, the accident, the wreckage left behind, it had all been a no-go zone for us. But if we truly wanted to mend things between us, we'd have to dig it all up and rip all those wounds open again.

Ford nodded. "When I woke up in the hospital, and they told me what had happened, that we'd lost Vi, the first thing I did was ask to see you. I needed to make sure you were okay. I was terrified. Scared to death that you were going to hate me forever, but I still needed to see you."

His body seemed to tremble as he took in another breath. "When I asked my parents to find a way for me to see you, they told me that your parents had refused them access. They didn't want us anywhere near you or them. When I pushed it, your mother came to my hospital room and informed me that if I contacted them or you, they'd sue me for wrongful death. God, Bell. I was so damn young. I thought I knew it all then. But looking back, I was just a kid. She said you didn't want to see me, and part of me believed her."

It was as if someone were tearing at my insides. Tears burned my eyes, trying to break free. "Ford…" I didn't know what to say after that, could only get out his name.

He shook his head. "So, I ran. Ran to school, and then LA, and tried to bury it all. The truth is, *I* blamed myself. If I had just been quicker, paid better attention, *something*, none of it would've happened. I thought you would blame me, too. But I was putting all my own thoughts and feelings on you. I was so damn focused on myself, so selfish. And I didn't think about everything you might be going through beyond losing your sister. I didn't even consider that you'd think I abandoned you."

The tears I'd been trying to hold back spilled over and ran down my cheeks. "Ford—"

"I'm so damn sorry, Trouble." The nickname was my breaking point. My knees gave way, and Ford caught me just before I hit the floor. He lifted me up, wrapping his arms around me in the tightest of hugs, whispering in my ear. "I'm so sorry." He whispered it over and over, rocking me back and forth as I sobbed.

I didn't know how long we stood there, Ford holding the majority of my weight. "It's going to be okay." He squeezed me tighter as my sobs slowed. "We're going to be okay."

"I'm sorry." I'd held so much anger in my heart for him. Thought him a coward and cruel for leaving the way he did. But he'd been broken too, and my parents had dealt a death blow on top of everything that had already happened. I gave a little jerk, startling out of Ford's arms. "Why didn't your parents tell me what mine had done?"

Ford winced. "They didn't think it was their place. And they didn't want to cause you any more pain."

That was so very Frank and Kara, never wanting to hurt me. And I'd been too scared to ask them about Ford, didn't want to hear that he was gone and never coming back. I threw my arms back around him, pressing my face into his muscled chest. His body felt different, the shape of it, the curves and edges, but the warmth felt just the same. "I'm sorry I was so angry with you. You're not the only one who's been focused on themselves."

I'd been so hurt by Ford leaving, by not having him to lean on when he was the one person I wanted, that I didn't stop to consider just how this whole thing might have warped his mind. Lies had taken root there, in his head and in his heart. And they had been screaming at him for over a decade. "It wasn't your fault, Cupcake." A tremor ran through him at my words. "Please hear me. It wasn't your fault."

Ford pulled me tighter to him, his heartbeat pulsing against my cheek. "I know. The rational part of me does, anyway. But I can't tell you how much it means to hear you say it. I never thought I'd hear those words from you."

I pressed my cheek harder against his pec. "Well, you're hearing them." Guilt took root in my belly and oozed outward. Ford had been through so much, and I hadn't once paused to consider all the ways he could be hurting beyond losing Vi. We'd both been too focused on our individual pain, drowning in it, unable to reach out a helping hand to anyone because we were struggling to simply keep our heads above water. But that season had passed, and we were stronger now. We'd healed. But in a way where some of the bones hadn't set right. We'd needed to rebreak them to ensure we walked without a limp, without pain. And now we were both broken wide-open.

"I'm so sorry my parents did that to you. I didn't know." The guilt flowed around muscle and sinew, making a home in my chest.

Ford rubbed a hand up and down my back. "I know you didn't, Trouble."

Tears threatened, burning the backs of my eyes. "I missed that."

"Missed what?"

My mouth curved into the barest smile. "You calling me 'Trouble.'"

Ford chuckled, the action sending vibrations through my body. "Never thought I'd say it, but I missed you calling me 'Cupcake.'"

My smile grew as I forced myself to release my hold on Ford and step out of his embrace. The loss of him was physically painful. His arms, his warmth, they felt too good. "I'll make sure to use it often and say it loud, especially in front of customers."

He grinned, shaking his head. "I'm gonna regret admitting that, aren't I?"

I pressed my lips together, trying to hold back my laugh. "You should've known."

Ford's smile turned gentle, a wistfulness filling his features as though he had lost himself in a memory. "I should've."

I wanted to know what he was seeing, the scene he was lost in. Was he picturing the girl he'd left behind? The one who had been all knees and elbows. Or something else altogether? I cleared my throat. "After the lunch rush, you wanna go somewhere with me?"

Ford studied me carefully. "Always."

My stomach clenched. "I'll talk to Caelyn and Darlene; see if they can cover for us." Ford nodded. "Don't eat lunch."

"Okay."

It was as simple as that for Ford. He didn't have the baggage that I did. Because I'd loved this man all my life. Adored him as a toddler when I'd chased him around the back yard, my little legs not getting me where I wanted to go. Crushed on him in middle school when I watched his football games with Vi. I'd fallen head-over-heels when he told me that I was worthy even if I didn't want to be a doctor like my sister and father. I'd loved him forever, and the price I'd have to pay now was the guilt. Guilt and knowing I'd never have the one thing my heart wanted above all others. Him.

Chapter Seventeen

Ford

I PUSHED OPEN THE DOOR TO THE PARKING LOT, HOLDING IT for Bell. "You sure you don't want me to carry that?"

"Nope." She smiled up at me with that mischievous grin I used to see so often on her face. But it affected me differently this time, stirred something deeper. And at the same time, there was a painful pleasure in it, regaining something I'd thought was lost to me forever.

"Want me to drive?"

"Sure, I'll play navigator," she said.

I headed towards my SUV, and Bell let out a low whistle. "Fancy."

Heat crept up the back of my neck. My family had always been solidly on the lower end of middle class. We never struggled to put food on the table, but my parents hadn't been driving Mercedes G Wagons either. It had always been the Kiptons with the nice cars and the elaborate home. Bell had never seemed to care much about that stuff, but I wondered how hard it had been to give it all up when she went her own way. "There's so much I want to know."

The words tumbled out before I could stop them, and Bell's steps faltered. "What do you mean?"

I pulled open the passenger door to my SUV, but Bell didn't get in, just kept staring at me, waiting for me to answer. "I've missed so much. There's just a lot to catch up on." I wasn't sure what her reaction would be to that. I'd missed so much because of my own stupidity and selfishness. Maybe she wouldn't want to spend the months I was sure it would take to catch me up on even just the important stuff.

Bell's expression gentled, and she reached out to lay a hand on my biceps, the warmth of the touch filling me with a peace that had been missing for far too long. "We've got all the time in the world…Cupcake." That devious smile was back. "Plus, I need to hear about all the famous people you've met. It sounds like you were friendly with at least a model or two."

I winced. I hadn't been a manwhore really, but if I'd needed companionship for a night or two, it hadn't exactly been difficult to get. It had waned over the years, though. The encounters had become empty, and yet I hadn't been willing to reach for more. Not even seeing my friends Austin and Liam find incredible women to settle down with had prompted me to take that risk. I cleared my throat. "Famous people are overrated."

Bell laughed. "Oh, you jaded LA soul."

I grinned and helped her up into the SUV. "It does get old after a while." I'd gotten restless over the past year, as if everything that gave me a thrill about running my bars had grown dull. I needed a new challenge or something. I just had no idea what that might be.

Bell buckled herself in but turned to face me before I could shut the door. "Maybe you've just been missing the things that give life heart. It's not always the big, glamorous accomplishments. Sometimes, it's the everyday things that have meaning."

She wasn't wrong. And I had basically crapped all over that everyday stuff. My parents. My brother. The Catch. Bell. I'd let them all down. There was nothing I could do to change the past, but I sure as hell could do something about the future. "You always were wise beyond your years."

Bell's nose crinkled as she gave me a mock scowl. "Always looking at me as the baby."

I closed her door, careful to do it gently. If there was one thing I was sure of in all of this, it was that I no longer saw Bell as anything childlike. It would be a hell of a lot easier if I did. I rounded the front of my vehicle and climbed inside. "So, where to?"

Bell nibbled at her bottom lip and twisted her fingers in the sack that rested on her lap. I turned in my seat so that I was fully facing her. "What's wrong?"

Her gaze lifted to meet mine. "I wanted to take you with me to do this thing I do every week or so. But now I'm wondering if that was a horrible idea."

"Why don't you tell me what you were thinking, and then I'll let you know if it's as bad of an idea as that one time you wanted to go cliff jumping in November."

Bell chuckled. "Hopefully, it's not that bad." She released her hold on the bag, her eyes never leaving mine, carefully assessing any reaction I might have. "I like to take picnics to Vi's grave." My heart stuttered in my chest, but I didn't say a word. Bell pressed on. "I miss her. Miss talking to her. Even when she didn't understand me, she was always *there*. So, I go and eat lunch and tell her about my week. Share crazy stories from the bar, what I'm reading, any whale sightings I've had."

"She always loved the orcas."

Bell pressed her lips together and nodded. "She did." We were silent for a brief moment. "Do you think it's weird?"

Some people might find it morbid, bringing a picnic lunch to a grave. I'm sure people in town gossiped about it like crazy. But I knew the heart behind it. "I went there for the first time yesterday."

Bell sucked in a sharp breath. "How was it?"

"A lot less painful than I thought it would be. It was kind of nice." I ran a hand through my hair. "That's not the right word. It was peaceful. Like there was another little piece of closure. I can see why you like going there."

"Do you want to go with me?"

The hope in Bell's eyes damn near killed me. "Yes, I want to go with you."

Bell let out a shaky breath. "Okay. I had Hank make your favorite." She lifted the bag in her lap.

"Turkey club, extra cheddar?"

"And fries with honey mustard." My stomach growled at her words, and Bell dissolved into laughter. "It's good to know some things haven't changed."

"Never have, and never will. I swear that turkey club has haunted me." I pulled out of the parking lot and started towards the graveyard where Violet rested, the music of Bell's laughter lightening the pressure in my chest as we razzed each other about past memories. God, I'd missed this. So much it seemed impossible that I'd stayed away this long.

I pulled to the side of the street opposite the church, and Bell grew serious. "You really don't have to do this if you don't want to."

I reached over and gently took her hand in mine, giving it a squeeze. "I want to." I studied her light green eyes, noticing the small flecks of gold that dotted their depths. "I promise."

"Okay. Let's go."

I released Bell's hand, immediately missing the comfort and warmth. I reached into the backseat for a blanket that was always back there and hopped out of my SUV. My heart took another stutter-step as I took in the headstones, that guilt eating at me a little more. I kept my feet moving as Bell and I crossed the street and headed into the graveyard. But I wasn't sure how I would be able to handle witnessing Bell's grief up close and personal. I didn't think I'd be able to not assume that blame.

A familiar pressure seized my chest, but I refused to abandon Bell again. I wasn't going to leave her alone in this, even if it hurt worse than anything I could imagine. I followed Bell as she wove through the headstones, each step cranking the vise around my rib cage a little tighter.

We came to a stop at the now-familiar marker. As I laid out the blanket, Bell bent and pressed her lips to the top of the head-stone. "Hey, sissy. Guess what? The trio of terror is reunited." The action was so like Bell, not caring in the slightest that someone might think her odd for kissing her sister's gravestone. But it was her tone that nearly knocked me over. It was happy, so damn joyful.

Bell had always surprised me, so I should've planned on her shocking me now too, but I hadn't. She wasn't angry or bitter that her sister had been taken from her far too soon. And she didn't blame me for the accident. She was simply happy to have the three of us together in the only way we could be.

Bell set the bag down on the blanket and immediately began tidying the potted flowers. She cleared away fallen leaves, popped off blooms that had passed their prime, and then pulled a water bottle from the bag and began to water the pots.

I settled onto the blanket and watched her work, marveling at the focus, the tenderness. "You did all of this, didn't you?"

Bell finished pouring the last bit of water into a pot. "I did." She surveyed the greenery and the blooms around her. "I like making it beautiful for her."

I sensed that was true, but also that she was holding something back. I didn't blame her. I hadn't proven myself to be a worthy holder of her secrets yet. But I would, eventually. "It's the prettiest one here."

Bell settled onto the blanket and started pulling things out of the bag. "I always was damn competitive."

"I'm not going to argue that one." Bell had always wanted to run faster, jump higher, and play with the big kids. I grinned down at my lap as I remembered that she'd tricked her mom into signing a permission slip to let her play flag football by telling her it was a form for cheerleading. Heather Kipton had been appalled when she and her husband showed up at the field, expecting to see their daughter dressed in a cheer uniform, and instead found her in football garb and playing with boys two and three years older than her.

"What are you grinning like an idiot about?"

I couldn't hold in my laugh. "Flag football."

Bell groaned, flopping onto her back. "I was grounded for a month."

"They let you keep playing, though."

She turned onto her side to face me. "Only because it would've meant admitting their daughter had tricked them if they pulled me out."

I bent forward and picked up one of the bar's to-go boxes. "That's true." I opened the lid and saw a panini. "No more grilled cheese?" That had always been Bell's favorite.

She sat up and swiped the box from me. "This is just a classed-up version of a grilled cheese. Mozzarella, tomato, basil, with a little balsamic."

"That sounds good. New menu item?" I hadn't perused the menu much since I'd been back. I'd been too focused on numbers and thinking up ways to bring more bodies through the door.

Bell nodded as she chewed a bite of her sandwich. "Yup. We wanted to add a few items that might speak to the Seattle crowd.

This was one of the first things Hank tried." Bell grinned as she shrugged. "Who knew I had fancy-schmancy Seattle tastes?"

I grinned and pulled out my club. "Variety is the spice of life."

"But it's the old favorites that always taste the best."

I swallowed hard, my bite of sandwich sticking in my throat. "I'm seeing that now."

"Good."

I cracked open one of the two Cokes from the bag and took a sip. "So, what do you usually do now?"

Bell glanced at the headstone. "Tell her about my week. Like I found an especially obscene piece of driftwood on my walk this morning."

I arched a brow. "Obscene how?"

"It looked like a hooked dick." Bell held up her finger, hooking it slightly to punctuate her point.

I nearly spit out the sip of Coke I'd taken. "I'm sorry, what?"

Bell laughed, pulling out her phone and showing me a photo she'd taken. It honestly looked like a crooked cock. It even had a bulge at one end that looked like balls. I laughed so hard, my eyes began to water. "Why did you take a photo?"

"I needed proof for Kenna and Caelyn. Kenna would've never believed me."

I shook my head, grinning. We kept talking, to each other, to Vi, trading funny little anecdotes about our past week or two. We never ventured into anything too serious, as if both of us were still testing the waters. But the warmth of the afternoon sun, the excellent food, laughter, and simply being together took root in my chest, clearing all the pressure that had made a home there. It was the first time in over a decade that the vise was totally gone.

Nothing but peace remained.

Chapter Eighteen

Bell

"**G**IRL, THOSE GUYS AT TABLE SIX ARE GIVING YOU the business."

I chuckled as I set a series of pint glasses down on Darlene's tray. "You know my rule about customers."

She waved a hand in front of her face as if shooing away a bug. "Yeah, yeah. If you need to get you some, go somewhere else."

"It's always worked out well for me." But now that I thought about it, it had been far too long since I'd come close to getting myself even a hint of anything. No dates, no kisses that made me long for more, and certainly no sex. I'd been too caught up in the bar, my restoration projects, and helping Caelyn with her siblings. Maybe it was time to take a night off and convince the girls to go out on the town. Perhaps even in Seattle.

"Heeeellloooo, Earth to Bell. You thinkin' about gettin' yourself some?"

I winked at Darlene. "Maybe I am."

She picked up her tray. "Good for you. Those guys at table six are hot."

"I'll take it under advisement." I turned and almost crashed into Ford. "Whoa."

He reached out a hand to steady me, his palm seeming to sear the skin at my elbow. "What was that all about?"

My brows pulled together. "What? Darlene?"

"Yeah."

I sidestepped Ford and began fixing a Jack and Coke. "Oh, nothing. She's just trying to get me to break my rule."

Ford stepped in closer, the heat of his body seeping into my back. "Your rule?"

I shot the Coke into the rocks glass. "Yeah. I don't sleep with customers." Ford let out some sort of strangled sound, and I glanced over my shoulder to see redness creeping up his neck. I clenched the glass tighter. "You know, I am a grown woman, Ford. I do have sex."

He cleared his throat. "I know you're not a kid, Bell."

"Good. Now, if that's settled, you have some customers waiting on you." I inclined my head towards his end of the bar. Ford opened his mouth as if to say something and then closed it again, heading for the patrons flagging him down. Ford might know that I was an adult woman in theory, but I was pretty sure he'd always see me as that gangly fifteen-year-old in his mind. And didn't that just burn?

I slid the Jack and Coke across the bar. "Here you go, Ethan."

"Thanks, Bell. Things look busier in here. Even after the dinner rush."

I scanned the crowd. There were a heck of a lot more people than usual, and I think that was in large part because a band was about to take the stage. Ford hadn't wasted any time getting a few different acts lined up, and it looked like his play was going to work. I glanced down the aisle to see none other than Lacey

Hotchkiss with her boobs resting on top of the bar as if they were a platter for Ford to feast from.

Lacey and I had never become friends, much to my parents' chagrin. But we'd mostly stayed on opposite corners of life on the island. She hadn't once been into The Catch since I'd worked here. Of course, now that Ford was back, here she was. I was honestly surprised it had taken her this long. My stomach roiled as the two of them laughed, Lacey flicking her long, blond hair over her shoulder. I gripped the edge of the bar and forced my gaze back to the man in front of me. "Uh, yeah. I think people are excited about the band."

Ethan nodded. "That was a really smart idea."

I busied myself wiping down the bar. "It wasn't mine."

"Whose was it?"

Ethan blanched, coming to the realization that Ford was behind the live music. "Don't worry. Ford and I have gotten over our bad blood."

Ethan studied me carefully. "You sure? It takes a lot to get you riled up enough to pour a beer over a man's head."

I grinned. "And let that be a warning to you to never piss me off." He held up his hands in surrender. "So, where's your boss?" I hadn't seen much of Hunter since we'd buried the hatchet at the bonfire.

Ethan took a sip of his drink, then set it on the bar. "He'll be here in a bit. Just wanted to stop by his parents' and see if they needed anything."

"Good. I miss seeing his ugly mug around here."

Ethan grinned. "Make sure you tell him just how ugly it is."

"Always do. Can't have all the attention the ladies lavish on him going to his head."

Ethan lifted his drink in a toast. "Amen to that."

"Speak of the Devil."

Hunter slid onto the empty stool, and Ethan gave him a

friendly slap on the back. "What? You guys talking about how amazing I am?"

I stepped up onto the shelf under the bar so I could lean over the counter. I grabbed Hunt's face in my hands and laid a smacking kiss on each cheek. "Actually, we were just talking about how ugly you were."

Hunter let out a deep chuckle. "That cuts deep coming from you, Bell."

There was a prickling sensation on the back of my neck as I stepped down from my perch. I scanned my surroundings, my gaze catching on Ford. A muscle in his cheek ticked wildly. Lacey reached out a hand, settling it on his biceps. I couldn't watch, it burned something deep in my belly as if acid were festering there.

I startled at the hand on my shoulder. I must've been staring for longer than I thought, because Hunter was now at my side behind the bar. "What's wrong? Is Ford giving you trouble?"

Something about the question had tears burning the backs of my eyes. I wanted to scream "*yes*," say that Ford was giving me the worst kind of trouble, the kind that reminded me of how I had pined for the boy who was my sister's. How I'd wished he were mine. I'd wanted it so badly that a part of that sixteen-year-old girl I'd been had worried that I'd willed my sister's death into being. God, it had been so long since any of those thoughts had taken root in my mind. I thought I'd banished them for good. But all it took was Ford walking back into my life for me to realize they were still there, just simmering below the surface.

"Bell?"

I looked up into Hunter's concerned eyes. "No, I'm fine. Ford and I made our peace."

"Then why do you both keep looking at each other like you're tempted to commit murder?" His gaze flicked back and forth between Ford and me, his jaw tightening. "Or…rip each other's clothes off."

Heat flared in my cheeks. Ford certainly didn't want to rip off my clothes. He probably just couldn't handle the idea of the girl he'd always looked at as a little sister talking to men. Heaven forbid. I had a sudden urge to lay one on Hunter just to make a point. And not only on his cheeks this time. "We're just figuring out our new normal, and Ford needs to get used to the idea that I'm no longer a sixteen-year-old girl. I can handle myself."

Hunter let out a chuckle and pulled me into a side hug. "He always was overprotective of you."

I grumbled a few choice profanities under my breath. Ford had always gone a little over the top when looking out for me. I was pretty sure he'd threatened bodily harm to all of the boys at the high school if they were to take advantage of me. It got so bad that none of them would even talk to me for the first year. And when I'd wanted to learn to skateboard, Ford had made me promise that I'd only do it with him and then had proceeded to buy every sort of protective gear the local sporting goods store sold. I'd looked like the Michelin Man waddling out to learn that first lesson.

"Well, he needs to learn that I can take care of myself," I grumbled.

Hunt gave me a hard squeeze and released me. "He will." He eyed his brother. "And if he gives you any shit, just let me know, and I'll pop him one for good measure."

Hunter looked a little too happy at the idea of punching his brother. I grabbed his biceps, bringing his focus back to me. "We're fine. And look how busy the bar is. That's all on Ford."

Hunter's mouth pressed into a hard line as he scanned the crowd. "We'll see if it lasts."

I sighed. Ford and Hunter needed to make peace. For their parents, if nothing else. But I really wanted that peace for both of them. I'd have given anything for just another day with my sister, and these two idiots were squandering the second chance they had right in front of them. "Give him a shot to make this right… for me?"

Hunter's expression gentled. "I'll try. But only for you." He bent, kissing the top of my head before he headed back around the bar.

I turned back to Ethan. "So, refill?"

"I think I'm good," Ethan said, holding up his still half-full glass.

"All right. I'm going to see if Darlene needs any help on the floor. Just flag Ford down if you need another."

Ethan grimaced, looking from Ford to Hunter and back again. He was probably debating if asking for another Jack and Coke would end in a fistfight between brothers. I really hoped not.

I wove my way through the crowded tables, flagging Darlene down. "You need any help?"

Darlene blew her bangs out of her face. "Can you get refills for table six?"

"Sure thing." I was halfway back to the bar before I realized that table six was the group of hot guys Darlene wanted to foist on me. I groaned but filled pint glasses and placed them on a tray before heading for the table in the back corner. I studied the men as I approached. Definitely tourists. Wealthy, from the looks of things. Collared shirts and sweaters that probably cost more than I made in a night here. Darlene was right, they were good-looking, but they weren't my type.

I unloaded the glasses, one at a time, onto the table. "Here you go, boys. Need anything else? Something to eat?" The last thing I needed was them getting shitfaced and making a scene.

A guy with sandy-blond hair and blue eyes gave me a grin. It was a smile I knew he'd used on countless women before. One that probably got him what he wanted nine times out of ten. But all I could think was that his eyes weren't quite blue enough, and his hair was too blond. "We could actually use some tips from a local."

I put on my polite hostess mask. "Sure, what are you looking for?"

Blondie leaned back in his chair. "Good restaurants. Places to hike. Anything that we shouldn't miss."

I tucked the tray under my arm. "The Mad Baker is my favorite breakfast spot. The General Store has great sandwiches, and they can pack you lunches for day hikes. I'd check out the trails around the bluff and maybe do a kayaking trip for some whale watching."

"Sounds like there's a lot of great stuff to do around here."

"There is. The General Store has tons of brochures for more activities, too."

"Thanks." The guy gave me another of those flirty smiles. "Want to take that kayak trip with us?"

Before I could open my mouth to politely decline, a heavy hand landed on my shoulder and sent shivers down my arm. "Excuse me, gentlemen. I need to steal Bell away."

Ford steered me away from the table and back towards the hallway. I was so stunned by his move that I didn't even fight him. But when we hit the hall, I shrugged out of his hold. "What the hell, Ford?"

His expression was relaxed, but the set of his shoulders gave him away. "I didn't like the way those guys were looking at you."

My mouth opened and closed like a fish on a line. "You didn't like the way they were looking at me?"

"No." The statement came out on a growl. "It—it was like they were undressing you with their eyes." He could barely get the words out, as if the idea were appalling to him. He might not want me, but some men did.

I threw up my hands. "News flash, Ford, this is a bar. Guys are going to check me out. Some girls, too. I'm used to it. And I know how to handle myself. If someone gets out of line, I'll remove them or have Hank help me do it. I don't need you swooping in and ruining tips for the waitstaff or me."

The muscle in Ford's cheek flickered. "There were five of them, and one of you. It's not safe."

I let out a growl of my own. "I have been taking care of myself for a long freaking time. I don't need any help doing it now." I forced myself to ignore Ford's flinch. "And you're not actually my big brother, you know."

I stormed past him, but not before I heard him mutter, "Trust me, I know."

Chapter Nineteen

Bell

I MOANED AS I TOOK A SIP OF THE COFFEE. "I NEEDED THIS way more than yoga this morning."

"Yoga would probably help that black cloud following you around a lot more than loading yourself up with caffeine."

I scowled at Caelyn. "I didn't sleep well last night. This coffee is keeping me from murdering people." The truth was that I'd tossed and turned all night long, replaying the argument with Ford over and over in my head. Now that I had him back in my life, I hated the idea of us being at odds. But there was so much baggage with our friendship, and part of me wondered if it was even possible for us to not blow up at each other.

Kenna tipped her face towards the early morning sun. "I'll take caffeine over yoga any day."

Caelyn twisted on the bench to face Kenna. "You're even worse because you drink all that fake sugar and fat-free creamer in your coffee."

Kenna kept her eyes closed. "Don't start with me on that crap, C."

"All right, you two. We each have our own ways of functioning, and let's just leave it at that."

Caelyn settled back in her seat, watching the boats load up for the day. "Fine."

Kenna let out a husky laugh. "You sound like a pouting toddler. Not everyone is down for your level of healthy living."

"I'm not that bad."

Kenna snorted. "You won't even let the kids have soda."

"I occasionally let them have cane soda."

"That's not the same thing, and you know it."

I grinned at my two best friends, trying to hold in my laugh. "You know, Will has a secret stash in the garage." The poor kid had hidden candy, soda, and chips out there. When Kenna and I found out, we started adding to his supply.

Caelyn straightened in her seat. "He does not."

Kenna choked on her laugh. "In the old army chest in the corner."

"That little bugger."

"Caelyn," I warned. "Do not throw out his food. He's fifteen, he needs a little junk in his life."

She sagged back against the bench. "Oh, fine." She looked back out to the water. "I did wonder why he never asked for dessert."

"Because your idea of dessert is some all-natural carob thing." Kenna eyed the whole-grain muffin in Caelyn's hand.

"Hey, carob is basically chocolate."

I held up a hand. "Not even close."

Caelyn's attention suddenly darted back to the dock, and she sighed. "I want to climb that man like a tree."

I let out a strangled sound that was part laugh and part cough. "What?" I followed her line of sight to a hulking frame striding down the dock. Not only was the man tall and broad, but he also wore an expression that threatened bodily harm to anyone who got in his way.

Kenna groaned. "What is it with you and the brooders?"

Caelyn shrugged. "Their waters look smooth and quiet, but they always pack a punch."

I shook my head as I watched the man disappear into the marina shop. "I think it's probably a good idea for you to stay away from Griffin Lockwood."

"Why?"

The look of hopeful innocence on Caelyn's face was reason enough right there. She always thought she'd be the woman to fix the broken guys, and it had burned her more than once. But she didn't need me to remind her of any of that. I forced a smile. "Because he could eat you."

Caelyn waggled her eyebrows. "Maybe I want him to."

"Gross. I do not need to hear about that," Kenna groused.

"No, you just need some sexual exploits of your own."

Kenna turned to face me. "I think we should talk about Bell's love life."

The mask slipped over my features without me consciously putting it in place. "I have no love life currently, you know that."

"Hmmmm." Kenna drummed her fingers along the side of her coffee cup. "So, what about the scene last night at The Catch?"

My spine stiffened. "Who told you about that?"

"I ran into Crosby when I was getting our coffees. He was at the bar last night, for too long judging by his rumpled state this morning." Kenna let out a little huff.

"What did he say?"

Little worry lines appeared between Kenna's brows. "He told me Ford pulled you away from a table full of guys. Said he didn't look too happy about the attention they were paying you."

This was the problem with living on a teeny-tiny island. Everyone knew everyone else. And they all loved spreading gossip. I was going to pour salt in Crosby's beer the next time I served him. It wasn't that I didn't want to share what had happened with Kenna and Caelyn—I told them everything—it was just that I hadn't wrapped my head around it yet.

Caelyn took a sip of her tea. "Ford does seem pretty protective of you."

"Yeah, like a little sister," I grumbled into my coffee.

"And the problem with that is?" Kenna asked.

Caelyn reached around me to smack Kenna's knee. "You know what the problem is."

Of course they already knew. They'd known since the day I first started having those butterflies take flight in my belly when Ford was around. They'd listened to my fears that I'd never feel for anyone the way I felt about him. And they'd held me as I sobbed when I learned that he was gone for good. So, of course, they knew those feelings wouldn't just up and vanish.

"Maybe I need to sign up for one of those online dating sites or apps." It's not like I had dated a lot in college and after, and it had to partially be a numbers game. If I put myself out there enough, there had to be someone who'd make my skin tingle and my soul feel at peace the way Ford did. I just hadn't tried hard enough to find them.

"Are you trying to get murdered?"

"Kenna," Caelyn scolded.

"What? Those places are a breeding ground for serial killers and sexual predators."

I grimaced. "I'll be safe. Meet in a public place, not give out my phone number."

"Everything's searchable these days, Bell."

"We could double." I looked to Caelyn. "Or triple?"

Caelyn held up her hands. "Oh, no. You're not dragging me into this. I'm perfectly happy with my fantasy life with Griffin the Greek god."

I grinned at her but underlying it was just a hint of worry. The last thing she needed was to build that broody man up in her mind to something he wasn't. "Okay, fine. But I have to try something, and it's not like there are a lot of options on an island of fifteen hundred people."

Kenna turned in her seat so she was facing me, tucking one long leg under her. "What's with the sudden desperate urge to date?"

Emotion clogged my throat. "I have to get over him. I thought I was. For the past eleven years, all I've felt was anger." Anger and maybe a little sadness for all that I'd thought Ford had thrown away. "But all it took was one look at him in the flesh to know I'd been lying to myself all along."

I looked out at the ocean, dark gray waters rippling and swirling. "At first, I was still so angry with him. He'd betrayed me. Spit on the bond we had. Left me in my worst moment. But when I realized what was happening, how much he'd been hurting, what my parents had done...I didn't have any anger left."

"I still can't believe they pulled that crap," Kenna muttered.

Caelyn made a hushing sound at Kenna, sensing that I needed to get this all out now. "When I didn't have my anger to hold on to, all I had left was my longing. That and my guilt."

"Oh, Bell." Caelyn wrapped an arm around me, squeezing in close.

"I thought maybe he'd turned into a fancy asshole in LA. But at the end of our shift, I saw him wrapping up the extra food to send home with Darlene. He knows she has two kids at home, and her ex is so far behind on child support it's ridiculous. He's kind to all the staff, he's working his ass off, and dammit, I *missed* him. I missed talking to him about the important stuff and about the things that don't matter. I thought I might've blown that out of proportion in my mind, romanticized it or something, but I didn't."

Caelyn gave my shoulder a squeeze. "Then you should go for it, honey. You know better than anyone that you only get this one precious life."

Kenna's gaze snapped to Caelyn. "No, she shouldn't. That man has done nothing but hurt her and leave her when she needed him the most. He doesn't deserve her."

I swallowed back the invisible razor blades that seemed to be crawling up my throat. "It doesn't matter, I can't."

"Why not?"

It was Kenna who answered. "Because she feels like she'd be betraying Violet."

Caelyn's head snapped back in my direction. "Is that what you really think?"

I gave a tiny nod. It was so much more complicated than that, though. There were so many layers of guilt and grief and anger and longing. And they all mixed together in an ugly stew that meant there would never be a happy ending for Ford and me. Not in the way I truly wanted anyway. I would have to settle for having him as my friend. I just had to make myself believe the lie that friendship would be enough.

Chapter Twenty

Ford

"FORD HARDY."

I looked up from my phone at the crisp tone, shoving it into my back pocket. I bit back a groan. "Mrs. Hotchkiss. Lacey."

"Hey, Ford." Lacey blinked up at me as if the fluttering of her eyelashes was sending some sort of Morse code.

Mrs. Hotchkiss's gaze narrowed on me. "I heard you were back."

"That I am."

"You should've stayed gone."

"Mom!" Lacey's cheeks heated as she gripped her mother's arm.

Mrs. Hotchkiss turned to her daughter. "It's the truth. He should hear it."

My back teeth ground together. "I'm just here for a few months, helping my family out."

Her gaze snapped back to me. "With no regard for the family

you destroyed, for how much pain it will cause them to see you here."

My gut twisted. "I'm not trying to cause anyone pain, but my family is here, so there's no way around it."

"You sure stayed away long enough before. But now you're back, and it's breaking Heather's heart. And I can't imagine how painful it must be for Isabelle to have to see you at work every day. You need to stay away from that girl, from her family. Grant them whatever semblance of peace they have left."

"I've got to be real honest, Mrs. Hotchkiss, this is none of your damn business." I sidestepped her as she gasped and then strode in the direction of The Catch.

"Ford, wait!"

A hand caught my elbow, and I spun around. "What?"

Lacey's cheeks were red, and she was out of breath. "I'm sorry, she's just very protective of Mrs. Kipton, and Mrs. Kipton has been really upset that you're back and working with Isabelle."

"Like I told your mother, it's none of their damn business."

Lacey reached out a hand, laying it on my forearm. "You're right, it's not. Why don't we go over to The Mad Baker? We can get a cup of coffee and talk."

I stepped out of her hold. "I've got to get to work."

"Violet would want you to be happy. Maybe if we talked, it would help you realize you can move on."

I didn't have words for the woman in front of me. She might've been Vi's friend, but I'd never liked her, and now, she was basically a stranger. If she thought I'd open up my wounds to her, she had another thing coming. Before I could tell her as much, Mrs. Hotchkiss called from down the street. "Lacey, get away from that boy. We need to go."

Lacey glanced at her mother and then back to me. "I'm sorry. I'll come by the bar soon. We can talk."

"There's no need." My words were cold, but it couldn't be helped.

Lacey let the hurt show in her expression. "You're hurting. I get it."

"No, you don't, and you never will." Before she could say anything else, I turned and headed towards the bar. This was what life on Anchor would always be like, some random person sticking their nose in my business and telling me how they felt about my life, what they thought I needed to do to *heal*. Or worse. Bell might've forgiven me, but there were plenty of people on this tiny island who hadn't.

As I reached the gravel lot in back of The Catch, my phone buzzed in my pocket. Pulling it out, I hesitated for only a moment before hitting accept. "Hey, man."

"Ford, how's island life?"

I paused for a moment, unsure how to answer that one. It was both torture and exactly where I needed to be. There were moments, like the one I'd just encountered, that heated my blood and brought back my worst memories. But there was also a sense of peace on Anchor that I'd forgotten about, something that I'd never find in LA. There was comfort in having my family close. And there was something altogether different about having Bell within arm's reach. Something that I both wanted to lean into yet didn't want to look too closely at.

The hesitation as my mind spun cost me, because as one of my closest friends, Austin knew when something was up. "What's wrong? Is your dad okay?"

I cleared my throat and started walking again, headed for the beach. "Dad's fine. There's just a lot of baggage in this place for me."

Austin was quiet for a moment. "Family stuff?"

Guilt gnawed at my gut. Austin had always been nothing but honest with me. Sure, he'd held his emotions close to the vest, but he'd never hidden huge events of his past from me. I'd hidden what felt like an entire other life from him and our other friend, Liam. "That's part of it. There's some stuff in my past…" I struggled with finding the right words. How did you tell someone something like this? "The summer before I left for college, I was in an accident. My girlfriend and her sister were in the car with me. Violet, my girlfriend, didn't make it." My voice grew hoarser with each word, catching on the syllables of Vi's name. "I haven't been back since."

The sound of a door closing came across the line. "Ford, I'm so sorry. God, that sounds like such a cop-out. Of course, you know I'm sorry. But I'm not sure what else to say. I just hate that you went through that."

I rubbed at the back of my neck as I stared out at the ocean. "Thanks, A." I could finally look at it and say I was sorry, too. None of us had deserved how the accident had torn our lives apart. Each in very different ways, but destruction and disease ensued nonetheless. Vi would never get to put her pieces back together, but Bell and I…we had to try.

"I'm fucking things up with her sister." The words were out of my mouth before I could stop them. I had been holding in all my feelings about Bell and the situation for more than a month now, and they were just dying to get out.

Austin sucked in a sharp breath. "What's going on? Were you guys friends?"

Friends seemed like such a bizarre term for what Bell and I had been. She'd always been more, though not in any sort of romantic way—I just hadn't seen her in that light. Bell had always been like another limb. She was simply a part of me. I didn't think about it much, it just was. This girl, who had always been wise beyond her years, had seen things about me no one else did, as if she lived inside the deepest parts of my mind. And, God, I had missed it when that part of me went quiet, when *she* went silent. Those phantom pains had never gone away.

I swallowed against the emotion building in my throat. "We were close."

Austin was quiet for a moment. "You have feelings for her." It wasn't a question, it was a simple statement of truth. We'd known each other for a decade, he could read between the lines.

"I can't." The two words hurt as I spoke them, as if they contained a ball of barbed wire, slicing through my body as it traveled up to escape my mouth.

Austin let out a low whistle. "Bet you're beating yourself up pretty hard right now."

I chuckled and bent to pick up a rock along the shore. "If you were here, I'd let you go a few rounds in the ring with me."

"You're worse off than I thought if you want me to kick your ass."

I put all the force I could into sending the stone in my hand out into the ocean. "It's so damn complicated. It's this mess of guilt and want and anger and so many other things I don't have a name for, and it's making me question everything."

Sleep had escaped me again last night, and as I'd lain awake staring up at the ceiling, I'd kept replaying the question, *have I missed what's been right in front of me this whole time?* over and over in my head. Sure, Bell had been two years younger than me, but she'd been adorably cute. Had I missed all that she brought to my life because I'd been distracted by Violet's classic beauty? Vi and I had made sense. Starting string of the football team and one of the varsity cheerleaders. It seemed so cliché now, so... empty. I'd loved her in the way an eighteen-year-old boy could, but we had no real depth. We knew each other's coffee orders and each other's bodies, but did we know anything that lay below the surface? I wasn't sure anymore.

"That's life, Ford. Nothing is as black and white as we want it to be. It's all shades of gray. All we can do is try to make the best choices with what's placed in front of us."

I started out down the beach, kicking a rock as I went. "That's the problem, I don't know what the hell to do. For the longest time, I thought Bell hated me because I was the one driving that night. I was sure she'd never be able to forgive me. So, I stayed away. Turns out it was the staying away that hurt her more than anything. She never blamed me."

"Of course she didn't. It was an accident."

"But now, we're in this weird space of getting to know each other again, and there are all of these landmines.. You never know if one false step will make one blow up in your face."

Austin sighed. "I know how that feels." He certainly did. Austin and his now-wife, Carter, had a falling out that had lasted a year. When they came back together, it had been more than a little dicey for him. "You just have to give her time. And more than anything, you need to prove that you aren't going to leave her again."

Austin's words cut. I'd hurt Bell when she was at her most vulnerable, and even though I knew she was happy that I was back in her life, I also knew she didn't trust it. Didn't trust *me*. I let out a muttered curse. "But I am leaving. In a few months, I'll be gone again. I just need us to be in a better place when I do. I don't want to lose her when I leave. That means the only thing that this can be is friendship." There was too much standing in our way to have more. I wasn't even sure Bell wanted more, but the way I caught her looking at me sometimes told me there might be.

Austin was quiet for a moment. "Ford, wasn't it you who once told me not to miss out on the best thing to ever happen to me? I fucked around for way too long with Carter, and I almost lost her. I can't begin to imagine the shell of a man I'd be without her. I don't want that for you."

I swallowed hard. "I don't either." Bell had always made me a better person. She challenged me. Asked the hard questions, even when she was a little girl. Bell never let me get away with anything, and I loved that about her. It wasn't easy with her, but it was real, and I'd had more than enough easy to last me a lifetime.

"It wouldn't be easy," Austin said as if reading my mind. "And I'm sure there are a million and one things that I don't know about that will make it even harder." He wasn't wrong. Fuck. My family. Hers. The gossipy people of this damn island. Not to mention the ten-ton monster on both our backs: guilt. "Just because it's hard, doesn't mean it's not worth it. Sometimes, the greater the difficulty, the sweeter the reward."

I tipped my head back to stare at the sun peeking through gray clouds. "I can't, A. It could ruin everything." Most importantly, my shot at keeping Bell in my life in any real way.

"Just think about it."

He didn't have to tell me that, it was all that consumed my mind.

Chapter Twenty-One

Bell

I LET OUT A COLORFUL SLEW OF CURSES AS THE SPRAY bottle full of cleaning solution tumbled to the floor.

Darlene bent to pick it up, eyeing me carefully as she handed it to me. "What's with you this morning?"

I sprayed the table with a little more force than necessary, scrubbing the wood surface as if I could clear away all my problems along with the bar grime. "I just didn't sleep very well last night." That was true, but it was more that my emotional unburdening with Kenna and Caelyn had stayed with me. And not just in the redness of my eyes. It had taken root deep in my chest as if I'd lost something profound. But that something had never been mine to begin with.

"This have anything to do with a certain boss of ours?" Darlene arched an eyebrow.

I bristled at the word *boss*. Ford hadn't pulled rank on me or any of the other staff, and I didn't think of him that way. But it still frustrated me that he had the trump card in his back pocket if he ever wanted to use it. "No." *Lies, lies, lies.*

Darlene chuckled. "Sure, Bell."

"Do you want bathroom duty today?"

Darlene held up her hands in defeat. "I'm just saying, you could do worse. And the way he was eyeing you last night… Girl, sign me up for that any night of the week."

I scrubbed an invisible spot on the table. "He's all yours."

"No, honey. He's all *yours*."

But Ford wasn't mine. All of these people were mistaking his overprotective big-brother routine for jealousy or interest. It only hurt more to know how wrong they were.

Boots sounded on the cement of the back hallway, and Darlene waggled her brows at me. I glared at her and then went back to cleaning the spots on the table only I could see. "I brought coffee and baked goods."

Just the low timbre of Ford's voice had those danged butterflies taking flight in my belly. It was as if the vibrations from his words crossed the room and skittered over my skin in a physical caress. Freaking great. I needed to get a grip.

"You know the way to my heart." Darlene abandoned me and went straight for the treats and the hot guy. Traitor.

"What about you, Trouble? Got room for a snickerdoodle muffin in your life?"

The man played dirty. His sexy morning voice *and* my nickname? Lethal. I cleared my throat. "I'll be over in a minute. I just want to finish this."

A few seconds later, I felt heat at my back. Too close. "I'm pretty sure that table was clean twenty passes ago."

"Can't be too careful about germs." My voice cracked halfway through, and I grimaced.

Ford plucked the spray bottle and rag from my hand, leaning in close to whisper in my ear. "Go get your breakfast. Can't have you fainting on me now." He straightened, and with a wink, strode off in the direction of the closet where we housed the cleaning supplies.

What the hell was with Ford and his winking? At me. He'd had that carefree teasing ease when he was younger, but I hadn't seen much of it since he'd come back. I guess it wasn't gone forever. I turned and headed for the bar where Darlene was fanning herself. "I'm telling you, this is better than porn and my teen dramas all rolled into one."

I slapped her on the shoulder as I headed for the bar sink to wash my hands. "I can't deal with your snark before I've had my coffee."

"Well, get over here and have some of this delicious latte that hunk of a man just brought you."

I ignored the latter part of Darlene's sentence and went straight for the coffee and muffin. "What'd he bring you?"

Darlene grinned. "The man knows me well. He got my favorite, a maple bacon bar. Gotta have my daily protein."

I let out a half-snort, half-laugh. "That thing is ninety-nine percent sugar."

"Hush, you. Calories don't count before noon."

I raised my coffee cup to her. "Amen to that."

The morning prep flew by with the three of us working. Still, I was a bumbling mess, dropping silverware and napkins, tripping over invisible dips in the floor. When I dropped a glass, sending it shattering into a million little pieces, Ford seemed to have had enough.

"All right, Trouble. You and I are taking the afternoon off."

"W-what?" I couldn't help the stutter in my words. "We can't. We have to work." Not to mention the fact that alone time with Ford in my current state was a horrible idea.

Ford stepped over the glass and lifted me effortlessly onto the bar top. I huffed. "I'm wearing Converse, it's not like I'm going to cut myself."

"Better safe than sorry. Stay here."

I scowled at his retreating back as he turned to grab the

broom and dustpan. "I'm going to get this cleaned up. You are going to go upstairs to put on whatever you wear hiking, and then we are getting out of here for the day."

My scowl deepened. "Are we now?" The nerve of this man.

"We are."

I jumped off the bar top as Ford finished sweeping. "Well, *boss man*, I don't leave my employees to handle a lunch rush on their own."

"We can totally handle it on our own," Darlene called from the other side of the bar. Such a little traitor.

"Yup, we've got it covered," Hank echoed from the kitchen.

"See?" Ford arched a brow. "You've got good people who can handle whatever tourist hordes come their way, and the new trainee will be here in an hour. Now, get changed, and let's go. We'll pick up lunch on the way."

My mouth opened and closed, searching for an excuse, but everything I landed on sounded like the ultimate cop-out. "Fine." I headed for the back stairs, stomping like a two-year-old the whole way.

⌒◎

Ford pulled his SUV to a stop in one of the parking spots on the outskirts of town. "The General Store? For lunch?"

I smirked. "Some things have changed since you've been away, and this is one of them."

He eyed me from the driver's seat. "I'm trusting you with the most important thing of all."

"What's that?"

"My stomach."

I let out a choked laugh. He'd always been highly motivated by food. "I promise I won't steer you wrong, but you're going to have to roll with me."

He switched off the engine and hopped out of the SUV. "Fine."

The man sounded like I was dragging him to his death, not a potential lunch spot.

I smiled down at the sidewalk, trying to hide my amusement. Just wait until he saw the menu. Ford held the worn screen door open for me. We'd been here countless times before. Riding our bikes from my house in the summer for a popsicle. Stopping on the way home from school for some candy.

Most of the store hadn't changed a bit, but Old Man Walters had built on an addition at the back of the shop that housed a small kitchen and a counter with eight stools. On the back wall was a chalkboard menu written in an artsy script that was as familiar as my own handwriting. "Caelyn."

She whirled around at the sound of my voice, her hair piled in a haphazard bun, the bracelets on her arms jangling. "Bell. What are you doing here?" Her eyes widened at the man behind me. "Ford. Hi." Her last sentence came out as a squeak.

I bit back my laugh. "We're going on a hike and could use a little sustenance."

Caelyn beamed at the two of us. *Shit.* She was going to get her hopes up. I could see it in her eyes, she was already writing some grand romantic end for Ford and me, and it would crush her when things didn't go that way. "That, I can do for you."

I turned back to Ford, who was studying the menu with a look of horror. "Sprout sandwich?"

I couldn't hold in my laugh this time. "What? Living in LA for over a decade, and you're still not into rabbit food?"

"That's not exactly my cuisine of choice." He glanced at Caelyn. "No offense."

She held up a hand. "None taken. We've got more carnivorous options, too. Tell you what, you tell me what you don't like, and I'll whip you up something special. I already know Bell's favorites."

"No sprouts. No mushrooms."

"Fair enough. Bells, you want the vegan BLT?"

I nodded. "That sounds perfect. We'll go grab some chips and drinks while you're cooking."

Ford studied me carefully as we headed down the cracker and chip aisle. "You've changed, Bell."

I halted at his words. "Well, it has been a while." I couldn't help the defensiveness in my voice. The idea that he didn't like the woman now standing before him, giving me the sudden urge to crawl into myself.

Ford grabbed my elbow, tugging me towards him so I was forced to look up into his eyes. They softened at my expression. "I just never thought my double-bacon cheeseburger girl would be ordering a *vegan* BLT. That should be illegal."

The stiffness swept out of my body, and I laughed. "You don't know what you're missing out on by not trying new things, Ford." And with that, I turned on my heel and headed for the kettle-cooked chips.

Chapter Twenty-Two

Ford

"I'M OUT OF SHAPE. HOW DID I NOT KNOW I WAS OUT OF shape?"

Bell's laugh caught on the breeze as she sank to a rock at the top of Mount Orcas. "That's because you're used to sissy LA workouts."

I sat on the rock next to hers and gave her a mock scowl. "I'll have you know that I spar with a professional fighter regularly."

She smirked. "Doesn't help you climb a mountain any better."

I dove for her sides, tickling the spot I knew was extra sensitive. She let out a high-pitched shriek that had a couple of birds from a nearby tree taking flight. "What was that?"

"You're a Greek god! So in shape, I could never compete with you!"

I stopped my tickling, but my hands stayed on her waist for just a moment longer as I relished the feel of the dips and curves. Bell's breath hitched as our gazes locked—her mouth such a short distance away. All I would have to do is lean forward and—

"So, what'd you think of Caelyn's sandwich?"

I released my hold on Bell and settled back on my rock. *Shit.* That was close, too close. "I told you, it was damn good." I didn't know what voodoo witchery the girl had, but she'd combined things I never would've thought of. My sandwich had prosciutto and some sort of apricot spread, along with things I didn't even recognize. But it had tasted delicious.

"I told you to trust me."

I met Bell's gaze. "I do trust you."

Her breath seemed to stutter in her chest. "Good."

With that one word, I knew that trust wasn't returned. It burned. That angry fire. Not at Bell but at myself, for destroying one of the most precious gifts I'd ever been given. But that was the thing about life. So often, we didn't realize that the rarest and most beautiful gifts were already in our possession. Sometimes, we didn't discover that truth before it was too late. I refused to let that be the case. I would do whatever it took to mend what I'd broken.

"Tell me about your bars." Bell tucked her legs up under her.

"What do you want to know?"

She smiled. "Everything. Why you started them. Which one's your favorite. What you're doing next."

I chuckled. Bell always did have a million and one questions. I'd always said that she could make conversation with a tree stump. "It just made sense. I'd grown up with Dad and Mom showing me the ropes at The Catch, so I knew the basics. I majored in business at UCLA, but I just couldn't get excited about working in some stuffy office. I wanted something different."

"I get that. Did you always want to start in LA?"

"It was another thing that was just logical. I had a few connections, people who were willing to invest. The first bar is still my favorite. It's the one that I spend the most time at, the one that was the hardest to hand over the reins to."

Bell's expression softened. "Who's looking after it while you're here?"

"The manager who's been with me the longest. I trust him, and he's doing a great job. I guess I'm still just a bit of a control freak with my babies." Though it had gotten easier over the past couple of weeks. When I'd first arrived, I'd called Luke every day, sometimes twice a day, to check on things. But now, I found myself waiting for his weekly reports instead.

"It must be hard."

I looked back to Bell. The sun had caught in her hair, blond streaks of her ponytail catching the light. Her cheeks were pink from the hike, and her green eyes seemed to dance and sparkle. She'd never looked more beautiful. "What must be hard?" There was a rawness in my voice that I couldn't disguise, a mix of emotions.

A flicker of sadness flitted across her features. "Being away from what you love. I bet you can't wait to get back."

Dammit. Austin had been right. Bell was waiting for me to leave her again. And she wasn't wrong to expect it. The entire three-day road trip from LA to the island, I'd been calculating just how long I'd have to be on Anchor. What would be the shortest stay I could get away with to turn the bar around and placate my brother. Now, I found myself looking for excuses to stay. I didn't know what the future held, but I knew I wanted Bell in it.

"I actually needed a break."

Bell's gaze flew up to mine. "Really?" I nodded. "Why?"

I leaned back on the rock, the rough surface digging into my palms as I looked out at the sea all around us. The view was breathtaking. The air around us silent. Still. I'd missed the peace of the place more than I wanted to admit. I searched for the right words to explain the restlessness I'd felt lately in LA. "I'm not exactly sure why. I'd been happy in LA for a long time. But over the past year or so, I started getting restless, like my skin was too tight for my body. The things I loved about the city had become things I hated."

I looked back to Bell. She listened intently as I spoke, nibbling on her bottom lip. "I think LA was what you needed at the time. It's so different from here." She let out a little laugh. "You couldn't find something more polar opposite if you tried. And you needed something that held no reminders of the past for you. But now, maybe you need something else." Bell's gaze bored into mine. "I think it's a good thing, Ford. I think it means you're healing."

My gaze traveled over her face. "I think it means I'm ready to move on." We sat in silence, the air dancing between us. I gave a forced laugh. "You always were a wise little Yoda."

Bell stuck out her tongue at me. "Leave it to you to compare me to a wrinkly green man."

It was her heart and soul that were Yoda-like. The rest of her was anything but. "What's the deal with you and Hunter?" I cursed the question that had escaped before I could consider what it might reveal.

"What do you mean?"

"Were you guys dating? Friends?" My breath hitched as I waited for her to answer.

Bell's eyes widened. "No, we're just friends. Always just friends."

Some invisible tension in me loosened, a feeling I didn't want to think too much about for a woman who'd taken over my mind.

"Let's grab an early dinner." I was pushing my luck, and I knew it. We'd spent the whole day together, and I only wanted more. More of her smiles, especially the ones where her nose crinkled. More of her laughs that turned husky at the edges. More of her insights into life. More of *her*.

She pulled out her phone and glanced at the screen. "I can do that. What are you in the mood for?"

"What about that new Italian place?"

"Rocco's?"

"Yeah." I'd seen it the first time I'd been brave enough to venture into town. The menu looked promising, and the setting appeared just a step above a pizza joint.

Bell glanced down at herself. "I'm not exactly dressed to impress...and I'm all sweaty."

"You look gorgeous." *Oh, shit.* I hurried on. "It didn't look fancy when I walked by."

Bell's cheeks had an adorable pink tint to them. "Okay. But if they kick us out, I'm blaming you."

"Fair enough." I pulled my SUV into a parking spot in the center of town. Hopping out, I went to open Bell's door, but she was already out of the vehicle. "I would've gotten that for you."

Bell pressed her lips together as if holding in a laugh. "You look like someone ate your last Kit Kat. I'm all grown now, Cupcake. I can open my own doors."

I scowled in her direction, and the laugh she'd been holding back escaped. "Maybe I wanted to be a gentleman."

"Forgive me. I promise not to open any doors for the rest of the night. And if I drop anything, I'll make you pick it up."

I grinned, pulling open the door to Rocco's. "You have to let me buy you dinner, too."

"Go right ahead, Mister Moneybags."

I groaned. "Are you ever going to stop giving me shit about living in LA and making a decent living?"

Bell drummed her fingers along her lips and squinted her eyes. "Hmm...that would be a no."

"Never lets me get away with a damn thing," I grumbled.

"And that's the way you like it."

I gave her long ponytail a little tug. "I do like it."

A man in his fifties appeared from the back of the restaurant. "Bella! You've come to see me again. And you brought a handsome date with you this time."

Bell blushed. "Pietro, this is my friend, Ford. Ford, this is the owner of Rocco's, Pietro."

Pietro took my hand in a hearty shake. "Any friend of Bella's is a friend of mine. Welcome, welcome." He then took Bell by the arms and gave her a kiss on each cheek. "You're too skinny. You need to come in more often."

Bell let out a tinkling laugh that settled somewhere deep inside my chest. "I'll see what I can do about that. We just hiked Orcas, so I'm sure I'll be eating my fair share tonight."

Rocco clapped. "We must hurry, then. Take any table you like. I'll bring out some appetizers, on the house."

Bell led us to a table against the wall towards the back of the restaurant, and I couldn't help but wonder if she didn't want any passersby to see us. I didn't blame her. I was sure people would talk if they saw us on what looked like a date.

I pulled out Bell's chair, and she grinned up at me. "*Such* a gentleman."

I chuckled. "I'm trying my best, but you don't exactly make it easy."

She shrugged. "Nothing easy is ever worth much."

She was more right than she knew. Bell and her Yoda wisdom. "Pietro seems like a character."

"He's the best. I come in once a week with Will, Ava, and Mia to give Caelyn a night off and to get some one-on-one time with them. Pietro always makes some special dessert for them and has little toys for Ava and Mia."

"Do you spend a lot of time with them?"

"The kids?"

I nodded. I wanted to know what had happened with Caelyn's parents, but I didn't want to pry.

"I do." Bell toyed with the napkin in her lap. "Kenna, Caelyn, and I kind of formed our own little family. The kind we always wished we'd had."

I swallowed against the burning emotion in the back of my throat. I hated how alone Bell must have felt. "I'm really glad you have those two. I'd like to get to know them again." If they were her family, I knew I'd have to win them over, too.

"They'd like that. And the kids would, too. Will could really use a good guy in his life. He doesn't have many."

I flipped open my menu. "I could come with you on your next weekly date here." I wasn't sure how Bell would react to that idea. Maybe it would feel too much like playing house. Maybe I was encroaching on her special time with Will, Ava, and Mia.

The smile that broke out across Bell's face told me those concerns were unfounded. "That would be great. The girls love new people, especially ones who pay a lot of attention to them. Will's more guarded, but you'll grow on him. It'll help that you played football."

"He's on the team?"

"Yup. Made varsity his freshman year."

"That's impressive."

Pietro appeared, laden with enough appetizers to make a meal out of. "Here you go. These are some of my favorites."

Bell tsked at him. "This is too much food."

He shrugged. "If there are leftovers, you take them home."

I chuckled as Pietro headed back to the kitchen to get our drinks. "I get the sense that there is no arguing with that man."

"None."

Dinner flew by far too fast, in a mix that was uniquely Bell and me. Part deep conversations about life and purpose, part stomach-twisting laughter and shared memories of the past. It felt good to bring Violet out into the light again. I was starting to realize that I could appreciate her for what she had been for me, and not force myself to think of her as something she wasn't. She'd been my first love, the perfect match for the boy who was growing into a man. But she was never going to be my life partner. It didn't make her any less valuable, it didn't mean it hurt any less to lose her. It just meant that I could stop blaming myself for losing my only shot at love. Because I hadn't.

"I'm stuffed." Bell groaned as she rose from her chair.

I patted my stomach. "I think that third cannoli might've been overkill for me."

Bell laughed. "I tried to warn you."

"They were too good." I placed a hand on the small of Bell's back, guiding her through the restaurant that had begun to fill over the past two hours. I'd felt eyes on us throughout the evening, even heard a whisper or two. But I'd forced myself to ignore it, to focus on the woman in front of me.

I felt Bell's body jolt before I saw them, the two people I'd been dreading running into since the moment I stepped foot on Anchor. Bell came to a dead stop right in front of the hostess stand. "Mom. Dad."

The sharp edge of my anger took me by surprise. For so long, I'd felt nothing but guilt when it came to the Kiptons. Even when Heather had threatened to sue me if I had any contact with their family, I'd excused it. I'd welcomed all the blame she'd wanted to place on my shoulders. After all, I'd been driving that night. If I would've reacted differently, maybe her daughter would still be here.

But now, there was a fire low in my gut. I knew they'd been grieving, but they'd hurt so many people with their actions. Their daughter most of all. And that was something I wasn't sure I could forgive.

"What—what are you doing here? What are you doing with *him*?" Heather spluttered.

Bell's jaw hardened. "I imagine we were doing the same thing you and Dad are. Having dinner. But we're done now, so we're heading out."

Bell took a step forward, but her mother moved to block her. "What are you thinking, Isabelle? This is a disgrace."

Bell met her mother's furious glare. "Well, that's nothing new, right? I've been a disgrace to you for a long time. Why change now?"

Heather opened her mouth to retort, but Bruce stepped in and gave her elbow a firm tug. "Heather, this isn't the time or the place. Let's get to our table." He gave me a stiff nod and then looked at his daughter. He studied her as if he hardly knew her at all. As if he were trying to place the woman who stood in front of him now. "Good to see you, honey."

"You too, Dad." Bell's words were a hoarse whisper, filled with so much pain it seemed to pull at the muscles in my chest.

I placed my hand firmly against Bell's back, guiding her forward yet again. Pushing open the door, the cool night air was a welcome relief. Neither of us said a word as I navigated us towards the SUV. I helped Bell in and then rounded the front of the vehicle to climb in myself. But I couldn't bring myself to start the engine.

"He never calls me by my name."

I looked over to see Bell staring blankly out the windshield. "Your dad?"

She nodded. "I told them I wanted to be called Bell. I explained why. I was so desperate for a fresh start, something to mark rebuilding my life."

"You needed your own version of what LA was for me."

Bell turned towards me. "I didn't see it then, but yes. I just needed to be someone else. Someone who wouldn't waste this one precious life I was given. I didn't want to be the person who let her parents push her around. Vi wasted so much energy worrying about what other people thought of her. Losing her made me see how we all waste so much time on unimportant things. I didn't want to ever look back and think I'd held myself back from the life I wanted."

"So, you asked them to call you Bell."

"I did. My mom flat-out refused." Bell scoffed. "I'm sure you're shocked about that. But it was my dad's reaction that hurt the most. It was like he understood why I needed it, but he didn't want to piss off my mom, so he just stopped calling me anything real. Only dime-store endearments that held no meaning."

Bell's voice tripped over a sob. "It's like I slowly disappeared for them. The person they knew doesn't exist anymore, and they have no interest in getting to know the new me. So, I'm just... *gone.*"

I couldn't hold back any longer. I pulled Bell against me, wrapping her in my arms as best I could with the console in the way. I hated this vehicle at the moment, would've given anything to pull her into my lap and rock her like I wanted to. "I see you, Bell. And everything about you is beautiful."

She cried harder then, pressing her face into my chest. I kept whispering the words over and over. "I see you."

Chapter Twenty-Three

Bell

I KNELT DOWN, STRAINING FOR THE PERFECT ANGLE TO GET in the final groove of the credenza. I folded the fine-grain sandpaper around my fingers, using my nails as the sharp edge required to refine each nook and cranny. I needed this today, this one simple thing I could control, one finite thing I could fix. My family might be beyond repair, my relationship with Ford a jumble of confusing emotions, but I had my workshop. I had my hands that could bring broken things back to life.

I moved my fingers back and forth along the groove, careful not to press too lightly or too hard. It was a delicate balance. There was always some pain involved in bringing a piece back to life. Layers of an old existence that needed to be stripped away so something new could emerge. Sometimes, I even found myself talking to the piece. Explaining that all of the hurt would be worth it in the end.

I didn't have those words in me to say today. They wouldn't have been believable, even to a piece of furniture. My sleep the night before had been fitful at best, peppered with nightmares and anxiety-filled dreams that had left my t-shirt and sleep shorts damp with sweat. I'd gotten up before the sun and had come out to the place where I always found solace.

It wasn't packing its usual punch of relief today, though. I blew on the groove I had just sanded, clearing away the dust. That would do. I straightened, arching my back in a stretch and glancing at the clock on the wall. *Shit.* I needed to get showered and changed for work.

My stomach hollowed out at the thought of seeing Ford. Last night, he'd held me for at least half an hour as I'd cried everything out in the front seat of his SUV. When I'd finally gotten ahold of myself, I hadn't known what to say. Things between us were changing, but I couldn't let it go where I wanted it to. *Friendship.* It had to be enough. And as much as it killed, that meant putting a wall around my heart. No more tear-filled embraces or anything of the like.

I quickly cleaned up my workspace and headed for the staircase along the back of the building. My muscles screamed with each step. A hike yesterday, crappy sleep, and four hours of restoration work might've been overdoing it a little bit.

As I reached the top step, I froze. I hadn't left the door to my apartment open, had I? My heart beat harder in my chest, seeming to rattle my ribs. I had been pretty out of it at five a.m., maybe I hadn't shut it all the way, and the wind had blown it open.

I eased forward a step, listening for any sounds coming from inside. Nothing. I blew out a long breath. "Get it together, Bell."

I pushed open the door and gasped. It looked as if a tornado had come through my apartment. Items had been torn off shelves and thrown about. My precious potted plants had been upended, and dirt was strewn everywhere. And there were feathers, so many feathers. From the pillows, I realized. Someone had taken scissors or a knife to the throw pillows on my couch.

The world seemed to go a bit wobbly at the edges, and I realized I was shaking. I needed to leave, to call someone, the police, but I couldn't seem to get my legs to obey my brain. I simply stared at the carnage around me. My eyes caught on something in the midst of it, and a strangled sob escaped my throat.

I rushed forward, my knees knocking against the hard floor as I went down. My scrapbook. I quickly flipped through the pages, every single photo was gone. When I reached the back page, there was a note written in angry black letters.

You don't deserve to have her. You never did.

My breaths came quicker, each one tripping over the last as they struggled to get out. I stumbled back, falling on my butt and then scrambling to my feet. I needed out of here. I needed to call the police. I shakily pulled out my phone, but before I could unlock the screen, there was a flash of movement in my peripheral vision.

The world seemed to slow down and speed up at the same time. A masked figure moving forward. I tried to turn, to head for the door, but a fist struck out, landing right on my cheek. Flashes of light danced across my vision as my legs lost their purchase, and I tumbled to the floor, my phone flying from my grip.

My hands caught the worst of my fall, jagged bits of a shattered pot cutting into my palms. My eyes watered as I blinked rapidly. Footsteps thundered past me and down the stairs. They weren't going to hurt me any worse. My chest heaved as I tried to catch my breath, and as I pushed to my feet, my vision swam. I darted for the door, but my steps were wobbly, as if I'd had one too many drinks and not enough dinner.

I gripped the railing as hard as I could as I rushed down the stairs. Two steps from the bottom, my feet tangled, and a startled scream escaped me as I began to fall. I collided with hard, muscled arms with an *oomph.*

"Whoa, Trouble. Where's the fire?" Ford righted me, and his

amused expression immediately turned to concern as he took in my face. "What the hell happened? What's going on?"

"M-m-my apartment. Someone broke in. They—they tore it apart. I thought they were gone. They weren't." The shaking was only getting worse. It was at least sixty-five degrees out, and I felt like I was freezing.

"Jesus, Bell. Your face. I have to call the cops. An ambulance. Are you hurt anywhere else?" His gaze ran up and down my body, searching for any other signs of injury.

I gave my head a small shake and winced. Ford began to release me, to reach for his phone, but my fingers dug into his arms. "No. Don't leave me." The words were out before I could stop them. I hated the sound, the meaning behind them. But most of all, I hated the weakness.

Ford wrapped his arms around me in a tight hug, resting his chin on the top of my head. "It's okay. I'm not going anywhere. I'm right here." He kept his hold on me with one hand while he fished his phone out of his back pocket with the other. He quickly dialed. "Yeah, I'm at The Catch on Anchor. There's been a break-in and an assault in the apartment above the bar." Pause. He loosened his hold on me just a bit so that he could look me over. "No, there's no one here now. I think she's okay, but she has an injury to her face."

Ford seemed to be looking at me as if to double-check. I nodded. Nothing in his body language relaxed. He was on high alert as he took in the surrounding area as if waiting for someone to jump out from behind a tree. A shiver ran through me at the thought. Had the intruder watched me while I worked?

Ford pulled me in tighter again. "Okay, thank you. We'll stay outside." He shoved his phone back into his pocket. "They're sending someone out, but it will be a little bit. Why don't we sit down?"

I nodded, but the action was wooden. I fisted my hand in Ford's shirt as he guided us towards one of the benches flanking the back patio. I couldn't seem to force myself to let go of him. I needed that point of contact more than my next breath.

Ford eased me onto the bench, quickly sinking down beside me and pulling me close. His hand ghosted over my face, stopping just shy of where I could feel my cheek and eye swelling. "Who was it?" His voice was calm, *too* calm, as if he'd shut off his emotions. I hated it.

"I don't know. They were wearing a mask."

A muscle in Ford's cheek ticked. "Tell me what happened."

"I didn't sleep well, so at four, I just got up and went out to the workshop to work on my credenza. I locked my door. At least, I thought I did. Maybe I didn't. I was distracted—"

"Bell." Ford gave my shoulder a squeeze. "Whether you locked the door or not, this isn't your fault."

I gave a quick, jerky nod. "I worked out there for a few hours. I didn't hear anything. No cars in the lot. No footsteps. Nothing. When I went up to shower and get ready for work, the door was ajar. I thought maybe I hadn't shut it firmly and the wind had blown it open. You know this building, it's old. I didn't hear anything, so I went inside—"

"Bell," Ford growled.

"I know, I know. It was stupid. But this is a small town, hardly anything criminal ever happens around here. I stepped inside, and it was just…*destroyed*. Whoever did this was so angry."

Ford pulled me even tighter against him, and I soaked up the feeling of warmth. "I thought I was alone. I stood up to call the cops, and it all happened so fast, just this blur of motion. Whoever it was punched me and ran out."

Ford's fingers flexed around my shoulder. "Fuck, Bell. This could've been so much worse." He rested his chin atop my head, his breathing ragged. I forced myself to try and pull back, but Ford just held firm. "Please. Let me have this. I need to know you're here, and you're okay."

I swallowed hard but nodded against his chest. I didn't know how long we stayed like that, but finally, Ford's breathing slowed, and his muscles relaxed a fraction. He released his stranglehold on me but kept one arm around my shoulders. "It's going to be okay. They'll figure out who did this." He studied my face, eyes zeroing in on my cheek, his jaw hardening. "Have you banned anyone from the bar lately?"

"Not since last year, I don't think it's that…" My sentence trailed off. I didn't know how to give voice to what I'd seen. If I spoke the words, then it was real, and the pictures…that felt like the greatest violation of all.

Ford gave my shoulder another squeeze. "What?"

I swallowed, my throat seeming to stick. "I have this scrapbook…"

"Okay."

"I started making it a few months after Violet died. It's all of my favorite memories with her. There are photos and drawings and collages. It became this living art piece." Tears began to fill my eyes. I'd poured so much into that book. Joy, pain, and everything in between. Every time I'd missed my sister, I'd worked on a page. Now, when I needed to remember her, I pulled it from the drawer and spent anywhere from a few minutes to a few hours laughing and crying as I went down memory lane.

Ford trailed a hand up and down my back. "That sounds beautiful."

"It was." His body stiffened at my use of the past tense. "Whoever broke in tore out every photo." My tears spilled over now, and my voice shook. "There was a note in the back that said I didn't deserve her, that I never had."

Ford spat out a curse, his gaze darting around the parking lot, then the beach. "We'll find out who did this, Bell."

Even if the police could find the person, I wasn't sure my apartment would ever feel like home again.

Chapter Twenty-four

Ford

THE EMT LOOKED UP FROM EXAMINING BELL'S FACE. "There are no broken bones that I can feel, or signs of a concussion. But I'd guess you're going to have one hell of a shiner."

I bristled at the man's tone. "It's not funny."

The man's eyes flared. "I'm not suggesting that it is."

"Everyone, calm down." Bell slid off the gurney. "It'll be funny when I tell everyone I went a few rounds with Rocky Balboa."

"No, it won't," I growled. I knew I wasn't helping, but I was on a knife's edge and about to lose it. One look at the inside of Bell's apartment had done that. The rage that amount of destruction would take…whoever the culprit was, they were angry enough to kill. I gave my head a little shake and forced my hands to unclench.

"Hey," the EMT started, "don't I know you?"

My gaze flicked to him. "I don't think so."

"Yeah, I do. I was a few years behind you in school, but the guys on my fire rescue crew still talk about it. That was one hell of an accident. It was a miracle you two walked away."

But we hadn't walked away. Not really. Our lives had been wrecked in a whole different way. I wanted to deck the man for bringing it up. But seeing as cops were milling about, that was a bad idea.

A man looking too young to be a sheriff strode up and placed a firm hand on the EMT's shoulder. "I think that's enough, Gil. Get your gear and get gone."

The EMT mumbled something under his breath but loaded the gurney into the back of his rig.

Sheriff Raines crossed to us. "All right, Bell. Crime scene techs are dusting for fingerprints. It's going to take them a while, but once they're done, you'll have full access to the apartment again."

"Yeah, an apartment that's destroyed," Bell muttered.

"We're going to figure this out. It might take some time, but we'll find who did this and put them away." Sheriff Raines patted her on the shoulder. It was friendly, almost familial, but I still didn't like it. He reminded me of the kind of guy Bell would end up with if I left Anchor. Someone entrenched in the community like she was. Someone who wouldn't constantly force her to face painful reminders. Someone who had never let her down.

I stepped forward, wrapping an arm around Bell. Instead of melting into my side like she had before, she stiffened. "What do you suggest in the meantime?"

Raines glanced up at the apartment. "I'd recommend replacing locks, maybe even the outside door completely, and I'd consider a security system."

I gave him a quick nod. "I've already called a security company in Seattle about a system, but I'll call the hardware store here about putting in a new door."

Bell turned, slipping out of my hold. "New locks are plenty, I don't need anything else."

My back teeth ground together. The shock was wearing off, and Bell had found her mad—or at least her annoyed. But I knew it was simply masking the fear that was bubbling underneath. "It was already on my list of things to do to get an alarm system for the whole building. This is just moving up the timeline a little." She didn't need to know that I was now getting the premium package instead of the basic, or that I was paying for it out of my own pocket.

Bell mumbled something under her breath about overprotective wannabe big brothers, and Sheriff Raines chuckled. "It's a good idea, Bell. And I'll be sending one of my deputies over on more regular intervals until Anchor's summer officers are in place."

The island didn't have a year-round law enforcement presence, but during the summer, the sheriff's department brought on extra staff, and each island in our small chain got its own dedicated officers to deal with the round-the-clock issues that came with an influx of tourists. I met the sheriff's gaze. "We appreciate that."

A truck pulled into the lot way too fast, sending gravel spitting. Hunter launched from his vehicle and jogged over to Bell, wrapping her in a hard hug. What was with all these guys touching her? God, I needed to get a grip.

"Are you okay? Holy crap, your eye!"

Bell extricated herself from my brother's hold, patting him on the arm. "I'm fine, Hunt. Promise."

His gaze traveled over her face and down her body as if checking for other injuries. "You're staying with me until they catch this guy."

"Oh, hell no." The words were out before I had a chance to even consider them. "If she stays with anyone, it'll be me."

Hunter's head snapped in my direction. "And why's that?"

"Have you forgotten that you're currently living in an

Airstream with one tiny-ass bed. I have extra rooms and an alarm system at my place." I hated that my brother had been the one to offer Bell refuge first. I'd wanted to, but I knew it wouldn't exactly go over well. I'd already been planning to get my mom to try and guilt Bell into staying with me by telling her how worried she'd be if Bell was staying here alone. It was underhanded, but I didn't care. I needed to know she was safe.

Hunter straightened to his full height. "I might not have the fancy digs that you do, but at least I stick around."

Bell threw up her hands. "I'm not going anywhere with either of you." She glanced up at Raines. "Will you find something to arrest these guys for? Maybe lock them up overnight?"

He chuckled. "I'll see what I can do."

"Thanks. I'll be in the bar getting set up for the day."

Bell headed inside, and Raines turned back to me and Hunter, all traces of humor gone from his face. "You two need to get your shit together. Bell does not need you going at it when she's dealing with everything else."

I swallowed hard. The man was right. I was acting like a jealous high schooler. "You're worried."

"Damn straight, I'm worried. This is clearly personal, and whoever this creep is, they're mad." A muscle in his cheek ticked as he looked up at the apartment again. "All the pillows on her couch were slashed. The perp used a knife. That does not signal good things."

Every muscle in my body tightened to the point of pain. "How long is it going to take to get fingerprints back?"

"I'm going to put a rush on anything we find, but I'm guessing we won't find any."

"Fuck," Hunter muttered.

I glanced at my brother. "I already called a security company in Seattle. I paid a rush fee, and they're coming out tomorrow."

"That's good." Hunter studied me carefully, his gaze seeming to try and read between the lines. "What's going on with you two?"

Raines cleared his throat. "I'm going to go check on my guys."

I never looked away from my brother. "None of your damn business."

Hunt's body gave a small jerk. "I'm the one who stuck by her side when you bailed. I'm the one who's been here year after year when you couldn't suck it up to face this place. So, tell me just how it isn't my business."

He loved her in his own way. And as pissed as I was in the moment, I had to appreciate that he'd been here for Bell all the times I hadn't. And he deserved the truth. "I'm figuring things out."

"You're also leaving," he challenged.

I wasn't so sure I could anymore. Not when leaving meant not having Bell in my life daily. "I'm figuring that out, too."

"She know that?"

"Not yet."

Hunter chuckled. "I wonder how that will go over."

I grinned. "Not well." If I told her now that I was thinking of staying on Anchor, at the bar, past this summer, she might try and throw me into the ocean. "I have a lot to make up for, Hunt. And not just with Bell. I know that."

Hunter's Adam's apple bobbed as he swallowed. "It's good you know."

"I'm sorry I left you to deal with everything." I'd placed so much on my little brother's shoulders when it should've been the other way around. I should've been protecting him, taking on his burdens.

Hunter glanced out at the sea. "I get it, Ford. I do. I can't imagine going through what you did at eighteen. I saw how it fucked with your head. Even at sixteen, I knew it was warping your mind. But it's like you lost sight of everything except your grief and your guilt. You couldn't see me or Mom and Dad or anyone, not even Bell."

"I know. And I'm so damn sorry."

Hunter nodded. "If you're thinking of going after Bell, you need to be damn sure you can handle staying on this island. Damn sure you're not going to let the ghosts from the past mess with your head. You cannot bail on that girl a second time."

I swallowed hard. "I know."

Hunter gave a jerk of his chin. "Good. I'm glad you're waking up." His gaze bored into mine. "I missed my brother."

I pulled him into a hard, back-slapping hug. "I missed you, too."

After a few beats, Hunter released me and gave me a shove. "All right, enough with this mushy shit. We need to figure out what we're going to do about Bell."

"I was thinking about siccing Mom on her."

Hunter burst out laughing. "You are brutal, bro."

I shrugged. I would do whatever it took to keep Bell safe.

Chapter Twenty-five

Bell

A KNOCK SOUNDED AT MY DOOR, AND I QUICKLY SWIPED at the tears under my eyes. "Who is it?"

"Ford."

My chest warmed as those damn butterflies took flight in my belly before I shoved them down. "Come in."

"Why the hell isn't your brand-new lock doing its job?" If Ford's words hadn't clued me in to his anger, the vein pumping on the side of his neck would have.

"Because…" I drew out the word. "Every five minutes, one of the staff members or patrons is coming up here to check on me, and I got tired of having to get up off the floor to go and unlock the door." I gestured to the mess I was attempting to sort through and clean up. After three smashed pots, I'd finally decided that trying to glue them back together was a lost cause.

Ford took a few steps forward, plastic bag in hand. "I don't think you should be alone with anyone right now. We don't know who's behind this."

I arched a brow at him. "Then what are you doing here? I clearly shouldn't be alone with you." My inner bitch was coming out, and I knew it. Ford had been nothing but kind and helpful and supportive in the past ten hours, but that sweetness was dangerous for my heart. I had to keep it at arm's length.

Ford scowled. "I don't count. Neither does Hunter, Crosby, Caelyn, Kenna, or my parents. Everyone else stays on the suspect list."

I gaped at him. "You have to be kidding me."

"Better safe than sorry."

"Whatever," I mumbled and turned back to placing pot shards in the thick plastic garbage bags we used to line our recycle bins in the bar—they could handle anything.

"Come on, Trouble, time for a break." I kept right on sorting. Ford chuckled. "I asked Pietro to make you whatever was your favorite comfort food."

My movements slowed as I sniffed the air. "Lasagna?"

"With parmesan garlic bread, and four different desserts."

I placed the pot shard in the garbage bag and pushed to my feet. "You play dirty."

"Never said I didn't."

I sighed, rubbing my temples. "The kitchen is an even bigger mess than the living room. We'll have to eat on the couch." While all the throw pillows had been destroyed, my couch cushions had miraculously remained intact.

"That's fine. I've got silverware, plates, everything we need."

I sank down onto the couch and tried to ignore the destruction I'd barely made a dent in. "Thanks for getting me dinner."

Ford reached over and grabbed my hand. The warmth of it felt so good, so reassuring, and I hated myself just a little bit for letting it rest there. This man had belonged to my sister for most of our lives. And even though my heart had claimed him, he hadn't been mine. "Come stay with me for a few days. At least until we can clean all of this up."

I shook my head and slipped my hand out of his. I couldn't. For a million different reasons. But most of all, because I knew that if I left now, I'd never come back. I needed to reclaim my space. Exorcise any nasty energy lingering around and make the place mine again. Maybe Caelyn could burn some of that sage she was so fond of. "I need to stay here."

"Not even my mom could convince you, huh?"

My gaze snapped to Ford's. "You're the one who had her talk to me, weren't you?" Kara had used her best concerned-mom voice and had made me feel awful for refusing to stay with Ford, but I'd known I needed to be here.

He shrugged. "I can neither confirm nor deny those allegations."

"You're the worst."

"No, I'm worried."

The concern in Ford's expression had my anger melting away. "I'm sorry. I just—I have to stay. I need to make it mine again."

Ford sighed, taking dishes out of the bag and spreading them out on the coffee table. "I get it. I really do. I just don't like it."

"Kenna and Caelyn are coming over later, and Kenna's going to spend the night. I won't be alone."

"That's something, I guess."

My lips curved into the first smile I'd cracked all day. "I'll be safe, Cupcake. I promise. I've got my mace and that bat from when I convinced you I wanted to try out for little league."

Ford shook his head and grinned. "You always did have a mean swing."

"This time, I'll just be aiming for an intruder's junk."

Ford let out a choked laugh. "I'll be extra careful to announce myself before entering this apartment."

"Smart man."

We ate, mostly in silence. If we spoke, it was about nothing serious. The food helped, but it also made me realize just how tired I was. I groaned as I pulled my legs up onto the couch. Ford caught one of my feet and then the other, tugging them onto his lap. He took the left one and began digging his thumbs into my sock-covered arch.

I bit back a moan. I wanted nothing more than to close my eyes and sink into the sensation. To forget all about one of the worst days in the history of days. To ignore the fact that the man bringing me comfort had once belonged to my sister, and that if she were still here, he likely wouldn't be rubbing my feet right now, he'd be rubbing hers.

The thought was like a bucket of ice water dumped right over my head. I quickly tugged my legs back, tucking my knees to my chest as if that would protect me from all of the emotions thrumming through me.

Ford let his hands drop. "Why'd you do that?"

I refused to look away. Couldn't even if I tried because those blue eyes of his seemed to hold me captive. "I can't touch you like that."

"Pretty sure I was the one touching you."

"Don't." The word cracked out like a whip.

Ford's gaze bored into mine. His eyes seeking, searching for something in the depths of my face. "What if I want more?"

My heart hammered in my chest, a freight train against my ribs. "You don't."

He arched a brow. "Shouldn't I be the one who gets to decide what I want?"

"We've been through the wringer today. Your emotions are just on overload. And even if you did want more, even if I did…I can't go there with you, Ford. For a million reasons."

He didn't say a word, but there was a pull to his stare, one that had me leaning forward instead of away. He slipped his hand under the fall of my hair. "Trouble—"

Before he could say anything else, the door swung open. Caelyn came to a screeching halt as she took in the two of us. "Whoops, I'm so sorry. Are we interrupting?"

I straightened in my seat, pushing to my feet. "Nope. Ford was just leaving. Thanks again for dinner." I said it all without once making eye contact with the man in question.

"Promise me you'll call if you see or hear anything suspicious."

"I will." I wouldn't. I'd get my bat, and I'd call Sheriff Raines, or "*Sheriff Hotstuff*" as Caelyn liked to call him.

Ford muttered a curse, knowing I was lying through my teeth. "I'll be downstairs until close."

Kenna let out a low whistle as soon as the door closed behind Ford. "That was…"

"Hot as hell?" Caelyn suggested.

"Don't," I warned and quickly gathered up Ford's and my trash, throwing it in the garbage bags along with the remnants of my ruined apartment.

"Bells, we don't have to talk about it, but something is going on between the two of you."

I tied the garbage bag opening into a knot, tugging on the ends a bit more harshly than necessary. "Nothing is going on between us. There will never be anything between the two of us." I opened a new trash bag and began stuffing things inside, not even bothering to consider if it was salvageable. If this creep, whoever they were, had touched it, I didn't want it in my apartment. I shoved item after item into the bag.

"Bell." I jolted as Kenna laid a hand on my shoulder. "Let us help you."

I bit my lip, trying to hold back the tears. "Thank you."

Caelyn wrapped her arms around both of us, bringing us into a huddle. "That's what we're here for. Anything you need. We've got you. You can move in with the tiny terrors and me for a while. You'd have to sleep on the couch, but you wouldn't have to stay here."

"There's no extra bedroom at the guest cottage, but you could sleep on my couch, too. Or I'm sure Harriet would give you one of the guest rooms at the main house."

I swallowed back the ball of emotion gathering in my throat. "Thank you." I released my hold on both of them. "But I need to stay here. I need to make it my safe place again. Get rid of all the bad memories and leave only the good."

Caelyn straightened. "I brought sage for just that reason. We can burn it after we clean up."

Kenna groaned, and I chuckled. "I was hoping you might."

Concern filled Caelyn's features. "Are you sure you don't want to talk about Ford? He cares about you, Bells."

I shook my head. "I'll never be able to go there. I can't."

Chapter Twenty-Six

Ford

I MUTTERED A CURSE AS I ALMOST DROPPED THE BOTTLE OF Jack for the second time.

"How's she holding up?"

I glanced up at Crosby for a split second before returning my attention to the drinks I was making. "She's hanging in there." Hanging in and making it really fucking clear that she had no need of me. Her support system was firmly in place, and I wasn't a part of that.

Crosby took a sip of his Guinness. "I can't tell if you're pissed at the psycho, Bell, or both."

I slid the Jack and Coke to the woman a few seats down and turned back to Crosby. "This sicko, Bell, myself, take your pick." Apparently, it was an equal opportunity day for my anger. Yet I didn't have a right to it, not where Bell was concerned, at least. I'd left her when she needed me most, and I knew a big part of her pushing me away was because she didn't trust that I was going to stick around a second time. Didn't trust that I would be there if she needed me now.

"You love her?"

Crosby threw out the question so casually, it took me a second to really take it in, but when I did, my muscles locked. "I've always loved her."

Crosby arched a brow. "That's a hell of a thing to realize."

"Not like that." My feelings for her had morphed over the years, sure, but the thing that was crazy was that they'd grown even while we were apart. I hadn't realized it at the time, but those feelings had always been there, steadily chipping away at my resolve. She'd always been the thing that tempted me to return. Even through my fear that she blamed me for the accident, I'd get hit with a memory of the two of us, the reckless kind, the kind that lit a fire in me to call her, to see her. Those reckless memories would almost bring me to my knees. I couldn't count the times I'd picked up my phone and hovered over her name in my contacts. Yet I'd always resisted.

"So…" Crosby let the word hang as he popped a French fry into his mouth. "What are you going to do about it?"

Wasn't that the million-dollar question? "It's a precarious situation." Who was I kidding? Moving Bell and me in the direction I wanted would be like trying to defuse a bomb with dozens of tripwires. One wrong move and I'd take us all out.

"Slow and steady, my friend, slow and steady."

It wasn't a bad plan. I knew the one thing I couldn't do was retreat. When Bell pushed me away, I needed to stand my ground. I had to show her with my actions that I was here to stay. Pretty words weren't going to cut it.

"Any updates?" Hunter appeared behind him, Ethan in tow.

I shook my head. "Not really. Kenna and Caelyn are up with her now, helping her clean up the mess. She'll be okay. But right now, she's freaked." I surveyed the men around me. "We all need to keep an eye out." The more people on the lookout for something suspicious, the safer Bell would be.

"How bad was it?" Ethan asked.

My back molars ground together as I remembered seeing the space for the first time. If the person responsible would've been in front of me at the time, I wasn't sure I wouldn't have killed them. "They destroyed just about everything."

Ethan looked around the bar. "Cops got any leads?"

"Not so far."

Hunter shook his head. "Goddammit. How could no one see anything? There are usually people out walking their dogs or jogging then. Someone must have seen a car, *something* that could help."

I began pouring half-pints of beer. "Raines is still getting the word out. His deputies will be back tomorrow to canvass the surrounding neighborhoods, see if anyone was out and about."

Crosby dropped a French fry back onto his plate. "Hell, the gossip mill will do a better job than they will. Word's already spreading, but we can make sure that folks are asking if anyone saw anything."

I slid two beers across the bar top to Hunter and Ethan. "That's not a bad idea." As much as I hated the way gossip spread in this town, people did genuinely care. They wanted to help whenever they could.

Crosby inclined his head to the dining area. "This is the perfect place to start. Have the waitstaff ask around as they're serving. And we can ask people at the bar."

Hunter nodded, giving Crosby's back a slap. "Good idea." Hunt looked back to me, lowering his voice as if the people around us couldn't still hear. "How's she really doing?"

My jaw worked. "Scared but determined."

"I'm taking that to mean she won't be coming to stay with either of us."

I chuckled despite my frustration with the situation. "Not even Mom's guilt trip could sway her." I glanced towards the back stairs. "I think she needs to prove to herself that she's not scared to stay here."

Hunter muttered a curse. "She's too damn stubborn and prideful."

"She's just used to handling things on her own now." And I hated that she'd had to become that way.

"She's letting Kenna and Caelyn help."

I shrugged. "They're family to her."

Hunter straightened. "So are we."

"It's different." I knew that Bell loved every member of the Hardy clan. But that didn't mean she'd completely let down her guard around us. We'd hurt her. Even though it had been her parents who had kept us away in the beginning, it didn't change the wound that was there.

Hunter glanced up at the ceiling. "I hate this."

"Me, too, brother. Me, too."

"Security company still coming tomorrow?"

"Yup." I poured another beer and handed it to Ethan.

"What about tonight?"

I gripped the edge of the bar, fingers digging into the glossy wood. I hated the idea of Bell staying here, even if Kenna was planning to stay. What would the two of them do if someone bigger and stronger broke in? "I guess I'll be staying in the office."

Hunter's lips twitched. "On that ratty old couch?"

"Dad's stayed there a night or two."

"When he was in the doghouse. And he always came home moaning about his back."

I chuckled. "But it was his pained looks that would always get Mom to forgive him."

Hunter shook his head. "She's always had a soft heart."

Crosby grinned. "Maybe your pained looks will get Bell to take pity on you."

Hunter snorted. "Yeah, right. She's not as easily won over."

And wasn't that the damn truth?

The night moved slowly and quickly all at the same time. We were busier than usual, but not because of any live band playing.

People were coming in to ask what had happened, if the sheriff had caught the intruder, how Bell was doing. I fought the urge to bite people's heads off. Instead, I asked them to spread the word that if anyone had seen something suspicious, to contact the sheriff's office.

I felt a little bad for Sheriff Raines. He had no idea the number of calls his office was going to receive tomorrow. Everyone from well-meaning citizens to nosy grandmas would be dialing him up. But maybe one of them had seen something helpful.

"Need anything else, boss man?"

I glanced up from wiping down the bar. "No, you go on home, Hank."

He shuffled his feet but didn't move towards the door. "You're staying, right?"

"Yeah. I'll sleep in the office, but leave the door open so I'll be able to hear if anyone tries to break in."

Hank's shoulders sagged in relief. "Good. Take care of our girl."

"I will." I was glad Bell had found good people like Hank who would have her back, who'd had it while I was gone. Now, I just needed to prove that I could be one of those people, too.

Footsteps sounded on the stairs, and Caelyn jolted as she came around the corner, hand flying to her chest. "Ford, geez, you scared the crud out of me."

I grinned, but it was half-hearted. "Crud, huh?"

She smiled. "Gotta try to keep the cursing to a minimum around the tiny terrors."

"Understandable. How are they?"

"They're good." Caelyn rested her palms against the bar. "How are you?"

There was genuine concern in her eyes as she asked, and my shoulders sagged in response. I was so damn tired. Exhausted from trying to prove myself to Bell, worrying about her, and now the nightmare of today. "I'm still fighting the good fight."

"Don't stop." She whispered the words as if Bell might be able to hear her a soundproofed floor away.

My spine straightened. This was the first bit of encouragement I'd gotten from Bell's inner circle. "I wasn't planning on it. You got any tips?"

Caelyn pressed her lips together, glancing back at the stairs. "You can't give up. Don't push, but don't back down either. I know that might not make sense—"

"No, it does." I studied her for a moment, light brown hair swept back in two braids that were tied off with colorful rubber bands, and so much hope in her eyes. "Think you could put in a good word for me?"

A mischievous smile stretched across her face. "Please, I already am." Her smile briefly turned to a grimace. "You might have more of a battle bringing Kenna over to your side, though. She's not one to forgive easily."

I sighed. "Thanks, Caelyn. I'll win you over one at a time." I set down the rag. "Let me walk you to your car."

She waved me off. "I'm fine, Ford."

"I'd feel a lot better if I did."

The humor fled Caelyn's face. "All right. You can just watch me from the door."

I led the way to the back door, unlocking it and holding it open for her. "Get home safe."

"I will. Hopefully, Will didn't sneak the girls candy while he was babysitting, and they're all asleep."

I chuckled. "Good luck with that."

She gave a little wave, her gaze catching mine. "Stay the course, Ford."

I nodded. I would stay the damn course if it killed me. But for the first time in a long while, something foreign invaded my chest. Something that felt a lot like hope.

Chapter Twenty-Seven

Bell

I STRETCHED UP ONTO MY TOES, STRAINING TO DUST EVERY NOOK and cranny of the light above the bar. I almost had it.

"What the hell are you doing?"

Ford's sharp voice caused me to shriek and jerk my arm back, sending my delicate balance off-kilter. "Oh, shit." My arms windmilled, but just as I started to teeter off to the side, strong arms caught me and tugged me in another direction. I landed with an *oomph* against a hard chest. Thankfully, it was my unmarred cheek that took the brunt on my landing.

"What. Were. You. Thinking?" Each word was gritted out as if it were its own sentence.

I struggled free of Ford's hold, straightening my t-shirt and tugging on the hem of my denim shorts. "I was thinking I was cleaning. What did it look like?"

"It looked like you were taking completely unnecessary risks with your safety."

I scoffed. "I was doing just fine until you scared the crap out of me."

A muscle in Ford's cheek seemed to flutter. "Don't do it again. It's a lawsuit waiting to happen."

"Fine. Since we're closed today, I'm heading out to the workshop." The security company had been here all morning but had realized that they needed more sensors than they had originally brought with them. Two of the guys had gone back to Seattle and would return late this afternoon to finish the job. I thought it was a waste to lose an entire day's business, but Ford had insisted, and he was the boss.

Ford glanced out the back door to the workshop. "Do me a favor and lock yourself in there."

My spine stiffened, but when I took in the genuine concern in his features, some of the tension melted away. "I will."

"Thanks."

I nodded, heading for the shop. I didn't know what to say to Ford anymore. But as I walked away from him, my body seemed to revolt, my stomach turned, and my heart sank. "Get used to it," I muttered to myself. Ford might be growing tired of LA, but he wasn't going to stay on Anchor either.

I unlocked the workshop and stepped into the space, relocking the door behind me. The scents of sawdust and sea air eased something in me. Sometimes, I blared music while I worked, drowning out the world. But today, I needed silence. Needed the space to let my thoughts cycle themselves out so I could finally release some of my worries.

I got to work putting my first coat of paint on the credenza, a gorgeous teal tone that was a little out there but perfect in my mind. I lost myself in the back and forth of the brush against the wood, in focusing on reaching every piece of surface perfectly. It was a meditation of sorts. A clearing of my mind. Nothing worked as well as this.

I lost all sense of time as I painted, losing myself in the work. I startled as I saw movement at the door, but sighed as I took in

Ford's form as he entered. "What is it with you sneaking up on me?"

"What is it with you and not paying attention to your surroundings?"

Ford's rough voice seemed to both make my anger heat and my skin tingle. "I locked myself in. I thought I was safe from distraction."

"I just came to tell you that the security company is gone. Everything's all set up."

I glanced outside. At some point, the sun had set, and we were now deep into twilight. I pushed to my feet, arching my back in a stretch. "That's good."

Little lines appeared between Ford's brows. "You hurting?"

"Just a little too much time hunched over."

He took a few steps forward. "You been working on this all afternoon?"

I nodded. It had been just the ticket. When I lost myself in making something whole and new again, nothing else existed, only the work in front of me.

"This is the piece we picked up from the garage sale?"

I laughed. "One and the same. It looks a little different, huh?"

Ford circled the credenza, hunching to get a closer look in places. "This is incredible. You could sell it for a nice chunk of change."

I shrugged. "Sometimes, I do. Other times, I keep them. But I'm never going to rip anyone off."

"I wasn't suggesting that. But you deserve to get paid for all of your hard work."

My cheeks heated. "Thank you."

Ford leaned against the shelves on the wall of the workshop, his gaze going from the credenza to me and back again. "You restored all the furniture pieces in the bar, didn't you?"

I pressed my lips together. It was moments like these when I felt a million miles away from Ford, like he didn't know me at all. Kenna, Caelyn, Hunter, they all knew how hard I'd slaved over bringing The Catch back to life. They'd brought me lunch or dinner as I worked through the day and into the night. They came to garage and estate sales with me as I hunted for bargains. They helped me haul and paint. And they knew how much it all meant to me. Ford had missed all of that.

"Most of the pieces in the bar are things I fixed up. But not everything." Who was I kidding? It was ninety-nine percent mine.

Ford swallowed hard, as if the information pained him in some way. "Why are you hiding from me?"

I reared back at the question. I wasn't hiding from him. I opened my mouth to say so and then stopped myself. Wasn't that exactly what I was doing? Ford Hardy terrified me. He was the tallest cliff I could jump off of, the greatest rush and worst potential for injury. I kept holding myself back from him because if he didn't have all my pieces, then maybe it wouldn't hurt so badly when he left. Or even worse, if he stayed and found someone else to love.

Gathering tears burned the backs of my eyes as I let out a shaky breath. "For so many reasons."

His knuckles turned white as he gripped the edge of the bookcase. "Maybe you could share some of those with me."

I let out a little laugh, but it was tinny in its falsehood. He wanted me to say it out loud? That I loved him but couldn't have him? That one day he would leave again? That I'd danced in my sister's shadow for most of my life, and I couldn't risk doing that in a relationship, too? My stomach turned at the thought of him comparing me to Vi. Her classic beauty and grace to my brashness and scarred body. I couldn't look into Ford's eyes and see the truth there.

"You don't trust me, do you?"

He never looked away from me as he asked the question, kept

his voice even and restrained, but the words made me wince. I trusted him. I trusted him with all of me except for my heart. I kept my gaze firmly locked with his. "No. I don't."

Ford gave a firm nod, pushing off the bookcase and striding for the door, not saying a single word. As the door slammed behind him, I slowly sank to the floor. Tears flowed freely and unchecked now. I bit down hard on my knuckle, silencing the sound of any sobs.

I was weak. So damn weak. Letting the fear of him leaving, of the possible comparison, the guilt over having always loved a boy who belonged to my sister eat away at my strength, at my bravery. And that weakness was going to cost me my one shot at happiness.

Chapter
Twenty-Eight

Ford

I LET THE DOOR SLAM BEHIND ME AS I STRODE OUT TOWARDS the beach. I was being a sulky asshole and knew it. But hearing Bell say out loud that she didn't trust me… It sliced deep, twisting and turning the blade as it went.

I blew out a harsh breath as I watched the waves crashing into the shore, darkening right along with the sky. Doubt crept in right along with the tide. Maybe too much was broken between Bell and me for this to work. Maybe I was crazy to think that she cared for me, too. But then I'd remember the flicker of heat in her eyes when I touched her, the quick catch in her breath. The way her voice cracked when she'd said that even if she did want more, she couldn't go there with me.

She was scared. Afraid because I'd hurt her. "Dammit." I'd done the exact thing I'd sworn I wouldn't do. I'd left the second things got tough. The only message I was sending her with that was that I couldn't handle her emotions, her hurt. Bell needed to feel free to share anything she was experiencing with me: her pain, her anger, her fear. I had to be strong enough to hold it right along with her, no matter how much agony it brought.

I let out another curse as I turned to head back to the workshop and make this right. Movement flickered in my peripheral vision, but before I could turn to find the source, pain cracked against the side of my head, light flashing behind my eyes before my vision tunneled. My legs seemed to go out from under me, unable to obey my brain's command to stay upright.

Darkness descended. The world flickered in and out. Rocks dug into my back, cutting into flesh as it felt like I was moving. My body *was* moving, but I wasn't responsible for the action. I tried to force my eyes open, but darkness engulfed me again.

Fire burned in my shoulder. Someone was pulling me, the grip on my wrist vise-tight. The pain in my arm stirred me back to consciousness. I groaned. The grip tightened, and the pull seemed to intensify. Then familiar darkness took me again.

Ice-cold water slapped at my face. I spluttered, turning my mouth away from the salty liquid trying to choke me. Someone cursed. There was pressure at my neck, pushing me down into the inky black water.

As my body submerged, it woke something in me—adrenaline similar to the kind that allowed mothers to lift cars to save their children. I pushed off the rocky seafloor, my shoulder screaming as I did. I clambered to my feet, my eyes stinging as I blinked the salt water out of them. The figure in front of me was only a blurry mass. I swung, aiming for the fuzzy middle, hoping to stun.

I caught ribs and flesh, and the assailant cursed. A male voice. I didn't pause, I went for a hook-shot to the jaw, and his head snapped to the side. But the move cost me. My body, already weakened from the assault, teetered off balance. The attacker used the moment to his advantage, delivering a brutal blow to my side.

I wheezed as I tried to straighten, praying I didn't have a broken rib or a punctured lung. A wave crashed into us both, sending more stinging salt water into my face and eyes. I straightened, steeling myself for another blow, but a deep voice from down the beach called out.

"What the hell is going on?"

The figure in front of me froze for a split second, and I tried to blink the water out of my eyes. Attempted to identify the man in front of me, but my vision wouldn't cooperate. The man tore off, moving out of the water and in the opposite direction of the guy jogging down the beach.

The adrenaline drained out of me in a flash. My body crumpled as I fell to my knees, my head staying just above the water.

"Are you okay?"

I pushed to my feet with the help of the guy who hadn't hesitated to help. "Thanks."

The man guided me to the beach where I could sit. "I'd offer to call the cops, but I don't have a phone, and I'm not sure I should leave you alone right now."

"Hey! Are you guys okay?" Crosby's voice broke through the night air.

"You got a phone on you?" the stranger asked.

"Yeah."

"Call the cops."

Crosby muttered a curse, crouching down as he pulled out his phone. "What the hell happened, Ford?"

"Someone tried to drown me." My throat burned as I spoke, the reality of the words hitting me as I said them. Someone had tried to drown me. Panic began to lick at my veins. "Bell." I pushed to my feet.

Crosby was at my side in a second. "Whoa. Slow down there. You need to sit."

"I have to make sure Bell is okay." The world wavered again, and then suddenly, everything went black.

And I didn't feel anything at all anymore.

Chapter Twenty-Nine

Bell

VOICES SHOUTING ON THE BEACH HAD ME DRYING MY eyes and forcing myself to stand. It was probably just kids. My friends and I had used the beach as our hangout all throughout high school. But the last thing The Catch needed was underage drinking going on a stone's throw from our doors.

I pushed open the door of the workshop to find that night had descended. I blinked against the darkness, trying to get my eyes to adjust. I didn't see any huge group of teens on the beach, only a few guys, one who looked to be passed out. *Great.* "Excuse me, this is private property. You're going to have to move the party down the beach."

"Bell?" The worry in Crosby's voice had my spine stiffening. "Are you okay?"

"I'm fine. What's going on?" I jogged towards the figures. My breath froze in my chest as my eyes focused on the man in the sand. Still. He was too still. And there was blood trickling from a wound on his forehead. "Ford?" The name felt as if it were made of a million tiny, frozen razor blades.

I sank to the sand. My hands moved rapidly over Ford's fallen form yet not touching. I was too afraid that any contact would cause more damage. "Is he breathing?" I didn't recognize the voice that asked the question, it was as foreign to my ears as a stranger's.

A hand rested on my shoulder. "He's breathing, Bell. And the EMTs are on their way."

"The sheriff?"

"He'll meet us at the hospital."

I reached out and gently took Ford's hand in mine. It was cold, too cold. Tears stung the backs of my eyes. This was not happening. Any second now, I'd wake up and realize that this was all some horrible nightmare. But the seconds ticked by, and no daylight streamed in. "What happened?"

A throat cleared, and I glanced up to see that the third man was Griffin Lockwood, and he was soaking wet. "I was walking back to my boat and saw two guys fighting in the surf. I thought it was just a couple of drunk tourist idiots, but I yelled, and one guy took off."

Sirens sounded in the background, and my gaze snapped back to Ford. "They're here. They're going to help you." They had to. I would not lose him, too.

"He's going to be fine, Bell."

Crosby held tightly to my hand as we sat in a sterile waiting room. I hadn't seen this room before, but I was all too familiar with the hospital itself. The dime-a-dozen nature pictures on the walls and the smell of antiseptic. *It's going to be okay. He's going to be fine.* This would not have the same ending as my last trip through these hallways.

"Should I call Hunter? The Hardys?"

"No." I flinched at the sharpness in my voice. "Maybe call Hunter, but don't call Kara and Frank. I don't want them to worry." If this news gave Frank another stroke, I'd never forgive myself.

"Okay." Crosby gave my hand a squeeze and then released it.

The muffled sounds of Crosby's call with Hunter only made me zone out more. My vision blurred on the empty chairs across from me as time faded in and out. I wasn't going to lose him. I said it over and over to myself.

A voice cleared, and a tall man with salt-and-pepper hair appeared in my line of sight. "I'm Dr. Park, and I've been treating Mr. Hardy."

I pushed to my feet, wobbling a little. "How is he?"

"He's going to be just fine."

My shoulders sagged in relief at the doctor's words, and Crosby gave my shoulder a squeeze. "Told you, Bell. His head is tougher than you think."

Dr. Park glanced down at Ford's chart. "He has a dislocated shoulder, bruised ribs, a wound that required eight stitches, and a concussion."

I reached out blindly to grab onto Crosby's arm. That was just fine? Crosby scowled at the doctor, who seemed impervious to his stare.

"He's regained consciousness, and we'll be releasing him tonight—"

I cut the doctor off. "Is that wise? Doesn't he need someone to monitor him?"

Dr. Park looked up from the chart. "He'll need someone to stay with him, yes. To wake him up every few hours and ask him simple questions. But, honestly, we've found that patients recover better in their own homes."

"I'll stay with him." The words were out before I could

consider how wise the offer was. I didn't care anymore. None of it mattered. I'd almost lost Ford, and the last words I'd said to him had been ones of hurt and anger. "Was he able to tell you what happened?"

"We were able to put most of the pieces together from his injuries. Mr. Hardy filled in the rest. We found bark in his head wound, so we assume he was struck with some sort of stick or branch. The abrasions on his back led us to believe he was dragged towards the water where the assailant then attempted to drown him. This is when Mr. Hardy came to and began to fight back."

My stomach pitched, all its contents revolting at the image painted in my mind. "Excuse me." I ran for the bathroom across the hall, just making it in time to empty my stomach into the toilet. I retched and heaved until nothing more would come up. My legs wobbled as I exited the stall and made my way to the sink. I rinsed out my mouth and splashed water on my face, patting it dry.

I studied the reflection staring back at me. Far too pale, with dark circles rimming my eyes, and a feral, panicked quality to my gaze. I needed to see Ford for myself. I needed to touch him. To make sure he was safe and real and not going anywhere.

The door slowly opened, and a nurse appeared with a gentle smile. She had a grandmotherly air to her and extended a travel-sized bottle of mouthwash. "Your friend thought you might want this."

"Thank you." My hand shook as I took it from her.

"You just let me know if you need some juice or crackers, and I'll rustle some up for you."

I nodded, and she left. I quickly rinsed out my mouth, relishing the relief the minty mouthwash brought, and headed back into the waiting room. "Can I see him now?"

The doctor's expression gentled. "Of course you can. I'll have the nurse bring in some discharge papers and instructions for home care. Mr. Hardy needs to take it easy for a few weeks."

I nodded and headed straight for the ER bay the doctor pointed to. My hand froze for a moment as I gripped the curtain, my heart seeming to trip over itself. I wasn't sure what I'd do if Ford sent me away. I took a deep, steadying breath and pulled the rough fabric aside.

Ford's eyes snapped to me. "Trouble."

I did the last thing I wanted to. I burst out crying. It was as if all the emotions I'd been holding back for the past twelve hours spilled out of me all at once.

"Trouble," he growled. "Get over here. I'm fine. I promise."

I hurried over to the bed, trying to get myself under control—and failing miserably. "I'm so sorry." I hiccupped between words.

His arm that wasn't in a sling reached out for my hand. I took it greedily. "You have nothing to be sorry for."

I couldn't seem to stop my tears. Ford released my hand and cupped my face. "What is all this about?"

"I-I-I almost lost you, and the last thing I said was that I didn't trust you." The sobs started back up in earnest.

"Bell." His face softened. "I shouldn't have walked out. I haven't earned your trust back, it's okay. I will one day."

I let my head fall to the bed, pressing against Ford's leg. He ran his hand over my hair, the feel of his fingers tangling in the strands the most comforting thing I'd ever felt. "Everything's going to be okay."

My head snapped up. "Did you see who attacked you?"

Ford grimaced. "I wish. It was dark, and the salt water messed with my vision."

I took his hand in mine, trying not to grip it too tightly. "What the hell is going on around here?"

"I don't know. But we're going to find out."

"We are."

I startled, turning to see a very pissed-off-looking Sheriff Raines. A nurse gaped behind him. I didn't blame her. He looked like some dark avenging angel. "Hi." My greeting came out as a squeak, but the man was seriously intimidating when he was this angry.

Raines gave me a quick nod and then turned his attention to Ford. "I'm really sorry this happened to you."

"You and me both." Ford chuckled but then winced, holding his ribs.

I stood. "Do you want me to get a nurse?"

Ford squeezed my hand. "I'm fine, Trouble. Just a little tender."

My eyes narrowed on him. "You forget I know when you're lying." I knew all of Ford's tells, and the shifting of his eyes was a dead giveaway.

"I'll take the pain meds when I get home." I let out some sort of growl, and he grinned. "I promise."

Sheriff Raines cleared his throat. "Did you see anything?"

Ford scowled. "Not much that will help, I'm afraid. A man. About my height and build. But I couldn't see any discernable features. It was dark. He was wearing a hat. And my eyes were full of salt water."

Raines pulled a notepad out of his pocket and began scrawling things down. "We found the branch that was used to strike you, but I'm afraid we won't have much luck with prints. It was waterlogged, and the bark was peeling off."

"So back to square one," I mumbled.

"Not square one." The sheriff met my gaze head-on. "I'll have as many men as I can afford canvassing the surrounding area tomorrow and asking stores in the vicinity if they have any cameras outside their properties. Maybe we'll get lucky."

I wasn't going to hold my breath. Anchor was a safe place to live most of the time. The crimes we faced were petty theft, underage drinking, and an occasional drug bust. Store owners weren't big on security of any kind. "I hope you find something." The doubt in my voice told him how unlikely I thought that was.

"I'll give you two a call tomorrow and stop by to update you and take a formal statement." Raines' gaze shifted to Ford. "If you think of anything new, write it down, and we'll go over it tomorrow. And I'll have deputies doing drive-bys of your place and The Catch."

A chill skittered down my spine. "Do you think this is related to my break-in?" I hadn't put the two together until that very moment, but what were the chances that two unrelated crimes would take place so close together on an island the size of Anchor?

The sheriff's face hardened. "I think it's likely. I'm just not sure why."

"Bell, you're staying with me tonight."

The sharp crack in Ford's words had me spinning around. "I was already planning on it." My eyes narrowed. "But you bark an order like that at me again, and I'll conveniently forget where I put your pain pills."

Ford's lips twitched. "Fair enough."

"You two want a ride back to the island? Or should I be worried that Bell is going to throw you overboard?"

I let out a little laugh. My voice sounded rusty, as if I hadn't used it in a while. "I think there's a fifty-fifty shot. But we'd love a ride if you can fit Crosby on the boat, too."

Raines grinned. "No problem. I'll get everything squared away and be ready to go when you're discharged."

"Thank you." I held the sheriff's gaze for a beat, wanting him to know just how much I meant those two words. He gave me a swift nod and headed down the hall.

I turned back to Ford, his face was serious again as he spoke. "I was so damn scared, Bell. Terrified that the guy was going to go after you next, or that he'd already hurt you."

My throat seemed to catch as I swallowed. "I'm fine. Totally and completely safe."

"I know. Can you do me a favor?"

I stared into blue eyes that I could get lost in forever. I'd promise him whatever he wanted to clear the fear that clouded those beautiful eyes. I nodded.

Ford reached out, grabbing my hand and tugging me towards the bed. "I need you to stick close for a while."

"I can do that." But I knew I'd be letting my heart go in the process.

Chapter Thirty

Ford

I GROANED AS I STRETCHED, MY RIBS TWINGING. I BLINKED against the light that was way too bright. Everything hurt. I swore my eyelashes somehow even held pain. I glanced around the room, everything coming back to me in flashes. The strike on the head. The fight. My fear for Bell. Her waking me up throughout the night to ask me my birthday and who the president was.

"Shit." I scrubbed a hand, the arm uninhibited by a sling, over my stubbled jaw then slowly swung my legs over the side of the bed and sat up, letting out a litany of curses. The ribs were going to be the death of me.

I'd agreed to half a pain pill last night, but hadn't wanted to take any more. Even with the high-quality locks and top-of-the-line alarm system, I'd wanted my wits about me. If the asshole came back, I wasn't going to be drugged out of my mind and leave Bell to fight him off alone. Just the thought had my chest seizing with the sudden need to lay eyes on her.

I strode barefoot down the hall, peeking into bedrooms as I went. Each time I came up empty, my heart beat a little harder in my chest. By the time I reached the living room, it felt as if the organ might fly right out of my rib cage. Right up until I caught sight of Bell curled into a tiny ball on the couch.

I scowled. "What are you doing?"

Bell startled, flying to a sitting position. "What? Oh, hi. Are you okay?"

"Of course I'm okay. Why are you contorting yourself into the world's most uncomfortable position on my couch instead of taking one of the four other bedrooms?"

It was Bell's turn to scowl now. "Because I didn't want to let myself sleep too deeply. I was afraid I wouldn't hear my alarm and would sleep through it when I was supposed to wake you up."

I sighed. "You need your rest. You've been through a lot."

"I'm fine."

God, I hated that word. It never meant what it was supposed to. "No, you're exhausted. Why don't I make you some breakfast, and then you can go sleep on a real bed?" I wanted to curl up beside her and hold her and never let her go, but that wasn't what she needed from me right now.

"How about I make *you* some breakfast, and then you can take a nap?" I bit back a growl, and Bell laughed at my expression. She held up both hands. "Okay, okay. Why don't we make breakfast together, and then we can both take a nap?"

"You're getting warmer."

Before Bell could respond, there was a knock on the door. She pushed off the couch as if going to answer it, but I pinned her with a stare. "Don't even think about it." I turned for the door. While the back of the house was comprised of windows that looked out over the bluff and ocean below, the front was designed for privacy and security. There was no way to see into or out of the home other than through the small windowpanes on the front door.

I glanced through the small opening to see Sheriff Raines. I quickly opened the door. "Sheriff."

"Morning, Ford. How are you feeling?"

I ushered him inside. "Like I took a particularly hard tackle in a game I hadn't been training for."

Raines chuckled. "That's not a fun feeling."

"No, it's not."

"Morning, Sheriff," Bell greeted.

"Please, call me Parker, both of you."

Bell nodded. "Okay, Parker, can I get you some coffee? Ford and I were just about to rustle up some breakfast."

He held a hand out to indicate that Bell should lead the way. "We can do this in the kitchen. And I will never say no to coffee."

Bell immediately set to work on breakfast while I started on the drinks. Pulling a few mugs down from the cabinet, I glanced at Parker. "So, you find anything?"

The sheriff scrubbed a hand over his face, drawing attention to eyes that clearly hadn't seen enough sleep. "Nothing that helps in any significant way. The bank caught a brief glimpse of someone on their security feeds, but it's from the back, and doesn't give us much more than we already had to go on."

I knew Bell had expected as much, but I'd been holding out hope that they'd get something usable. Parker cleared his throat. "I need to talk to you both about something, and it's not going to be pleasant."

I stiffened, moving closer to Bell, who'd stopped whisking eggs. "What is it?"

"I did some research last night and saw that Ford was driving the night your sister was killed, Bell."

Her muscles visibly tensed as she set down the utensil. "What are you trying to say?"

"I'm wondering if there's anyone who was especially angry after the accident. Not just upset, but truly angry."

Bell's mouth opened and closed as she tried to wrap her head around what Parker was asking. I cleared my throat. "I'm not sure I'll be much help on that front. I left for college right after the accident and haven't been back here until now." Saying it outright like that made me realize just how cowardly it had been. I'd tucked tail and run.

A small, smooth hand slipped into mine, our fingers interlocking. The peace and comfort it brought nearly sent me to my knees, but I couldn't bring myself to look at her. "There were lots of folks who were sad, and there were more than a few who were angry."

My gaze flicked up to Bell. She swallowed hard. "At the top of that list would be my parents. They threatened to sue Ford if he had any contact with me or them."

Parker straightened on his barstool. "Do your folks know Ford is back in town?"

Bell nodded. "We ran into them a few days ago at Rocco's."

"And how did that run-in go?"

Bell's body gave a small shudder, and I released her hand, pulling her against me. I needed more contact. Felt like if I had that, I could protect her in some way. My ribs screamed in protest, but I ignored them. "It wasn't great."

Parker nodded. "I'm going to have to talk to them. Is there anyone else that you can think of? Someone who expressed thoughts or feelings that seemed odd or out of place?"

A faraway look overtook Bell's face, one that included flashes of pain every few seconds. She was back in the past, the time that had hurt her so badly. I had the sudden urge to deck the sheriff for forcing her to go back there, even though I knew he was only trying to help. "I know there were people who thought Ford should've been at the funeral, shown his support, but it's honestly all a bit of a blur."

Those people weren't wrong. I should've been there, no matter what Bell's parents had threatened. A toxic mix of anger and guilt swirled in my gut. "I'm so sorry, Trouble." I whispered the words in her ear, but I was sure Parker heard it.

Bell turned in my arms. "No. You will not let judgmental assholes make you feel guilty. You were hurting. You were eighteen and scared. We both made mistakes, but we're not going to let people who have no place in our lives make us feel bad for something they know nothing about."

The corners of my lips tipped up. "Sometimes, I forget how fiery you can get." It was a dangerous thing to forget because when fire was pointed at you, the burns could be lethal. But it was so damn beautiful to watch.

Bell scowled at me, and both Parker and I burst out laughing. She threw up her hands. "No one takes me seriously."

I pulled her back against me with my good arm, pressing my lips to the top of her head. The scents of jasmine and that thing that I'd always associated with Bell but had never been able to identify filled my senses. I breathed her in, letting the fragrance soothe my frayed nerves. "We take you seriously, Trouble. Trust me."

Parker cleared his throat. "I'm going to keep looking into who might have a grudge against Ford. Bell, have you noticed anything odd either before Ford returned or after? Anyone paying you attention that felt off? Anything at all?"

Bell gave a small jerk in my arms. "The gifts."

"Gifts...plural?" I'd almost forgotten about Vi's scarf that had been left on Bell's doorstep, but had there been more that she hadn't told me about? I fought the clench in my hands as I did my best to keep my frustration in check.

Bell nibbled on her bottom lip. "Every year around the anniversary of Violet's passing and around her birthday, I get gifts. It's usually flowers and a photo of her or the two of us together."

My blood went cold, and my heart rate seemed to slow. "And you didn't tell anyone?"

Color hit Bell's cheeks. "I honestly thought it was a friend. Someone who wanted to show their support but didn't want to make it awkward. There's never been a name, but they were never threatening. It only got weird with the scarf."

"What scarf?" Parker had taken out his notebook again and was furiously scribbling.

I adjusted the strap on my sling, wanting to tear the damn thing off. "Someone left Violet's favorite scarf on Bell's doorstep with a note telling her not to forget her sister."

"It was weird. And it almost felt a little mean. Like I could ever forget her."

I slipped my hand under the fall of Bell's hair, giving her neck a squeeze. "It felt threatening to me. I asked the staff to keep an eye out, but no one's seen anything."

Parker jotted down a few more things. "Do you have the scarf? Any of the gifts?"

Bell nodded. "At my apartment. They're in a box at the bottom of my closet."

Parker pushed to his feet. "I'd like to get those processed, just in case there are prints."

"Of course. Caelyn is running the bar today. She has an extra key to my apartment, and I can give you the security code."

Parker studied Bell for a moment. "How many extra keys are floating around to your place, and who has the security code?"

Bell stiffened, and I hated that Parker was forcing her to look at everyone in her life with suspicious eyes. "Hunter, Caelyn, and Kenna have keys, but none of them have the security code. I haven't needed to give it to them since Ford had the system installed."

Parker nodded. "Let's keep it that way. I want both of you to be careful. Stick with other people as much as possible. No solo runs on the beach or anything like that. Keep an eye out for anyone who's acting suspicious. If you notice something, no matter how small, call me."

We both agreed. Bell gave Parker the security code, and then he was on his way. She sagged against the door as it shut. "What the hell is going on, Ford?"

I reached out with my good hand, tucking a stray lock of hair behind her ear and trailing my hand down her neck, giving her shoulder a squeeze. "I don't know, but we're going to figure it out." She didn't look especially hopeful. And God, I hated that. "Let's eat breakfast, and then my mom gave me a box of stuff she saved for me. I think there are yearbooks in there. We can look through them and see if it jogs any memories for you."

"That's not a bad idea." A flicker of hope lit Bell's eyes. Trouble always did better when she could take action. She needed a sense of purpose, to feel like she could change her circumstances.

We ate quickly, neither of us having much of an appetite after our meeting with the sheriff. I took my plate to the sink. "The box is in the garage."

Bell took my plate and placed it in the dishwasher. "Don't even think about trying to get it. You sit on the couch. I'll get the box."

I grumbled but obeyed. My ribs weren't exactly happy at the moment, and I refused to take another pain pill.

Bell was gone and back in a matter of seconds, placing the worn box on the coffee table in front of us. She flashed me a devastating smile. "I really hope there aren't old *Playboys* in this box."

I chuckled. "If my mom found *Playboys* in my childhood room, I *really* hope she threw them out."

I pulled open the top flaps that were tucked into one another. There was a total mix of items peeking out, and I suddenly felt like any of them could be a live grenade. I pulled out two football trophies, setting them on the table.

"State champs your junior year. I remember that game." Bell picked up the trophy, dusting off the plaque.

I smiled. "I remember you bedazzled your shirt with my number on it."

That gorgeous pink flooded Bell's cheeks. "I was such a nerd."

My gaze caught hers. "I loved it." The color in her cheeks deepened, and I began to see those years growing up through a different lens. All the time she'd spent with me, the way she'd been my biggest cheerleader and staunchest defender.

"What else do you have in there?" Bell stood, leaning over the box, and pulled out a framed photo. Her thumb traced over the glass. "You two looked so perfect that night."

It was Violet and me at our senior prom. She'd coordinated my bowtie to her dress color and given the florist strict instructions for the corsage and boutonniere. Everything looked perfect from the outside looking in. But we'd gotten in a huge fight that night. I'd wanted her to consider going farther away than Seattle for college, and she'd refused to even entertain the idea. She'd ended up crying in the bathroom, and I'd felt like a grade-A jerk. "Nothing is as perfect as it seems."

I set the photo on the coffee table and pulled out the first yearbook. "Here we go."

Bell settled back on the couch, and we began flipping through the pages. I stalled on one that held a picture of Bell, Kenna, and Caelyn, their arms wrapped around each other and their faces dotted with paint. Bell looked adorable, and something more. She just had more life in her eyes than anyone I'd ever seen before. I couldn't explain it.

"That was community service day. We were on the team that painted benches at the park, and I'm pretty sure we ended up with more paint on us than on the benches."

I grinned. "I remember. I had to wrap you in two beach

towels before putting you in my SUV." My gaze caught Bell's. "You looked like an adorable burrito."

That gorgeous shade of pink was back in her cheeks. "All the girls were jealous that you came to pick me up. If only they knew you saw me as a burrito."

"An adorable burrito, there's a difference." Something shuttered over Bell's gaze. I pushed on, trying to get through it and back to those gorgeous greens. "And I don't see you as adorable now, Trouble. You're so much more than that."

Something that looked a lot like hope flared in her eyes before she tamped it down. "What's next?"

I bit back a growl and turned the page. A strangled laugh was startled out of me. On this one was a photo of Hunter and Ethan dressed in full cheerleader garb, complete with wigs, pom-poms, and skirts. Their arms were wrapped around Violet, who was caught in mid-laugh.

"Ohmigosh, the powder puff game. I'd totally forgotten about that."

Once a year, the cheerleaders and football players switched places for a round of flag football. Hunter had made sure he and his friends had gone above and beyond, and everyone had lost it when they'd seen the boys all decked out. "You know he had Mom sew those uniforms for them."

"No, he didn't." I nodded, and Bell shook her head. "Kara is such a trooper."

"She loved it. But Hunter drew the line when she offered to share her lipstick."

Bell dissolved into laughter. "I would've paid good money to see that."

"Me, too."

Bell's finger ghosted over the photo of Hunter and Ethan. "I think they both had a little crush on her."

My brows rose. "Really?"

She let out a scoffing sound. "Come on, pretty much every guy did."

"She had a light that drew people to her."

Bell's finger stopped just under Violet's face. "She really did."

We kept flipping through pages, lost down memory lane. The photos of Vi and me didn't hurt as much anymore. It was more of a dull ache. Not a sadness for what I'd lost, but for a life that had been cut far too short. And there was a healthy dose of joy mixed in too, at all of the memories we'd never lose.

I shut the book with a thud. "Did it bring back anything that might be useful?"

Bell tucked her legs up to her chest, resting her chin on her knees. "After it all happened, and I realized you weren't coming back, I was really angry." Bell didn't look away from me as she spoke, didn't hide herself from me, but I could feel the regret pouring off her in waves. "People felt bad for me. I'd lost my sister, and they all knew that you and I were close. I think they said things to make me feel better, to show they were on my side, so to speak, but I don't think most of them meant it."

I scooted closer, wrapping my free hand around her calf. "You had a right to be angry."

"So do you." Bell pressed her lips together before speaking again. "You didn't deserve all those people whispering about you behind your back, even if you weren't here to see it. I'm so sorry I fed that machine."

I gave Bell's leg a squeeze, pulling myself even closer to her. "Enough apologies. We were both hurting. Neither of us handled it in the best way. What matters now is that we don't waste the time we have left."

Bell's gaze locked with mine. "I don't want to waste a moment."

Chapter Thirty-One

Bell

THERE WAS A ROARING SOUND IN MY EARS, AS IF I HAD suddenly been submerged in water. I was frozen to the spot as Ford leaned in, hesitating for just a moment before his lips met mine, as if he were giving me one last chance to pull away, to tell him that I didn't want this. But I couldn't. Almost losing him had torn that last little bit of restraint and self-preservation away.

Ford's lips met mine in a slow, heady enticement. They were so warm and surprisingly smooth, but the bite of the stubble lining his mouth sent a warring cascade of sensations over my skin. I wanted to sink into the feeling, into the kiss, into Ford. I wanted to lose myself in everything that was uniquely him.

His tongue darted between my lips, and I welcomed it, tangling mine with his in a rhythm that could only be ours. I'd never experienced anything like this. It was a mixture of adrenaline and homecoming, of racing hearts and peace. It was like everything else about Ford: a potent and powerful juxtaposition.

Ford's hand slipped beneath the fall of my hair, his fingers tangling in the strands. As his mouth broke away from mine, I let out a mewl of protest. He kept his hand at my nape, studying my face as if looking for signs of panic.

My chest heaved as I willed my heart under control. "That was—"

"I don't think there are words to describe that kiss, Trouble."

I bit my lip as heat hit my cheeks. "But you stopped."

Ford chuckled. "There's only so much torture I can take when I know I'm not going to be able to have you. And as much as I hate to say it, my ribs and arm aren't up for what I want from you." His gaze roamed over my face. "*If* you want the same."

The roaring in my ears was back. This was a moment I'd dreamt of since I'd first realized that boys might be more than schoolyard playmates and cootie-filled classmates. My heart seemed to rattle in my chest. I was at war with myself. I wanted Ford more than my next breath, yet I was terrified. "I want you. Us. But—"

Ford's hand tightened in my hair. "But what?"

"But I think we should take things slow." The words came out in a rush, but I felt relief as soon as they were released. Slow and steady. That's what I needed, a chance to ease into things. I wanted to laugh, like I could ease into anything where Ford Hardy was concerned. My heart and soul were already tumbling down an incline I doubted I'd have any control over.

His lips twitched. "I can do slow." He swept his mouth against mine in a barely-there kiss. "As long as I can touch you." Another brush. "Kiss you." His hand teased the back of my neck. "Feel your skin."

I was practically panting. I scrambled to my feet. "We should get out of here." If I stayed locked up in this house alone with Ford much longer, I'd end up naked and making poor life choices.

Ford's eyes twinkled. "Can't resist me, huh?"

I grabbed a pillow and hurled it at him, but Ford batted it away with his good hand. I picked up another one and pointed it at him. "You have a real problem with self-esteem."

"I really do." He pushed to his feet, closing in on me. "Kiss it better?"

I held out the pillow to keep him at bay. "Oh, no, you don't. I'll punch you in your bad shoulder, don't think I won't."

Ford chuckled but sidestepped me and went for his keys in the dish by the door. "Come on. I'll buy you an ice cream cone."

I blinked rapidly at the quick turn of events. "Mint Oreo?"

"As if I would deign to get you anything else."

I grinned. "Smart man."

"Remember when that dweeb you dated in middle school brought you regular Oreo instead of mint?"

I bit back my laugh at the memory but tried to arrange my face into a scowl. "He wasn't a dweeb. He was perfectly nice. One of the few boys you didn't put the fear of God into."

Ford snorted. "You certainly sent him packing quick enough when he brought you that ice cream."

I rolled my eyes. He wasn't wrong. Jim had only lasted a week after that stunt. I grabbed my sweatshirt, and we headed for the SUV. I made a motion for the keys. "You're not driving anywhere until you get that sling off."

Ford's footsteps faltered. "You've got to be kidding me."

I held out my hand. "You heard what the doctor said, no driving for two weeks." Ford didn't budge. "Don't make me call Sheriff Raines and have you arrested."

Ford groaned but dropped the keys into my open palm. "You put a scratch on my baby, and we're gonna have problems, Trouble."

I chuckled as I climbed in and started the engine. Ford's fancy SUV drove like a dream, no...more like driving a cloud. The ride into town didn't take long, but by the time we pulled into a parking space near Two Scoops, it was almost as if the kiss hadn't happened. We'd descended back into the normality of our bantering friendship.

I reminded myself that this was good. I needed that normality right about now. Ford wrapped an arm around my shoulders as we walked towards the ice cream shop, and any semblance of normality vanished in a few beats of my heart.

He pressed his lips to my temple. "Breathe, Bell. Just breathe." I took a deep breath and willed my muscles to relax. "That's it. It's just you and me. Things have only changed a little."

I fought back the urge to laugh. A little? More like my world had been turned upside down.

A bell tinkled as Ford pulled open the door to Two Scoops and ushered me in before him. Mrs. Green looked up at the sound and grinned when she caught sight of me. "Bell, it's been too long. I'm so glad you came in. Ethan told me what's been going on. My boy's worried about you, and I am, too."

"It's good to see you, Mrs. Green. I'm fine, I promise."

"I've told you time and again, call me Cathy. You're not a little girl anymore." Her eyes flickered as Ford's arm wrapped around my shoulders. She cleared her throat. "Ford, welcome back."

"Thank you. It's good to see you."

"You, too…" Her voice trailed off as she looked from Ford to me and back again. "You two aren't…?"

Ford's grip on my shoulder tightened, his eyes hardening a fraction. "We aren't what?"

"You aren't dating. That's what she's too scared to say." The voice came from the back as Mr. Green, a hulking man in his late sixties, stepped out. He'd never made sense to me as the owner of an ice cream store, he looked more like a linebacker or a mobster. His gaze narrowed on us both but then locked with mine. "But you wouldn't do that, would you, Bell? That would be too weird."

I swallowed hard, my skin suddenly becoming too tight for my body. "I—I—"

"What she's too polite to say is that it isn't any of your business." There was a hard edge to Ford's voice. "But I can see that you aren't all that focused on keeping customers, so we'll just be going."

"No, please," Cathy started. "We're sorry, it was just a shock, that's all. Please stay."

My steps faltered, but Ford gave my hand a swift tug as he continued towards the door. I gave Cathy what I hoped was a sympathetic smile, but I couldn't bring myself to glance in Mr. Green's direction.

Ford strode quickly towards the SUV, and I almost tripped over my feet. "Would you slow down?"

He whirled on me. "That doesn't piss you the hell off?"

I took an instinctive step back, the anger seeming to roll off Ford in waves. "Mr. Green? Yes. Cathy? She was just surprised." I paused for a moment, taking in every detail of Ford's form, the tense muscles, the blazing eyes, and my heart sank. "That kind of thing? It's going to happen more than once. This is a small community, and people think it's their right to share their opinions on your life. Us dating, or whatever you want to call it…people are going to talk. If you can't handle it, we might as well call it quits before either of us gets hurt." The words burned my throat as I spoke, and I knew that the loss of even the possibility of what Ford and I could be would break me.

A muscle in his cheek ticked, but his blazing eyes didn't look away from mine. "I'm not calling it quits."

But I wasn't sure he'd ever be at peace with what the people of this island said about him. And what did that mean for our hope of a future?

Chapter Thirty-Two

Bell

"WHERE ARE YOU GOING?"

"To the pantry to get more napkins. Is that allowed, warden?" Each word came out through gritted teeth. The past two weeks, my life had turned into a jail cell. Every single person in my orbit seemed to have taken overprotective to a new level.

Hunter brought his crew in for lunch every single day, sometimes coming back for dinner, too. Kenna came by to check on me before and after work. And Ford had instructed the entire Catch staff to not leave me unattended for a moment. This was why Caelyn was giving me the evil eye as I headed down the hallway.

"Does no one else see how sexist and ridiculous it is that I can't be left unattended for sixty seconds? But, apparently, it's just fine for Ford to be out on his own?" He'd left this morning to pick up supplies for the bar in Seattle, and he'd gone completely alone. "He's the one that someone tried to kill." As soon as the words were out of my mouth, tears filled my eyes. "Shit, shit, shit!"

My emotions were on overdrive, and I seemed to cry or yell at the drop of a hat. Maybe I was PMSing. I hoped that was it, because I refused to become this crazy person forever. Caelyn pulled me into a hard hug. "I'm sorry, honey. I know this is a lot. We're all just worried."

After I'd stayed in one of Ford's guest rooms for two more nights, and he was free of his sling and on the road to recovery, I'd told him I was going back home. Ford hadn't been happy. In fact, he called nightly to make sure I had locked all my windows and doors and set the alarm. We'd gone from sharing a scorching kiss to me feeling like he saw me as a little sister again. Sure, he touched me, even brushed his mouth against mine, but those lip touches only came in private, away from anyone who might cast judgment. And they were missing the heat of that first embrace.

Part of me was relieved by the sudden reprieve, but mostly there was a crushing sense of disappointment, of loss, for the thing I'd never had to begin with. I stepped out of Caelyn's embrace. "I'm going to shut myself in the closet for at least sixty seconds and get my shit together. Do you think you can keep the sharks at bay in the meantime?"

Caelyn grinned. "I think I can handle sixty seconds. Much longer, and Hunter's going to start asking where you are."

I groaned. He was just as bad as Ford. "Do what you can." I strode towards the closet, shutting myself inside. I leaned my forehead against the cool brick wall, taking a few deep breaths. "Get it together, Bell." Maybe it was time for a vacation. I could empty my barely-there savings account and get myself as far away as that money would take me.

My stomach twisted at the idea of leaving Ford when all of this was going down. Sheriff Raines still didn't have any leads. And while nothing else suspicious had happened, everyone was still on edge. I straightened, knowing if I didn't get out there soon, Hunter really would come looking for me, and I didn't want to bite his head off, too.

I grabbed the package of napkins and headed out. When I reached the bar, my steps faltered. Waiting there, and looking supremely pissed, were my parents. Okay, maybe my dad didn't look pissed, but my mom made up for it. "Hey."

I wasn't sure what else to say. They had to have heard through the grapevine about my apartment being vandalized, and I hadn't even gotten a call. It was a reality check. They weren't a part of my life anymore, and chances were they never would be.

"Isabelle." My mother spat my name like an insult. And it was.

I tried to hide the flinch but knew a flicker of it showed. "Can I get you a drink? A menu?" The entire half full restaurant had grown silent, taking in the show.

"As if I would eat here. It probably isn't even up to code."

"Heather..." my father warned.

Her head snapped in his direction. "What? It's probably not."

I clasped my hands in front of me, refusing to give in to her games. "All right. If you're not here for a drink or a meal, why don't you tell me what it is I've done to piss you off now. I can then tell you I don't care, and you can get even more mad and leave."

My mom's mouth opened and closed again and again. "You— you are—did you know the sheriff came to speak with us?" I shrugged. "He wanted to know our whereabouts the night that your apartment was vandalized and the night that—that boy was attacked. I know that he's asking because of something *you* said."

I gave another shrug. "That's what happens when you threaten innocent people with lawsuits. That's what happens when you lie and manipulate." She had made me believe that Ford wanted nothing to do with me. Had said he couldn't live with the guilt of killing my sister and that he never wanted to see my face again. I could forgive her for a lot, for pressuring me to be someone I wasn't, for not being able to love me for who I was, but I didn't think I'd ever be able to forgive her for that.

My mother's face reddened to an unhealthy level. "That Hardy boy never should've shown his face here again. And *you*—you will have nothing to do with him. That's an order."

I chuckled, but it was low and ugly. "Mom, I have everything to do with him. I always have."

She gasped. "You didn't. You wouldn't." She was assuming something that wasn't exactly true, but I didn't care. Ford was going to be in my life for the rest of it. It didn't matter in what capacity. He was my *family*, more so than the woman in front of me ever was or would be. Her eyes narrowed. "You might as well spit on your sister's grave. He killed her."

"No, the rain killed her by making the road slick. That deer killed her by darting into the street. The truck killed her by driving at that exact time and not stopping fast enough." My voice hitched. "I killed her because I sat in the front seat. No one killed her! *It was an accident!*" I screamed the last words so loudly, I swore plates rattled.

Heat blazed in my mother's eyes. "It should've been you. Both of you." Her voice cracked. "Not my beautiful Violet."

Hunter appeared at my parents' backs. "I think it's time for you to leave, and I'm going to have to ask that you don't return."

"This-this is my daughter's place of employment. I'll come anytime I like," my mom blustered.

"I'm not your daughter." I said the words low, but everyone heard them. "You already lost one child. Congratulations, now you've lost another."

My mother gasped and I couldn't even look at my father. His reaction didn't matter. He was too much of a coward to stand against his wife, so none of it mattered at all.

I took off towards the back door. Hunter jogged after me, grabbing my elbow. "Where are you going?"

"I need to be alone." Hunter opened his mouth to argue but I cut him off. "Please—I'll stay within sight of the back windows, but just let me pretend I have some sense of privacy. I just need to fool myself into thinking I can be alone for five minutes."

He released his hold on me. "Okay, Bell."

With a jerky nod, I headed out the back door, trying to escape walls that felt as if they were closing in all around.

Chapter Thirty-Three

Ford

I PUSHED OPEN THE SIDE DOOR TO THE CATCH. STRIDING down the hallway, I slowly became aware of how quiet it was. I could hear every lyric to the seventies rock song drifting through the speakers. A flicker of dread trailed down my spine, and I picked up my pace.

The main room was about half-full, but all the conversations were happening in muted whispers. I scanned the crowd. Darlene was behind the bar filling a pitcher of beer. Caelyn was weaving in and out of tables. I didn't see Bell anywhere. My rib cage seemed to tighten, making it just a little harder to breathe.

My gaze caught on Ethan and Pete at a table. I hurried over. "Where's my brother?"

Ethan gestured to the back doors, and I saw Hunter standing there, staring out at the beach. "Hunt," I called as I headed his way. He glanced briefly over his shoulder and then returned his stare to the ocean. My annoyance ratcheted up a few notches. "Where's Bell?"

Hunter inclined his head to the beach. There was a figure sitting on a worn piece of driftwood, staring out at the water. "Why the hell is she out there alone?" I growled. "I asked you guys to do one thing. To not leave Bell alone. The cops have no idea who's behind all this and we have no idea if they want to harm Bell, too."

Hunter didn't even give me the courtesy of his attention, just kept his eyes firmly fixed on Bell. "Her parents showed."

The space between my shoulder blades tightened. "What happened?"

"What do you think happened? They made a scene. That mother of hers is a real bitch."

Dread, thick and insidious, crept through my gut. Nothing and no one got in Bell's head like her mom. It had always been the case. Why a mother couldn't see her daughter for the incredible, beautiful, unique being that she was, I'd never understand. Part of me had hoped that losing Violet would wake Heather Kipton up to what was right in front of her. Apparently, that wasn't the case. "What'd she say?"

A muscle in Hunter's jaw flexed. "She was pissed the sheriff came to talk to her. Berated Bell. Accused you of killing Violet. Told Bell she was spitting on her sister's grave." That dread intensified, adding itself to a healthy dose of guilt. Guilt for leaving Bell alone, now and eleven years ago.

"Don't you dare take that shit on." My brother spat the words in my direction.

"Take what on?"

"Vi's death. It was an accident."

"I know." For the first time, the guilt I was feeling had nothing to do with Violet's death. I knew that it wasn't my fault. I'd done what I could to avoid the deer, the cliff, the oncoming truck. I'd done the best I could with what I had. It hadn't been enough, but it wasn't my fault. It was no one's fault.

Hunter's startled gaze jumped to me. "You do?"

"I do."

"So you're not going to run?"

Shit. I had messed things up so badly with my brother. He was just waiting for me to bail on him again. Just like Bell. I clapped him on the shoulder. "I'm not going anywhere, Hunt. I'm actually thinking about staying." It had been circling around in my mind for weeks now. Bell had forgiven me, she was giving me a chance, and I could put up with nosy, judgmental islanders if it meant I had her.

His eyes widened. "Staying?"

"I'm trying to figure out a way to make it work." It would take some creative configuring, some back-and-forth travel to LA, but I could do it.

"Does Bell know that?"

"I don't want to tell her anything until I've got it all figured out." The last thing I wanted to do was promise Bell something and then go back on my word. I didn't think we'd survive it. Not to mention, the past two weeks had been hectic, to say the least. The bar had been packed, more with nosy locals wanting to know what had happened than anything else, but I'd take their money with a smile. I'd had to make trips to another island for follow-up doctor's appointments since I didn't think it was a good idea to make an appointment with Anchor's only doctor—Bell's father. My parents needed assurance that their son was safe and recovering. I'd hardly had a moment alone with Bell.

"I think you should tell her."

"I will." When the moment was right.

My brother gave me a slap on the back and then took hold of my shoulder. "I love her, too. And if you hurt her..." Pain flashed in Hunter's eyes. "Just don't."

I stiffened. "There's not—there was never anything like that between you two, right?" Bell had said there wasn't, but something about my brother's tone set me on edge.

Hunter scoffed. "No. Nothing like that." His gaze drifted back to Bell's form on the beach. "That doesn't mean I don't care about her, though. Just don't hurt her."

I swallowed hard. "I'll do everything I can to prevent that from happening."

"Good."

I pushed open the back door and headed to Bell. My eyes scanned the surrounding beach and the trees that lined the shoreline. I hated how exposed she was, that anyone could've snuck up on her. I didn't care how angry she was at her parents, it didn't mean she could take risks with her safety.

My back teeth ground together in a steady rhythm as I got closer to Bell. I eased down next to her on the log, not trusting myself to speak yet. She didn't even look at me, just kept staring out at the sea. I could feel a mix of energies coming off her in waves: pain, confusion, longing. I wrapped an arm around her, drawing her close. The twinge in my ribs barely registered now.

"How was the mainland?"

The question was so normal, so evenly stated, I almost laughed. "Is that really what you're going with?"

Bell gave a little shrug and kept right on watching the crashing waves. "What did you want me to say?"

"Oh, I don't know. Maybe, 'my mom is a crazy bitch, and I'm really hurting right now.'"

Bell was silent for a moment. "Saying it out loud doesn't change anything."

I sighed, rubbing a hand up and down her back. "It might not change anything, but naming it can take away some of the power." Her eyes flicked up to mine for a brief moment before returning to the water. "I had a long talk with Vi at her grave after I got here. It didn't change the fact that she was gone, but naming that guilt, saying out loud all the ways I'd fucked up…it took away some of the power the guilt had over me."

Bell's body melted into mine at my words, that release, the fact that she was leaning against me, it eased something in me. "I'm glad that helped, Ford."

"But you don't want to talk about your parents." My heart broke for her, and I had the sudden urge to shake her mom and dad until they woke up and realized the damage they were doing to the one daughter they had left.

Bell toyed with a string that had come loose on her denim shorts, twisting it around her finger. "She'll never understand me. She doesn't want to. She just wants to hold onto her anger, because if she holds onto that rage, she doesn't have to feel the hurt." My heart cracked a little further, for Heather Kipton too, a woman who simply wasn't equipped to handle this kind of loss.

"I'm sad for her, honestly." Bell gave voice to the thoughts forming in my head. "But I can be sad for her, feel empathy for her, and still not want her in my life." Bell looked up, unshed tears glittering in her eyes. "It hurts too much. I can't do it anymore. Not even these casual, polite conversations when we run into each other in town. It's all so fake, and when the real stuff bubbles up like it did today, when her true colors show, it's just too painful."

I pulled her closer against me, pressing my lips to her temple and leaving them there for a moment, needing to say all the things she wasn't ready to hear. "You're allowed to choose yourself."

A single tear tipped over, cascading down her cheek. "Am I?"

"You are and you should. You don't have to punish yourself by letting them spew venom into your life."

Bell pressed her cheek into my chest. "Every time I take a step back from them, I feel so damn guilty. But today was the straw that broke the camel's back. Mom's mind…it's too twisted, she's created this story to stoke her anger, to keep it burning, and I refuse to be a part of it."

"Good."

"You don't think I'm a horrible human?"

I pressed my lips to Bell's hair, that scent that was hers alone mixing with the sea air and giving me my peace. "I think you're the best human I know."

She let out a little laugh, the action sending pleasant vibrations into my chest. "Let's not get crazy."

We stayed like that for a long time. Bell's cheek against my chest, her body wrapped in my arms, just listening to the waves crash into the shore. I soaked in everything I could: her smell, the feel of her pressed against me, the sound of her breathing barely audible against the backdrop of the waves.

"I missed you, Bell."

"I'm right here."

She'd been right here these past two weeks but still felt so damn far away. "Will you do me a favor?"

"Depends on what it is."

I chuckled. "Stay with me for a while."

Bell groaned. "I don't know…"

"Please. I need this. To know you're safe. That your parents won't be able to show up unannounced and blindside you again—" My words cut off because I realized that all of the overprotective worry had gotten me nowhere with Bell. She didn't want to be sheltered, protected. "Bell, I *want* you with me. In my life. In my space. Yes, I want to make sure you're safe, but I also just want you close."

Bell was quiet for a moment before she spoke. "People are going to talk."

"Let them."

She tipped her head up to take in my expression. "Are you sure you can handle that?"

The ghost of my explosion outside Two Scoops still hung over us. I couldn't lie and say it didn't piss me off, but Bell was what mattered, not anyone else. "I don't care about them. I care about you. Stay with me." I held my breath as I waited for her answer.

"Okay." She leaned in, pressing her lips to my stubbled cheek. Then she rose and headed towards the bar. "Come on, we've been slacking long enough."

I shook my head as I stood, chuckling to myself. I guess honesty really did pay off in the end.

Bell

"DON'T YOU DARE EVEN THINK OF LIFTING THAT," I barked at Ford as he reached out for the bucket of ice I'd set in front of our ice bin.

Crosby chuckled. "Watch out, man, don't want to get smacked with a ruler."

I scowled at him. "He's still recovering. The doctor said he needs to be cautious about lifting for another week."

The smile on Ford's face startled me. I expected him to be annoyed that I'd told him not to lift something, like it might be a threat to his manhood. Instead, he had the biggest, dopiest grin I'd ever seen. He pulled me to him, my arms instinctively going around his waist. He pressed his lips to my forehead. "You're worried about me."

My cheeks heated as I quickly glanced around the bar. We definitely had folks' attention. I slipped out of his embrace and immediately felt the loss. Ford might have said he wasn't worried about what other people might think of us together. Still, I didn't want to risk someone else sharing their ignorant opinion with us. "Of course I'm worried about you. You have three bruised ribs and a dislocated shoulder. Not to mention the head injury."

"You kinda like me, Trouble," Ford called in a singsong voice as he poured a row of shots.

"Not for long," I muttered.

"Watching you two is better than a soap opera."

I arched a brow at Crosby as I grabbed his empty pint glass to refill it. "You a big *Days of Our Lives* fan?"

"Never miss an episode."

I laughed. "It's good to have a variety of interests."

"Brown Eyes! Where have you been all of my life?"

Kenna glared at Crosby as she walked up to the bar, Caelyn following behind her. "Doing everything I can to avoid you."

I choked on the laugh that escaped me, and Caelyn's eyes bugged. Crosby grinned as he took a sip of his beer. "You're just trying to hide your true feelings behind your insults. I know I'm your favorite."

"Favorite what? Barfly? Part-time lawyer, full-time slacker?"

He arched a brow in her direction. "Sometimes, it's good to let your hair down, have a little fun."

"Whatever." Kenna turned her attention to me. "Can you and Caelyn take your break?"

I glanced over at Ford. "You got things under control?"

"Yeah, just…" He glanced around the bar. "Will you stay close?"

I would've given him a hard time for pulling the overprotective act, but I saw the genuine worry in his eyes. "We'll just grab a table on the back patio."

Relief lit his features. "Thank you."

I rounded the bar, and Caelyn immediately hooked an arm through mine. "He's looking out for you."

I said nothing in response. What was there to say? All

afternoon, the touches had been frequent and lingering. Each brush of Ford's hands had refilled my strength stores a little bit more. I hadn't wanted to admit just how much my parents' visit had shaken me, hadn't wanted it to show. And I sure as hell didn't want to *need* someone else to help me recover from it. But that's exactly what Ford had done. Without me telling him, he'd somehow known exactly what I needed.

"What the hell is going on?" Kenna whirled on me as soon as we reached an empty corner of the patio. "Did your mom seriously show up here and rant at you? And why am I having to hear about that from Caelyn and not from you?"

I blinked rapidly. "She did show up, along with my dad, who, of course, said nothing. And I didn't call because—because…" I searched my brain for why I hadn't sent Kenna a text. Normally, that would've been my first move, to let her and Caelyn know. But I hadn't because—

"Because she had Ford here." Caelyn gave me a gentle smile. The hopeless romantic in her was shining through.

Kenna scanned my face as if looking for an injury or trying to find the truth. "Was he there for you?"

"He was." A flash of fear tore through me so fast and strong, I almost gasped. Sure, he'd been there for me today, but that didn't mean he'd be there tomorrow or the day after. I'd built a safe and secure support system. It was small, but I knew I could count on the people in it. Ford was still an unknown.

"He loves you, Bell."

My head snapped in Caelyn's direction. "You don't know that."

She reached out and took my hand. "Yes, I do. It's written all over him. And not just how he looks at you, but in his actions. And actions are always more important than words."

My heart seemed to trip over itself as it struggled to beat faster. I wanted so badly to believe her words.

Kenna took a step closer to Caelyn and me, her face grave. "Just be careful. I know he's been good to you lately, but I just don't trust that he's going to stick around."

I swallowed hard. Ford had made me no promises about the future. Hell, he hadn't made me any promises about tomorrow. But I didn't want to lose this shot at even just a moment of happiness because I was too caught up in what might happen weeks or months from now. I was done playing it safe. I didn't want to miss out on all life had to offer because I was scared of getting hurt. But if I genuinely wanted to live my life to the fullest, I had to let myself love the person my heart wanted above all others. Even if it was the scariest jump I'd ever make.

$\sim\!\!\odot$

My fingers drummed in a staccato beat along my thighs, and my stomach seemed to pitch with each turn Ford's SUV made on the climb back to his house. I really hoped I wasn't going to have to ask him to pull over so that I could puke on the side of the road.

"You're quiet."

I swallowed back the nerves climbing up my throat. "Just tired, I guess." I was the opposite of tired. My anxiety seemed to be doubling by the second. I'd have to run around the island three times to be able to sleep tonight.

I felt Ford's gaze on me for a split second. "If you're so tired, then why does it seem like you're about to crawl out of your skin?"

I pressed my lips together in a firm line. He knew me too damn well. Even after over a decade apart, he still remembered all my tells. I said nothing, just let the silence in the vehicle dial my anxiety up another degree. I wasn't going to hold myself back from Ford any longer. I wasn't going to try and convince myself that friendship or a slow build into something more would ever be enough for me. I was going to let myself love him and not allow myself to drown in fear or guilt because of it.

Just as the thought traveled through my brain, an image of Violet flashed in my mind. I pushed it out. I couldn't think about her right now. But what kind of sister did that make me?

Ford pulled to a stop in front of his house, turning off the car. I moved on autopilot, unbuckling my seat belt and grabbing the small duffle bag at my feet. I followed Ford into the house, my insides seeming to twist themselves further into a knot with each step.

I stopped in the living room, looking out at the dark sea below. Where was I supposed to go next?

Ford suddenly appeared in front of me, gently grasping my shoulders. "Bell, you're scaring the hell out of me right now. Tell me what's going on in that head of yours."

"I'm scared." Scared that when he left in a few months, I'd be crushed. Scared what giving in to this thing between us meant.

"What's scaring you right now?"

"I love you." The words were out before I could think better of them. And once I started, I couldn't seem to stop them. "I've been fighting it for so long." Tears began to gather in my eyes. "I didn't want to love you. And I feel so damn guilty, like it's gnawing away at my insides because some part of me has *always* loved you, and giving in to this feels like I'm saying I'm glad Violet's gone. That I pick you over her, and I can't. I can't choose because I love you both."

A fire blazed in Ford's eyes, a blue flame that meant the deepest of burns. He cupped my face in his hands. "You don't have to choose. You're allowed to love us both."

It was the right thing to say. Perfect in its simplicity. I launched myself at Ford, legs wrapping around his waist as my lips met his in a bruising kiss. It wasn't delicate or graceful, it was pure need.

Ford's hands gripped my ass, digging into the flesh. I tugged on the strands of his hair, forcing his head back so I had better access to his mouth. The moment his lips met mine, I wanted to sigh, as if some part of my soul had finally returned to me. His tongue darted in, stroking my own, stoking the fire that was starting to burn low in my belly.

Ford growled as I pulled back. "Bedroom," I panted. "We need a bed."

Ford chuckled, his eyes flashing. "I can get you a bedroom." Instead of setting me down, Ford simply strode down the hall with me wrapped around him like a spider monkey. I pressed my face to his neck, inhaling deeply. The woodsy cologne smelled so damn good, but it was the scent that lay underneath, the one I'd known forever, that I truly loved. I ran my tongue along the side of his neck, giving his ear a playful nip.

"Do you want me to drop your ass in the middle of the hallway?"

I released his ear as I laughed. "I think I'd prefer you to drop me on a bed."

Ford did just that. After pushing open the door to his bedroom, I was soon sailing through the air and landing with a small *oomph* as I hit the soft mattress. Ford stared down at me, his gaze tracking over my face and down my body. Each flick of his eyes felt like a promise of what was to come.

"I have been dreaming about this since the second I saw you butchering that beer behind the bar."

My lips curved up. "Then what are you waiting for?"

Ford shook his head, toeing off his boots and pulling his t-shirt off. "No. I'm taking my time with you."

My eyes traveled over his broad shoulders and the sea of lean, tanned muscle. I swallowed hard as my palms began to itch with the need to touch that skin. Ford unbuttoned his jeans, and I watched in fascination as his cock sprang free. God, it was beautiful. Such a weird thing to think about a penis, but it was true.

I suddenly realized that Ford was utterly naked, and I was still fully clothed. I sat up, ready to even the playing field. Ford reached out, stilling my hands. "No. I get that pleasure."

My arms fell to my sides as Ford knelt on the floor in front of me. His fingers went to the buttons on my shirt. Slowly and methodically, he unbuttoned each one, his eyes never straying from his task. My heart rate seemed to pick up with each button. As he reached the last one, he carefully slipped the shirt from my shoulders. His fingers trailed down my back and unhooked my bra, sending shivers of anticipation down my spine the whole way.

My breasts fell free, and Ford's gaze burned into me, tracing the tattoos and scars that lined my side, curving around my breast and lining my collarbone. I suddenly felt self-conscious and exposed. I must've made some small move because Ford cupped my face, staring into my eyes. "You are so damn beautiful." He kissed the corner of my mouth. "Perfect." His lips skimmed the column of my throat and moved down my chest, landing on the start of my tattoo. His lips and tongue traced my scars and the designs I'd created to make peace with them.

Ford looked up from where they stopped on my rib cage. "They're beautiful too, because they're a part of you."

My breath caught as tears gathered in the corners of my eyes. "Need you, Ford. Now."

His eyes blazed with that blue heat I was beginning to love. Ford slipped his fingers into the waistband of my shorts and panties, pulling them down over my hips, leaving them in a puddle on the floor, along with my sandals.

Ford tucked his hands under my knees and gave a quick tug, sending me falling back onto the bed with my center on full display for him. He groaned as he dragged his nose along my inner thigh, stopping and pressing a kiss to the small triangle of hair at the apex of my legs. "You smell like heaven."

I shivered in response, and Ford's hold on my legs tightened. "I need to taste you."

"I need you inside of me," I argued. I wanted to experience it all with Ford. Explore every last inch of his body. But right now, I needed to feel him moving in me, with me, more than anything. "Please." I didn't even care that I was begging.

Ford pushed to his feet. "Only because you asked so nicely."

I grinned, but it stalled as I took him in, standing before me, looking so devastatingly handsome. "I'm on the pill. And I've been checked."

That blue flame was back. "I'm clean. I had a doctor's appointment right before I left LA." He trailed a single finger along my center, teasing.

I whimpered. "Please."

Ford leaned over me, hovering, toying with me. "I love it when you beg. One of these days, when my patience is stronger, I'm going to see just how long I can draw out that first orgasm. How loudly I can make you plead for it."

I hooked my legs around Ford's waist, my heels digging into those divots of muscle right above his ass. "But not tonight."

A muscle in Ford's jaw tensed. "Not tonight." His tip bumped my opening, and his gaze locked with mine. "You're sure?"

"I'm sure." I had never been more sure of anything in my whole life. I didn't care if losing myself in Ford meant that the world around us burned. I needed him, needed this, needed to let myself be free to fall.

He entered me in one long, smooth glide. I couldn't hold back my moan. I'd never had sex without a condom, and it seemed perfectly fitting that Ford would be my first. I didn't want anything between us, nothing that would inhibit a single sensation.

Ford let out a muttered curse. "So perfect. How do you feel so perfect? Like you were made for me."

I reached up, my hand cupping his stubbled cheek. Ford

swept his lips against mine and then deepened the kiss as he truly started to move. With each thrust and stroke, the heat low in my belly built.

I gripped Ford's shoulders, fingers digging into flesh as my hips rose up to greet each movement. The angle of his thrusts changed, and I gasped as something deep inside me tightened, an invisible cord drawing tighter.

I wanted to keep my eyes open to see every possible expression on Ford's face, but I couldn't seem to do it. His thrusts picked up their pace, his cock delving impossibly deeper, hitting that spot inside me over and over. Pinpricks of light and sensation danced across my skin, sparking as they embedded themselves there, digging in until my body came alive. For the first time in my life, I felt everything.

A flick of Ford's thumb across my clit struck the final match of something I had no idea how to name. It was a black hole of sensation, the way a star explodes and then collapses in on itself. Ford came with a shout, filling me impossibly fuller and then collapsing on top of me as I struggled for breath.

He rolled, taking me with him. My chest heaved as I tried to regain my equilibrium. I started to laugh. I couldn't help it. It was as if all my circuits had misfired, and the only thing that could escape me was laughter.

"You know," Ford said low in my ear. "The sounds you're making right now could be a real hit to my manhood."

I laughed even harder. "I think I blacked out mid-orgasm. I've never experienced anything that intense before."

Ford grinned against my face, then pressed his lips to my temple. "I'm glad you didn't pass out on me."

My laughter slowly subsided, and I tilted my face up so that my chin rested on his sternum. I nibbled on my bottom lip.

"What is it, Trouble?"

My stomach twisted. "Was it, um, good for you?"

In a flash, I was on my back, Ford on top of me. "I am still inside you after the most mind-blowing sex of my life, and you're asking if it was *good*?" I swallowed and nodded slowly. "No, it was not *good*. It was the best I've ever had." His gaze bored into mine. "Because it was you and me, it'll always be the best I've ever had."

Tears pricked the corners of my eyes. "I think my emotional responses are going a little haywire."

Ford chuckled. "You're adorable, Trouble."

I grinned, even if it was a little wobbly. "You're pretty adorable, too, Cupcake."

Ford gave me a mock scowl. "She calls me Cupcake after I fucked her so hard she almost passed out." He shook his head. "Looks like I'm just going to have to try again." He slipped out of me, and I whimpered at the loss. Pushing to his feet, Ford swept me up in his arms.

"Ford, your shoulder," I warned. All this lifting me couldn't be good for the still-healing joint.

"It's fine. More than, actually. Now, it's shower time."

I wasn't going to argue with that.

Chapter Thirty-five

Bell

I MOANED AS SOMETHING LONG AND HARD PRESSED INTO MY backside. I arched my back. My muscles felt as if I'd just taken a brutal boot camp class after not working out for months. Warm lips pressed into my neck. "Morning."

"Feed me," I groaned. Ford chuckled and rolled his hips against me. "I didn't mean feed me your dick. Though I would take that for course two."

A strangled, husky laugh escaped him. "That feels wrong on so many levels, but I'm also oddly turned on by you talking about my dick as a meal."

I grinned, turning to face Ford. "Feed me pancakes, and then I'll see what I can do about making your weird fetishes a reality."

"Deal." He pressed his lips to the corner of my mouth. "Love waking up with you in my arms."

My heart tripped over itself in my chest. "Me, too." It wasn't an *I love you*, but I'd take it.

"Okay." Ford pushed to sitting and then stood. "Let's get you some food." I stared at his tight ass as he strode to the dresser and pulled out some boxer briefs. He glanced over his shoulder when I didn't respond. "Trouble...are you staring at my ass?"

I nodded, there was no shame in my game. "I'm taking full advantage of being able to ogle you."

Ford shook his head, grinning. "I feel so used."

"Oh, you love it."

He threw a balled-up t-shirt in my direction. "Yes, I do."

I got myself as presentable as possible while Ford cooked breakfast. My teeth were brushed and my face was washed, but there was only so much I could do with my hair. It was a rat's nest. But every time I glanced at it in the mirror, I smiled. It was in this intricate series of knots because Ford's hands had been in it all through the night. A pleasant shiver swept through me as I remembered the feel of him tugging it to give him better access to my mouth as he took me. "Get it together, Bell." I opted for a giant messy bun on the top of my head and called it good.

I padded down the hallway and through the living room to the kitchen. The house Ford had rented was beautiful. One of those high-end vacation rentals that cost a pretty penny in the summer months, but that didn't have a lot of character. It was all glass and modern furnishings. My stomach flipped at the reminder that this wasn't a permanent home. It was all so very temporary.

I wanted to ask him what his plans were, but that felt a little too serious after having sex for the first time. We were just starting to find our way. I didn't need to put added pressure on Ford.

"I don't have pancake mix, but will you settle for an egg and cheese sandwich?"

I slid onto a stool at the counter. "Sounds perfect. Can I have—?"

"Extra cheese on yours? Already done." He placed a plate in front of me with a bagel sandwich that looked like it had more cheese than egg.

"You know the way to my heart."

He grinned. "You want OJ or coffee?"

"OJ, then coffee."

"Coming right up."

Ford set down a tall glass of orange juice before settling onto the stool next to me. "So, what do you want to do before work today?"

I tore off a bite of bagel and then proceeded to rip it into small, even shreds on my plate. "I was thinking about going to visit Violet. Maybe you could come with me?" I flicked my gaze up to Ford. "Is that too weird? I just don't want to feel like we're hiding something."

He reached over and squeezed the back of my neck. "It's not weird. I'd love to go with you."

The tension in my shoulders eased a bit. Maybe this wouldn't be as hard as I'd thought. I had been sure that I would be swamped by guilt this morning, but I hadn't. I felt…happy. At peace. Like so much of my life was slipping into place. But I wanted to make sure Violet was still a part of that life, even if she was gone. "Thank you."

"We'll stop at the florist and pick up some flowers to take."

I picked up my sandwich. "They have to be potted."

Ford turned, studying me. "Why?"

"I kind of have a thing about cut flowers."

"Okay…" Ford took a sip of coffee and waited for me to explain.

I set my bagel back on the plate. "After Violet died, our house and my hospital room, they were full of flowers. So many, I lost count. Don't get me wrong, it was kind of people to send them. But they all started dying around the same time. And soon, my hospital room, and our house, they looked exactly like what they were. Shrines to the dead and damaged. Every time I looked at them, I remembered that Vi was gone. What I had lost. I wanted to remember the life she lived, not everything else." I gave a little shrug. "So, no more cut flowers."

"That's why you put all of the pots at Vi's grave."

I nodded. "I like having something to tend there, too. It gives me something to do while I talk to her. And it feels like, I don't know, like I'm taking care of her somehow."

Ford placed a hand on my thigh, squeezing. "You're honoring her, Bell. It's beautiful." He glanced down at the small piece of my tattoo that peeked out of my tank top. "Your tattoo is honoring her, too, isn't it?"

I smiled. "Violets and bluebells."

"And you designed it, didn't you?"

I placed my hand over his, linking our fingers. "I drew it out, and the tattoo artist put it on me." As much as Ford had said he thought my scars were beautiful because they were a part of me, I knew they still hurt him. Hurt him because they marked the pain I'd been through. "I didn't want to cover up the scars. I wanted to make peace with them. With all that had happened. This was my way of doing that."

Ford slid off his stool and wrapped his arms around me. "You are so damn brave. And always so wise beyond your years."

"I'm healed, Ford. I'm safe. Those scars aren't your fault."

He held me tighter, and I wrapped my arms around his waist. "I know it's not my fault. I really do. But I hate that I wasn't there to help you through it. It's hard for me to forgive myself for that one."

I fisted my hands in his t-shirt. "But you're going to have to. Just like I have to forgive myself for my anger towards you. We were lost in our own world of hurt. And doing our best with what we had at the time. Now, we're doing things differently because we have new tools."

Ford pressed his lips to the top of my head. "I can promise you this much. You'll never have to face the hard stuff without me again."

It wasn't a promise to stay on Anchor, but it was close.

I'd take it and run.

Chapter Thirty-Six

Ford

"I DON'T THINK ALL OF THESE ARE GOING TO FIT, CUPCAKE."
I looked at the back of my SUV, full to the brim with potted plants. They were all different sizes, shapes, and colors. Bell was right, they would never all fit at Vi's grave. "I might've gone a bit overboard."

Bell laughed, the sound catching on the breeze and taking root in my chest. "Might've?"

I gave her a mock scowl. "We can put the rest at my place."

She smiled, the movement causing the green in her eyes to catch the light. "I like the idea of having plants to tend at your house."

"You're going to have to teach me how to keep them alive. I have a black thumb when it comes to growing things. My gardener back in LA actually asked me not to do anything to the plants there. I kept killing them."

Bell choked on a laugh and patted me on the back. "I'll teach you how not to be a plant murderer."

"Thank you." We each took two pots from the SUV and headed for the church. As we wove our way through the headstones, there was no unease this time, simply peace. I'd like to think that Vi would be happy that Bell and I had found each other in this way. That was the kind of girl she'd been, wanting everyone she loved to be happy.

My footsteps faltered as we approached Vi's grave. All that peace that had been building inside me was ripped apart in a single breath. Every pot and plant that Bell had so tenderly cared for had been destroyed. Smashed into a million little pieces.

"What in the—?" Bell couldn't even finish her sentence.

My eyes immediately began scanning the area, looking for anyone who might still be lurking nearby. I saw nothing. But as my gaze tracked over the destruction on the ground, it caught on a piece of paper amidst it all. A worn piece of notebook paper with thick, angry slashes for handwriting. *They're liars. The flowers are lies. They betrayed you, but I'll always love you.*

My gut twisted. This wasn't just someone angry. This was someone sick. I set down the pots I was carrying, careful not to contaminate any evidence. Then I took Bell's plants and did the same. She stood in shock, just staring at her love for her sister shattered on the ground. I wrapped an arm around her. "We need to get back in the car and call Sheriff Raines."

She nodded woodenly, letting me drag her away. My eyes kept scanning the cemetery the whole time, looking for anything out of place. I kept one hand wrapped around Bell and used the other to pull out my phone. I hit Parker's contact. "We have a problem." I quickly filled him in. When I was done, I shoved the phone back into my pocket.

"He's on the island, so he'll be here in five." I opened the passenger door for Bell, helping her in. She nodded again, that same stiff movement that had my gut twisting. I stood at the side of the vehicle, not able to leave her, even to just walk around the damn SUV.

Bell turned to face me, but her eyes weren't focusing. "Who's doing this, Ford?"

I reached out, cupping her face, and Bell let her head fall to my chest. "I wish I knew, baby. I wish I fucking knew." My back molars ground together. The creep wasn't slowing down, and his anger was escalating, I knew that much from what my friends Austin and Carter had gone through back in LA. The twisting in my gut deepened. What if this guy hurt Bell again? Tried to kill her? The vise around my chest was back. No more easy breathing just because Bell was with me. I could lose her. And if I did, I knew I'd never recover. I pulled her tighter against me. "Maybe we should get out of town for a little while. Just until they find this guy."

Bell jerked back. "We can't do that. The bar is just starting to pick up business. We'll lose all of the progress we've made."

I felt a muscle in my jaw tic. "I don't give a flying fuck about the bar. I care about your safety."

Bell's expression hardened, her hands fisting in my tee. "I'm not letting someone scare me away from my home. And what happens if we leave? They stop doing this, and we're no closer to finding out who they are." She paused for a moment, studying my face. "Would you be okay with staying away forever? With never coming back?"

Bell seemed to hold her breath, waiting for my answer. I swept her hair back from her face. "No. I'm not looking for reasons to run. I just want you safe."

Her shoulders eased a fraction. *Shit.* She was still worried that I was going to take off on her. I needed to tell her I was going to stay. It was the worst possible timing for sharing the decision, but I couldn't handle the doubt in her eyes a second longer. I pressed my lips to her forehead. "I'm moving back to Anchor."

She pulled back, gaze boring into mine. "What? How?"

"I'll either have my manager take over the day-to-day of the bars permanently, or I'll sell." I'd do whatever it took so I didn't lose Bell.

"You can't do that. You worked so hard to build those bars into what they've become."

I had. There'd been blood, sweat, and probably some tears along the way. But Bell was more important. She always had been. It had just taken me way too long to see it. "They're businesses, Bell. You…you're everything to me." It was on the tip of my tongue to tell Bell that I loved her, but the words seemed to get stuck in my throat, anxiety gripping me.

Her expression softened, and she pushed a lock of hair away from my face. "I love you, Ford."

I wrapped my arms around her, guilt eating at me for not being able to give her those words in response. I forced levity into my voice. "Glad you do, because I'm going to be stuck to you like glue."

She gave a hint of a laugh. "And that will be such a hardship."

I grinned against her hair. "It will definitely have its perks." My head snapped up at the sound of an approaching car. My muscles relaxed a fraction when I saw the lights atop the SUV. "Sheriff's here."

Bell sighed. "I bet we're his two favorite people."

"It's his job, Bell. He doesn't mind."

Parker climbed out of his SUV. "You guys okay?"

I gave a quick nod. "We're fine. I can't say the same for Violet's grave."

"I'm going to check it out really quick, and then I'll be back to talk to you and wait for the crime scene techs."

I inclined my head in assent and rubbed a hand up and down Bell's back. I wanted the right words to give her, ones that would ease her mind and bring comfort, but nothing I came up with seemed adequate. I could only promise one thing. "I'll keep you safe. I'm not going anywhere."

She tipped her head back to look me in the eyes. "I need you to be safe, too. Promise me."

"I'll be safe, too."

Within a few minutes, Parker was striding back towards our SUV. "I'm really sorry you two had to find that."

"Thanks." Bell's voice was soft, almost timid, and I hated the tone with everything I had in me. There was no sass or spunk, none of the usual life force that ran through everything Bell did and said.

I met Parker's gaze. "It's safe to assume now that this is definitely about Violet."

"I'd say so." He scrubbed a hand over his jaw. "Have you two come up with names for anyone I should talk to?"

Bell nibbled on her bottom lip. "No one seemed angry enough to do something like this. Or hurt Ford. But maybe I'm just not seeing things clearly." She paused for a moment. "Did my parents have alibis?"

My heart broke for the girl who had to ask that question. I hated that there was enough doubt in her mind to think they were capable of it.

Parker rested his hands on his gun belt. "They said they were both home on the nights in question."

"Can anyone verify that?" The question had to be asked.

He shook his head. "Neighbors can't confirm either way."

"And are you talking to anyone else? Any other suspects?" I was losing my patience with how slowly this investigation was moving. I needed Bell safe, and I needed it now.

"I'm afraid I can't share a list of who we've talked to, but we're working our way around to some classmates of Vi's, plus teachers, coaches, anyone who had a relationship with her that still lives on the island."

My jaw hardened. "And what the hell are we supposed to do in the meantime? Just wait around like sitting ducks?"

"Ford." Bell placed a hand on my chest, trying to calm me. But not even her touch could ease me right now.

"Tell me, Parker. How am I supposed to keep Bell safe when I have no idea who's coming at us? When it could be someone we trust? Tell me."

A muscle in Parker's cheek flickered. "Trust me, Ford. I know how you feel. It's the worst feeling in the world when you can't protect the ones you love. But we're doing everything we can. I've got two deputies on the island 'round the clock, and they're doing regular drive-bys." He paused for a moment. "You know how to shoot?"

Bell bristled. "Oh no. No guns."

I quirked a brow at her. "Trouble, there's a Glock in a gun safe in my bedroom."

She sighed, rubbing her temples. "At least it's in a freaking safe."

Parker met my gaze. "Good. You might look into getting a concealed carry permit. I'll do what I can to fast-track it for you. In the meantime, get both of you Tasers."

"I already have one in my purse."

I glanced at Bell. "Really?" It surprised me. Bell had always been a bit of a pacifist. Hated guns and violence of any kind. I couldn't picture her picking up a Taser.

She grinned at me. "Your mom gave it to me before I went away to college. She didn't want me without protection in a big city."

God, my mom was the best. I pressed a kiss to the top of Bell's head, soaking in the way her body fit perfectly against mine, trying to grab hold of that peace she gave me. Bell would be safe. There was no other option.

Chapter Thirty-Seven

Bell

My head thrummed in a steady beat as Ford pulled out a chair. "Sit." I scowled at him. He glowered right back. "Please." It sounded like the word pained him. I sat.

Caelyn's eyes jumped back and forth between the two of us as if she were watching a tennis match. "Soooooo...Anything you want to tell us?"

I turned my scowl on her. "Oh, you know, the usual. Vi's gravesite being vandalized, threatening notes being left calling Ford and me betrayers."

Caelyn winced. "Sorry."

"Bell," Kenna chastised.

My shoulders slumped. I was such a jerk. My friends did not deserve me biting their heads off just because my day had been a nightmare. How a morning that had started off so perfectly could turn into such a disaster, I wasn't quite sure. I reached out and squeezed Caelyn's hand. "I'm sorry. It's just been a shitty morning."

She gave me a small smile. "I know." Her eyes flicked to Ford, who was heading to the side door of The Catch, and then she looked back at me. "It just seemed like there was some new energy brewing between the two of you."

Heat filled my cheeks, and I bit my bottom lip. There was definitely something new and different between Ford and me. I glanced over my shoulder, taking the man in as he pulled open the door. I didn't want to lose him. Didn't want to lose this new thing between us.

"They slept together," Kenna said matter-of-factly, but worry streaked across her expression.

My head jerked in her direction. "How do you know that?"

Caelyn gasped, and Kenna's lips twitched. "It's written all over both of you. If you want to hide it, you're both going to have to work on your poker faces."

"I don't want to hide it." But did Ford? I didn't think so. He'd been more than openly affectionate around the sheriff. But would that change around the people we knew?

Caelyn leaned forward. "What's wrong, Bell?"

I rubbed my temples, trying my best to clear the tension gathering there. "So, so much." It felt like more and more was being piled onto my plate, and I had no way to deal with it all. There was no release valve for my life. And as wonderful as last night and this morning had been with Ford, it had only raised the stakes. Instead of enjoying this newfound relationship between us, I was second-guessing every word and action, worrying that one wrong move would send this house of cards tumbling to the ground.

"You have got to be kidding me," Kenna muttered. "What is *he* doing here?"

"I missed you too, Brown Eyes."

I pressed my lips together to hide my chuckle as I waved at Crosby and Hunter. "Hey, guys. You know you're welcome anytime"—I arched a brow at Kenna—"but aren't you supposed to be working?"

Kenna scoffed. "Hunter maybe, but we're probably just interrupting one of Crosby's paddleboarding sessions."

Crosby sent Kenna a grin that even I had to admit was devastating. "You know you're always welcome on the back of my board."

She gave an exaggerated shudder. "No thank you. I prefer to stay disease-free."

"Don't worry, Brown Eyes. Safety first. My board and I are always disease-free."

Caelyn choked on a laugh, and I felt the color rise to my cheeks. Ford pulled out a chair next to me, handing me a bottle of water. "Enough with the circus act, you two. Crosby and Hunter are here because I called them."

Hunt pulled out a chair on my other side, giving my shoulder a squeeze as he sat. "You hanging in there, Bells?"

I nodded. I hated the worry that creased Hunter's brow, and the dark circles under his eyes. "I'm fine, Hunt. Promise." He didn't look like he believed me.

"I need your help." Ford slipped a hand around the base of my neck, massaging the muscles that might as well have been made of stone. "This asshole isn't slowing down, and I'm worried he might hurt Bell."

My stomach twisted as flickers of anger and worry began to build. "He hurt you, too. And you're the one he actually tried to *kill*." My heart began to pick up its pace. If Ford was too focused on my safety, he was going to neglect his own.

He gave my neck another squeeze and pressed his lips to the side of my face. "Yes, he tried, and he failed. He'll think twice about coming at me again."

"Or he'll come at you with a gun or a knife or some other weapon."

"That's why I'm getting a concealed carry permit. I'm going to be safe. I promise."

Hot, angry tears began building at the backs of my eyes. "You don't know that. You can't promise."

"Bell." In one fluid movement, Ford pulled me from my chair and into his lap, wrapping his arms around me. "I'm going to be fine. I'll be careful. But it really is you I'm worried about."

I buried my face in his neck, not even caring what the others thought. I needed Ford's scent, his feel. I wanted to be surrounded by him and never come up for air.

"We need to watch out for both of you. But my brother's right, Bell. We need extra eyes on you. You're not exactly evenly matched when it comes to a fight."

Ford nodded. "That's exactly why you're here. You're the only people I trust other than my parents. I want you to keep a lookout. And I also wanted to ask if you'd noticed anyone acting suspicious."

Kenna grumbled something about Crosby not being trustworthy. Ford must've silenced her with one of his looks because she quieted right down.

"I can ask my crew to keep a lookout, too," Hunter offered. "We're on projects on Anchor for the next few weeks at least, and we're grabbing lunch and dinner at the bar almost every day."

"No." I straightened at Ford's words.

Hunter bristled. "You don't trust my crew?"

"I don't trust anyone that's not at this table, other than Mom and Dad, but we can't put this shit on them. They're dealing with enough. Whoever this is, they were around when Vi died, and they're close, Hunt. It could be *anyone*."

Color leached from Hunter's face. "Shit, Ford. How the hell are we supposed to keep Bell safe when this creep could be coming into The Catch every single day and us not know it's him?"

"That's what we're going to talk about today. We're going

to figure out a plan so that neither of us is alone at the bar. I'll be with Bell as much as possible, but I'd like another person as backup."

I scoffed. "And what makes you so sure I want you around, buddy?"

My snarky question elicited just the reaction I'd hoped for. Ford's lips twitched. "Oh, I'm pretty sure you want me around."

A giggle came from Caelyn's direction. "I'm happy to be backup whenever I can, but I fully support Ford being your main bodyguard."

I stuck my tongue out at her. "Of course you do."

"If I can take over one of the tables, I can work here in the mornings," Kenna offered.

"I can take afternoons," Crosby chimed in.

"And I'll take evenings," Hunter said last.

That familiar emotion was back, building in my throat. But this time, it was entirely made up of gratitude. I had created an amazing family. It didn't matter that my parents couldn't accept me or love me for who I was; I had people in my life that did— and not in spite of who I was, but because of it. "Love you guys," I whispered, my voice going hoarse.

Ford rubbed a hand up and down my back. "Thank you. Truly. I had hoped this creep's attention would stay on me since I was responsible for the accident, but something in my gut just keeps telling me he's going to set his sights on Bell."

I stiffened in Ford's lap, turning slowly to face him. "What did you just say?"

Ford's brow furrowed. "That I'm worried he's going to come after you?"

My hands fisted in Ford's shirt. "The accident was not your fault."

Ford's face gentled. "I know, Trouble. I just meant that whoever's doing this *thinks* it was my fault."

I studied Ford's face carefully, my gaze searching every muscle and micro-expression. All I saw was the truth. "Good. Don't make me put the smackdown on you."

Ford chuckled, and Crosby let out a low whistle. "You've got a spitfire on your hands, buddy."

"Don't I know it."

$$\infty$$

I groaned as I looked up from the spreadsheet printout, cracking my neck.

Ford glanced up from his laptop. "You tired? Want me to take you home?"

Warmth flooded my chest at the word *home*, but doubt followed quickly on its heels. How long would a home on Anchor last for Ford when he was constantly being questioned and attacked? My parents, nosy islanders, this creep following us around. I closed my eyes briefly. *One day at a time.* I didn't want to ruin what we were building with worry about the future. He was trying, and that was all I could ask for. "Not yet. I need to finish this."

Ford rose from the couch. "Why don't I help you relax a little then."

My belly gave a little flip as that blue heat flared to life in Ford's eyes. I swallowed, hard. "What did you have in mind?"

Ford carefully gathered up the papers in front of me and set them to the side. The slow and methodical movements lulled me into a false sense of security. As soon as the printouts were on the opposite side of my workspace, he moved with a speed that had me gasping. Ford's hands were around my waist, and he was lifting me onto my desk faster than I could blink. "Ford."

He grinned down at me as he went for the button on my jeans. "Yes?"

"Um, uh, the door? Our employees?" I was grasping at straws I didn't really want to hold onto all that badly.

"Door's locked." He slowly brought down my zipper.

"O-okay." I couldn't disguise the shaking in my voice.

Ford grasped the waistband of my jeans and panties, tugging them with enough force that they came free, even though I was sitting. "I think I've been patient enough. It's time for me to taste you." My breaths came quicker. "Would you like that?" I nodded, wetness gathering between my legs as heat spread low in my belly.

"Lean back." I did as instructed. "Grab hold of the edge of the desk." My fingers dug into the wood as Ford slowly pulled my jeans down my legs. As his knuckles dragged along my thighs, I shivered. "So smooth. So soft." He pressed a kiss to my inner thigh. "Perfect."

My jeans and sandals came off and thudded to the floor. Ford knelt before me, spreading my knees wide. I fought the urge to squirm. The bright overhead lights meant that I was completely on display for him. Ford looked up at me. "You want to come?"

I nodded. I had somehow lost the ability to speak. He grinned. "Good. I want to make you come, but you have to stay still. You're not allowed to hide from me anymore." He trailed a finger down my center and then slipped it inside. "There is no part of you that's hidden from me. Understood?"

I nodded quickly.

"I need the words, Bell." His finger crooked inside me, making a come-hither motion.

I whimpered. "No more hiding."

"Good." Ford brought his face closer to my center, inhaling deeply. "God, I can't get over your scent."

My legs wanted to close around him. It was too much, too intimate, made me feel too vulnerable. Ford crooked his finger again, and I fought the urge to squirm. I took a deep, shaky breath.

Ford's tongue made a long, languid stroke, and I almost bowed off the desk. He immediately stopped. "Still, baby."

I let out a sound that was a cross between a whine and a moan. Ford chuckled, sending a wave of delicious sensation through me. "You're going to kill me," I muttered.

"But it would be a hell of a way to go."

"You're not wrong."

Ford's tongue darted out again. Teasing. Toying. Exploring every part of me. He slipped another finger inside, and my breaths came faster yet. My hands itched to move, to thread through Ford's hair, to touch him, but the second I shifted, Ford stopped all movement. "Don't make me withhold your orgasm, baby."

I growled in frustration, and he laughed. "You can do it, Trouble. Just stay still."

My hands gripped the edge of the desk so hard, I thought it might break. "I'm freaking still."

Ford's tongue flicked across my clit, sending millions of tiny sparks scattering along my nerve endings. "So well behaved, hardly any trouble at all." I would've kicked him if I didn't need him so damn badly.

"Please."

"I love it when you beg." His fingers teased and twisted, moving faster and deeper, and then his lips latched on to that bundle of nerves. It was no longer a slow build of sensation; I came apart at the seams. It was as if my body simply exploded into a million little pieces before they slowly came back to each other and reassembled themselves.

I was panting, my hands had gone numb. "That was..." I couldn't even finish the sentence. The man had fried my brain.

Ford gave me a wicked grin as he stood. He swiped a thumb across his lower lip and then licked it clean. "You taste delicious."

Holy...I didn't know what. That was hot. I leaned forward, going for the button of Ford's jeans, but he stepped out of my reach, shaking his head. "That was just for you."

I stuck out my bottom lip. "But I want to."

Ford chuckled. "Tonight. When we really have time to play."

"Fair enough." I jumped off the desk, my legs a little wobbly, and quickly pulled on my panties and jeans.

When I stood, Ford swept his lips against mine. "Thank you."

I grinned up at him. "I'm pretty sure I should be the one thanking you."

"I'll let you do that later." I let my head fall to Ford's chest. "What?" he asked.

I couldn't stop laughing. "I'm never going to be able to look at that desk the same way again."

Chapter Thirty-Eight

Ford

I KNOCKED ON THE GUEST ROOM DOOR. "YOU READY?" THERE was some grumbling from inside, and I had to clench my teeth to keep from laughing.

"I really don't think this is necessary," Bell called through the door.

"I think it's plenty necessary." Proving to Bell that I wanted a real relationship with her was not going to be an easy task. Words weren't going to cut it. Because even though I'd told her I was planning to stay on Anchor, I could still see the shadows of doubt in her eyes. She needed my actions. I wanted to show her that I wasn't hiding from anyone's judgment. And I wanted all of Anchor to know that she was mine. No more locals sniffing around her at the bar and making me want to bash their heads in. I wanted the world to see that she was taken.

The door swung open. "We left Caelyn and Darlene with a full house at the bar."

I wanted to say something about the fact that Hunter was

going to be helping them out, but I couldn't seem to form words. Bell was absolutely breathtaking. She wore a simple black dress that must've been made out of magic material because it hugged every valley and curve. Layered necklaces dipped in and out of her cleavage, and her blond hair hung in waves around her face. My gaze kept traveling up and down her body, trying to take it all in, but it was the cowboy boots that almost did me in. All I could imagine was Bell in nothing but those boots.

"Ford? Ford, are you okay?"

I started at the sound of worry in Bell's voice and shook my head, grinning. "I'm pretty sure you just pickled my brain."

She quirked a brow. "Pickled your brain?"

"Trouble…" I slid an arm around her waist, pulling her against me. "You look…incredible."

That adorable pink hit her cheeks. "Thank you. You clean up pretty good yourself."

I took her mouth in a slow, lazy kiss. "Come on, let's get out of here before I carry you to the bed and forget all about dinner."

Bell nibbled on her bottom lip. "I could get behind that idea."

"Nope. I am taking you on a proper date. Tonight."

"Oh, fine," Bell grumbled.

I chuckled. "Only you would complain about me taking you on a date." I led her down the hall and out towards my SUV.

"I don't need all that fancy wining and dining."

I pulled open the passenger door and helped her in. "I know you don't *need* it, but I want to give it to you." I paused, taking in the worry in her features. "Unless you're scared about this guy still being on the loose." For the past few days, our friends had stuck close. The only times we were alone were at my house and on the way to and from work.

Bell gave a quick shake of her head. "No, it's not that." She leaned forward, pressing her lips to mine. "Thank you for wanting to spoil me a little."

The tension between my shoulder blades eased a bit. "I'm just getting started."

Bell groaned and pushed me away. "Come on. Feed me."

I chuckled and rounded the hood. The drive into town was uneventful, but Bell was antsy, twisting the little strap on her clutch, straightening invisible wrinkles in her dress. Something was up with her.

I pulled into a parking spot outside one of the two fancier restaurants in town. The Cove was an old Victorian home on the water that had been transformed into a B&B and restaurant. Reservations were hard to come by, but promising tip to the maître d earlier that day had secured me a table.

I opened Bell's door and offered her my hand. "My lady."

She shook her head, smirking. "I'd say 'thank you, kind sir,' but you're no gentleman."

I gasped in mock affront. "How could you say such a thing?"

Bell laughed just as I'd hoped, and I guided her through the parking lot and up the stairs. "I haven't been here in years. And their crab bisque is my favorite."

I traced small circles on her lower back. "Let's get you fed, then." She shivered, and I grinned.

The maître d led us to a table by a window with a view of the harbor, lit by lights along the docks and the boats bobbing in the water. It was perfect. I helped Bell into her seat, pressing a kiss to the top of her head and soaking in her scent, the jasmine just a touch heavier tonight. I couldn't help myself, I dropped a kiss to her bare shoulder. "Thank you for coming with me tonight."

Pink tinged Bell's cheeks. "Thank you for inviting me."

We ordered drinks and debated over the best dishes. I insisted on ordering way too much food so Bell didn't have to choose. We laughed and talked about nothing too serious. The whiskey and Bell's company warmed me from the inside out. "So, tell me about the furniture."

Bell grinned and ducked her head. It was rare that she became bashful, and it only intrigued me more. "I love bringing forgotten pieces back to life. Giving them a second chance."

Bell had always been able to see what others missed, what lay beneath the surface of an object or a person, the potential of what could be. "That piece in the workshop is stunning."

"Thank you. It came out even better than I hoped." She took a sip of her wine, scanning the restaurant.

"You should start a side business. Or even open a shop." I wanted more for Bell than just helping my family's bar stay afloat. I wanted her to have something that was all her own.

She twisted the stem of the wine glass between her fingers. "That's the dream. But I don't really have the time to dedicate to it right now."

My hand tightened around my glass. She didn't have the time because she was so caught up with The Catch. She needed freedom to pursue this dream, and she needed someone to have her back while she did it. I was going to be that person.

Before I could ask another question, Bell did. "What about you? How are your bars doing without you in the city?"

"They're doing great." I grinned down at the table. "Better with me gone, actually. Maybe I was micromanaging too much. I'll need to take a trip to LA soon to discuss turning them over to Luke permanently. But I think he's up for the task." I studied Bell's face as I spoke, that doubt still underlying her features. I fought the urge to curse.

She took another sip of her wine, her gaze going over my shoulder. "That's great. I'm glad it seems to be working out for now."

"What are you looking at?" I turned slightly to take in what Bell was. A middle-aged couple sat at a table near us, making quiet conversation but blatantly staring our way. When they met my gaze, they immediately turned back to their meals.

"People are staring."

Bell's voice was quiet, almost timid, and I hated the tone. I looked around the restaurant. She wasn't wrong. Each time my gaze landed on another table, the people there turned away as if caught in the act. Only a handful of diners seemed to be immersed in each other's company. A muscle in my cheek ticked.

Whispers and stares. There was so much I loved about Anchor, things I'd forgotten and rediscovered, but the small-mindedness would always be a struggle. One I was more than willing to overcome if it meant having Bell in my life. "Small towns," I grumbled.

Bell smoothed the napkin in her lap. "They have their good qualities and their bad."

"You mean they have their nosy gossips."

She took another sip of wine. "They do. And you've been away a while, you're probably not used to it."

That much was true. I loved the anonymity of city life. But it had grown lonely, almost empty, over the past couple of years. No place was perfect. But Anchor…it held my family, Bell, the business I wanted to make sure left a legacy for generations to come. When I thought of making a home here, it brought about a peace that I hadn't thought I'd ever feel. "I'll get used to it." She nodded but said nothing.

Our waiter appeared at the table. "Can I tempt you with our dessert offerings for the evening?"

I opened my mouth to say yes, but Bell answered first. "I don't think I could eat another bite."

"Just the check. Thank you." I studied Bell. Something was off. Her eyes were pinched as if she were trying to find the answer to some ridiculously long calculus problem in her head. Or maybe she simply didn't feel well. "Are you all right?"

Her head snapped up, and she nodded. "I've just got a little headache. I think I'm overdue for a good night's sleep."

"Let's get you home and into bed, then." She smiled weakly at me. Somehow, I didn't think a headache was the full story.

Chapter
Thirty-Nine

Bell

"**I** WOKE UP, AND YOU WEREN'T IN BED."

Ford's words were more of a growl than a statement. I gave him my best smile and handed him an omelet that I'd started making the second I heard him stirring. "I woke up early and didn't want to wake you." More like I'd barely slept. I'd feigned sleep until I sensed Ford had dropped off next to me, and then I'd tossed and turned the whole night.

Ford took the plate I handed him as his gaze traveled over my face, searching. "You should've woken me."

My lips twitched. "Okay, grumpy."

He scowled at me. "I'm not grumpy. I just like waking up with you in my arms. I panicked when I woke up and you were gone."

My heart clenched. Which was it? That he loved having me in his arms, or that he was simply worried something would happen to me? I couldn't seem to grab hold of any sort of perspective when it came to Ford. I'd told him that I loved him, but he'd not once returned the sentiment. He'd said he was planning to stay, but something in me doubted he could handle what life would look like day after day. My stomach churned. What was the truth?

Ford slid onto a stool at the kitchen bar. "Anything you want to do before work?"

I twirled my cell phone between my fingers. "Actually, I've got a date with your mom."

Ford paused with the bite of omelet halfway to his mouth. "Okay…"

"She thought you could go with your dad on his daily walk while we baked."

"I don't know, Bell."

I leaned a hip against the counter, meeting Ford's gaze. "We'll be fine. Doors will be locked while you're away." I hated the worry in Ford's eyes. Loathed what it might mean. The idea that Ford might have confused concern for love had landed in my head somewhere around three a.m., and I hadn't been able to let it go.

∽⊙

Kara's gaze bounced from my face to Ford's and down to our clasped hands. She gave a little squeal. "I heard some talk around town, but seeing it…you two just make me so happy."

She threw her arms around Ford, and he released my hand to pat her back. "Okay, Mom. Let's dial it back."

Frank chuckled. "Come on, Kara, let the kids breathe."

She turned on her husband, giving him a mock glare. "You will not steal my joy in this moment. My boy is dating a girl I love like my own daughter. I'm allowed to be excited."

Frank grinned. "Just don't strangle them with one of those overexcited hugs."

"I'd never." Kara wrapped an arm around my shoulders. "You two go for your walk. And take a long one. I need time with my girl."

Warmth flooded me at Kara's words, but a sinking dread followed closely on its heels. So many people would be affected if this relationship blew up in my face.

"Make sure you lock the door, Mom."

Kara waved her son off. "I will, I will." We stepped inside, and she flipped the lock. "He's protective of you, huh?"

I grimaced. "Just a little."

Kara laughed. "You'll get used to it." She glanced out the window. "And it should ease when they catch whoever's doing this."

"I hope so."

Kara led me into the kitchen, where ingredients were already laid out for chocolate chip cookies. I smiled at the familiar sight. I'd spent countless afternoons in this kitchen growing up, making these very cookies. There was a lived-in warmth here that had always been absent at my own home. There was never a rebuke for making a mess, but you'd always be expected to clean it up. There was never criticism for making a mistake in the baking, just a gentle hand showing you the way. Tears pricked the corners of my eyes.

Kara gripped my shoulders. "What is it, honey?"

The flood I'd been trying to hold back spilled over. And once it started, I couldn't stop it. The tears tracked down my face faster and faster. I didn't know how to answer her, couldn't put into words what was wrong. I gasped for breath. "I'm scared." The words were out before I could even consider what they meant.

"Sit." Kara eased me into a chair before quickly running for a glass of water, setting it in front of me. She rubbed a hand up and down my back. "That's it. Just let it all out. You've been holding too much inside."

I hiccupped as I nodded, the tears still coming. Kara was so different from my mother, not telling me to stuff things away, but instead encouraging me to let every last thing I was feeling out into the open. She'd always been this way, gently probing, asking questions that led me to honestly think about what I was feeling. Without her, I didn't think I would've handled Vi's death at all. I simply would've detonated at some point.

I wasn't sure how much time had passed while we sat at the worn kitchen table, Kara rubbing my back and me letting the tears fall freely, but eventually my crying slowed and then stopped. I pulled another tissue from the box on the table. "I'm sorry."

Kara made a tsking noise. "You know we don't apologize for feelings in this house."

I gave her a wobbly smile. "I love that about your house."

Kara patted my hand and pushed my glass of water closer. "Drink some of this, and then we are going to talk this through. Feelings aren't as scary when we know why we're experiencing them." I nodded and took a drink. "Is this about the man who's been harassing you and Ford?"

She hid her worry well, but I could hear it sneaking into her tone. "I think that's part of it."

"But not the biggest part."

I shook my head.

"Ford," she whispered. It wasn't a question. It was a statement. She knew me way too well.

"He said he wants to stay, but I just can't keep myself from doubting it's even possible. I love him so much, but he hasn't said those words back. I'm worried he's confusing care and concern with something more." The words spilled out in a speedy jumble, the thoughts that had been tangling in my head all night bursting free. I'd twisted Ford's every word and action forwards, backwards, upside down, and inside out. I'd twisted them to the point that I was driving myself just a little bit insane.

"Oh, honey." Kara grabbed my hand. "I wish I could give us both a guarantee that he'll stay. I wish I could give you a promise that everything will work out perfectly, but I can't. I do know that my boy loves you. He might not be saying it with his words, but he's showing it with his actions. He never would've even considered coming back to Anchor permanently before you."

I swallowed against the tears that were gathering at the back of my throat. "It hurt so bad when he left before. And I wasn't in love with him then. Not like this." I hadn't known what it was like to truly have Ford. Now, I did. The touch of his fingers on my skin, how safe I felt in his arms, how understood and *seen* he made me feel just in the way he listened.

Kara squeezed my hand. "I wish I could protect you from all the hurts in this world, but the only way to do that is not to live, and I don't want that for you."

I bit down on my bottom lip, nodding. "I'm just so tired of all the unknowns. Tired of being scared that I'm going to get hurt. I realized I've had my walls up so high." I lifted my head. "Kara, I don't let anyone new into my life. It's you, Frank, Hunter, and my girls. That's it. Sure, I'm friendly with other people, but I don't let them in. I don't want to live my life in fear all the time."

"Then you're just going to have to let yourself fall."

"I already have." I only hoped the landing didn't kill me.

Ford

"**M**OM SAID YOU AND BELL CAME BY FOR A VISIT."
I handed Hunter his local ale and Crosby his
Guinness. "We did. But they kicked Dad and me
out so they could have their girl talk."

Hunter chuckled. "Pouting isn't a good look on you, bro."

I grimaced. I was pouting, and it was pathetic. "I think being with Mom helped. Bell seemed a little better after their time together."

"Mom always knows how to tend to any wound."

I grabbed a rag and wiped down the bar top. "I just wish she'd give me a clue how to do the same." When Dad and I returned from our walk, it was clear that both my mom and Bell had been crying. I'd pulled Bell into my arms and given Mom a dirty look. She'd just laughed and told me not to be so overdramatic. But neither of them would tell me what the hell was going on. I'd even cornered Mom alone in the kitchen to ask her, and she'd said that the conversations between Bell and her would always be private.

Hunter chuckled. "She wouldn't tell you what they talked about, would she?"

"No," I growled.

Crosby grinned as he took a sip of his beer. "Your mom is the best."

"Not when she's keeping secrets and won't tell me why Bell's been upset for the past few days."

"There has been a lot going on, brother. Cut her some slack."

My hand fisted around the towel, pushing it harder into the wood of the bar. I knew that Bell had been through the wringer lately. The past couple of months had been a rollercoaster for her, and now someone was lurking around and making her feel unsafe. But it was more. I couldn't put my finger on it exactly, but she looked as if she were expecting the whole world to fall out from under her at any moment. And there was nothing I could think to do to make her feel safe, steady. The feeling of powerlessness that brought had me snapping at people all day. Hank and Caelyn had given me a wide berth since lunch, but Bell was still lost in her own world.

"Maybe you two should take a getaway. Some distance might help," Crosby offered.

"I don't know if that's a good idea," Hunter argued.

I hung the towel back on its hook. "I already tried to get her to go away with me. No dice."

"Get who to go away with you?" Ethan asked as he eased onto an empty stool beside Hunter.

"Bell, who else?" Hunter eyed me. "Unless you've got another girlfriend we don't know about."

I threw a coaster frisbee-style and hit Hunter in the chest. "Don't be an asshole."

"Yeah, and definitely don't let Bell hear you say anything like that," Crosby muttered.

Ethan took a pull on his beer. "So, you two are officially together?"

"We are." The whispers and stares had only intensified since our date. It seemed every local that came in was here for the Ford and Bell show more than the alcohol and food. At least Ethan had the decency to come out and just ask, instead of talking around the subject.

He glanced around the bar. "How are people taking it?"

Hunter shifted on his stool. "Mostly just staring and whispering like nosy assholes."

I scanned the tables surrounding the bar, over Caelyn chatting up some more of Hunter's crew, my eyes not stopping until they reached Bell. She smiled down at a family as she took their orders, but the expression was forced. What the hell was going on?

"You're making that face like you want to kill someone," Crosby said, taking another sip of his beer.

Not someone, just circumstance. I had half a mind to kidnap Bell and take her away from here no matter what she said. We needed time, just the two of us. "Hey, Caelyn," I called over the din of the bar noise.

She shoved her notepad in her pocket and headed my way, not looking too happy. "What did you do to my girl?"

I arched a brow. "*Your* girl?"

"Yes, my girl. She was all sunshine and roses even though the world was going to hell around her. But now, she's got the sad eyes. I haven't seen those in a very long time. So, what'd you do?"

My back molars ground together. "I don't know."

Caelyn threw up her hands. "Seriously? Then how are you going to fix it?"

I glared at her. "I'm going to ask if you and Hank can close so I can take Bell home early and get to the bottom of this." She was going to tell me what was going on, even if we had to stay up all night. My girl was stubborn, but so was I.

"I like the sound of that. Maybe have some nice make-up sex to round out the night?"

Hunter groaned. "I do not need to hear that."

"Caelyn…" I warned.

She held up both hands. "All right, all right. I can close." Her stare seemed to bore into me. "Just bring that smile back."

"I'll do my best."

The night seemed to drag, more and more locals pouring in, more and more questioning stares. I was about two seconds away from biting someone's head off.

"Hey, Ford." The tone was meant to be seductive, but it grated on my nerves.

"Hey, Lacey. What can I get you?" The last thing Bell needed tonight was Lacey goading her into a fight. Bell hadn't mentioned her since I'd returned, but the brief encounters I'd had with Lacey a few weeks ago had told me that nothing had changed in her world. And that meant she was probably still giving Bell shit. I'd suffer through taking her orders and making her girlie drinks all night if it meant she left Bell alone.

"How about a daiquiri?" She leaned over the bar, making sure I got a nice view of her ample cleavage, and plucked up a cherry from behind the bar.

"We don't serve frozen drinks here, Lace. How about a vodka cran?"

She gave a pout that was supposed to look cute but just looked ridiculous on anyone over the age of ten. "Not even for me?" Lacey popped the cherry into her mouth, pulling out the stem.

"Not even for you. Vodka cran?"

A hint of annoyance flickered in her gaze. "Can you handle a cosmo?"

"That I can do." I got to work pouring ice into a shaker.

"So, Ford…" Lacey let her words dangle, and I braced myself

for what was to come next. "The rumors aren't true, are they? They must be something Isabelle started."

I stiffened but forced myself to pour the cranberry juice into the shaker. "What rumors?"

"That you two are dating." She said it as if the idea were disgusting.

I added a squeeze of lime. "This is the one time I'm happy to say the rumor mill got it right." I shook the drink before pouring it into a cocktail glass.

I turned to see Lacey gaping at me. I ignored her reaction and set the glass down on the bar. "Here you go. That'll be fourteen even. You want to start a tab, or cash out now?"

Lacey reached out, grabbing my arm. "You can't, Ford. What would Violet think? That's her sister."

I stepped out of Lacey's hold but held her stare. "You don't know a damn thing about what Violet would think. And you know even less about me. Now, cash or tab?"

Chapter Forty-One

Bell

I COULDN'T UN-SEE IT. THE IMAGE WAS BURNED SO CLEARLY in my mind, it was as if a branding iron had put it there. Lacey's hand resting gently, almost lovingly, on Ford's arm. She'd had worry written all over her face. What did she know about Ford that required her concern?

I'd forced my gaze away quickly, but it wasn't fast enough. My stomach roiled. I jumped as a hand landed on my shoulder. I squealed.

"Shit, I'm sorry, Bell. I just wanted to make sure you were okay. You looked upset."

I rested a hand on my chest, breathing heavily. "Sorry. I was in another world."

Hunter's face hardened. "Someone giving you trouble?"

I shook my head. "No, I promise. Just spinning my wheels about something." When Ford had bailed, Hunter and Ethan had taken it upon themselves to look out for me. I appreciated it, but it wasn't necessary.

"Is everything okay with you and Ford?"

Apparently, Hunter wasn't giving up. "We're fine. It's just weird having people whisper and stare."

Hunter scanned the crowd. "People are gonna talk. You and Ford? No one thought they'd ever see it happen. That's fodder for gossip for years to come."

Hunter was right. On an island the size of Anchor, people would always talk, and I'd always be faced with Lacey coming into the bar and putting her hands on my boyfriend. Was that even the right term? Ford and I hadn't made any formal agreements. Maybe he thought he was free to take someone else to bed. I gave my head a little shake. That wasn't Ford.

"Bell, are you sure you're all right?"

I nodded. "I just need to run to the ladies'. See you later." I barely made it into one of the stalls before my stomach emptied its contents. I braced myself against the wall as I heaved. I knew my brain was twisting things, but I couldn't seem to stop it.

When my stomach was finally empty, I struggled to my feet. "Get ahold of yourself, Bell." I made my way to the sink, splashing some water on my face and rinsing out my mouth. Thankfully, we kept mouthwash and little cups under the sink.

I took a deep breath and met my reflection in the mirror. I was paler than usual, dark circles rimming my eyes. There was no spark there like there usually was. I pressed my palm to my chest, where the tattoo and scars peeked out of my t-shirt. "What am I doing?"

I closed my eyes, straining to hear an answer, begging for some sort of reassurance. All I got was silence. I'd have to figure this one out myself. I opened my eyes and let my hands drop to my sides. *You have to let yourself fall.* I heard the echo of Kara's words in my mind. Maybe falling meant telling Ford exactly how I felt and why I was terrified. No more second-guessing or twisting his motives in my mind, just lay it all out there. I let out a long breath. I could do that.

My hand shook as I reached for the bathroom door. Pulling it open, I almost stumbled back again.

"What's the matter, Trouble?"

Ford stood leaning against the opposite wall, and the look of confusion and concern blanketing his expression pricked at the anger simmering just beneath the surface. Did he honestly think it wouldn't bother me to see Lacey flirting with him? That it wouldn't kill me to see that he'd let her touch him?

I straightened my spine, my shoulders rolling back. "You looked pretty darn cozy with my good friend Lacey."

Ford gaped at me. "Are you serious right now?"

Heat flushed my cheeks. "You know how I feel about her."

Ford ran a hand through his hair, giving it a good tug at the ends. "I was trying to keep Lacey away from you. To distract her from giving you shit. I know you've had a rough few weeks, and I didn't want her adding to it."

It made sense in theory. Ford's protectiveness had never been in question. My shoulders slumped. I felt like I was losing my mind. "She touched you."

"Trouble…" Ford eased forward, brushing the hair back from my face. "I stepped out of that in a split second and told her to mind her own business."

Maybe he had. I'd seen the exchange for no more than a few breaths. I couldn't stomach looking at them any longer and had immediately looked away.

Ford sighed, his jaw working. "You are never going to completely trust me, are you? What do I have to do to prove myself?"

I bristled at his words. "Trust you? I've laid myself bare for you. Told you things that I haven't shared with anyone. You've invaded every last piece of my life. But I don't even know how you truly feel about me. I tell you I love you, and you dodge and weave. Do you have any idea how much that hurts?"

Ford's mouth fell open. "Bell—"

I held up a hand to silence him. "No. Don't." I turned on my heel and headed for the side door. I needed air. Whatever Ford would've said in that moment, whatever promises he'd been about to make, I wouldn't have been able to believe them. Not a single word.

I pushed the door open, the cool ocean air a balm to my flushed skin. I strode towards the beach. I needed the sound of the waves, maybe even the feel of the water on my feet. My heart cracked a little more. I was so tired of having to battle to get those I loved to show me they cared. To show me that they'd stay, even when things got hard. Maybe Kara was wrong. Maybe I'd let myself fall too early and without investigating what was at the bottom of the cliff. Now I was on my way to the rocks below.

I passed by my workshop's overhang. Maybe I'd lose myself in restoration work after my walk. That would be just the thing to help me get through the night. With a sudden jerk, I was flying backwards. My breath caught in my throat as a hand covered my mouth. A cloth choked me. I thrashed, doing my best to elbow the guy in the gut the way I'd learned in my self-defense classes. But my world was going slightly fuzzy around the edges, and my movements became clumsy, as if all of my limbs carried an extra twenty pounds.

I tried to bite down on the hand through the cloth. Someone cursed. Sweetness filled my mouth and made me gag. I did my best to yell for help, to call Ford, but it only came out as a whisper.

Chapter Forty-Two

Ford

I WHIRLED, SLAMMING MY FIST INTO THE WALL. LUCKILY, MY knuckles landed on a wooden beam and not the brick. I cursed. I had royally fucked things up. And yet, as I tried to get the words to curve around my tongue, even in the silence of the hallway, I couldn't seem to force them out. I hadn't told anyone I loved them in…a memory hit me with a force that had me stumbling back on my heels. Since the day of the crash. I'd told Vi that I loved her seconds before that deer had jumped in front of my SUV.

I leaned forward, pressing my hands against the brick wall, trying to dig my fingertips into the stone. Fear. Some subconscious yet insidious monster had been twisting my mind, making me believe that if I didn't say the words, I'd never have to hurt the way I had when I lost Vi. But holding back had hurt Bell in the worst way imaginable. I *did* love her. Whether I said the words or not didn't change that. I loved her with everything in me. It was more than love, it was raw and real, some unnamed life force that lit my soul on fire.

I shoved away from the wall. All I wanted was to fix this, but anything I said now would feel like empty platitudes. I would fight tooth and nail to make her believe, though. I would beg and plead until she saw the light and believed the truth of it.

I ran a hand through my hair and started towards the side door. My steps faltered as I got closer. Bell wanted her space, needed it. My chest tightened. I couldn't give it to her, though. She couldn't be alone. My hand landed on the doorknob and stayed there. Maybe I could just keep an eye on her from afar. Give her space but not too much.

She was going to rain hell on me if she saw me following her. I sighed, pushing open the door. Her anger was just a risk I would have to take. Cool night air hit me, and tires screeched as someone pulled out of the parking lot way too fast. I really hoped it wasn't a drunk patron.

I scanned the parking lot, lit by the antique-looking streetlamps my parents had put in. I didn't see Bell anywhere. My heart picked up its pace, and so did my feet. I strode across the lot, scanning in between cars as I went. No Bell.

I headed for the workshop. Maybe she'd gone to find her peace there. I tried the door. Locked. "Bell?" I called through the door. There was nothing. No sounds or flicker of light.

That vise around my chest grew tighter. Maybe she'd gone to the beach. The crashing waves had always calmed her. That's where she was. She had to be.

I picked up a jog, jumping over a piece of driftwood and making my way to the water. I scanned the shore. The moon was close to full, giving me just enough light to see by. Bell was nowhere. I looked north and south but saw nothing. No one. The beach was completely empty.

No. No. No. This wasn't happening. I couldn't lose Bell when I'd just found her. I pulled my phone out of my pocket, hitting the sheriff's contact as I started to run back to the bar.

"Sheriff Raines."

"Bell's gone. She stepped outside, was out of my sight for less than five minutes, and now she's gone."

Parker let out a slew of curses. "I'm on my way, but it's going to take me at least thirty minutes. I'm sending the on-island deputies now, though. Stay put."

I couldn't promise him that. I'd do whatever I thought might get me Bell back. "See you soon." I hung up and pulled the door to the bar open. I went straight for the cabinet that housed the stereo system, cutting the music.

There were yells of complaint and muttered confusion. I didn't think, I just moved, climbing up onto the bar. "Can I have your attention, please? Has anyone seen Bell? Isabelle Kipton. Has anyone seen her? Blond hair, green eyes, about yay high." I motioned to my shoulders.

Caelyn hurried up to the bar, Crosby hot on her heels. "What happened? Where's Bell?"

I looked back out at the crowd. "If everyone could stay put, we'd appreciate it. Police will be here in just a bit to ask you some questions. The next round of drinks will be on us." I hopped off the bar, meeting Caelyn's gaze. "I don't know. She's gone." Just saying the words out loud killed something inside me.

Crosby let out a litany of curses. "Where'd you last see her?"

My jaw worked as a burning sensation gathered at the backs of my eyes. "Heading out to the parking lot." This was all my fault. Bell was gone, and someone could be hurting her right now. None of this would've happened if I hadn't been a stupid idiot and just told her how I felt. That I loved her.

Darlene appeared at Crosby's side. "Why the hell was she alone?"

Crosby's hand landed on Darlene's shoulder. "The why doesn't matter. We just need to find her now. What did Parker say?"

"To stay put." The front door swung open, and two deputies strode in. I waved them over. "I told everyone not to leave in case you had questions."

"Thank you," the older officer, Deputy Shepard, said. "Deputy Hughes, will you start taking statements?" The younger female officer nodded and headed to the closest table. "Okay, walk me through it."

I did just that. By the time I was through, Kenna had arrived. She was unnaturally pale but wrapped an arm around a crying Caelyn. Deputy Shepard closed his notebook. "Raines will be here any moment, but it might be worth you guys checking her regular haunts just in case she was upset enough to bail altogether."

That wasn't Bell. She wasn't selfish. She wouldn't have left without a word because she knew it would terrify the people she loved. But I'd take any excuse to get out of here. To do something. Anything. "Okay, we'll check out my house and a few other places."

The officer nodded. "Just keep your phone on you and stick together, just in case."

"Will do." I pulled out my phone and hit Hunter's contact. It rang and rang before finally clicking over to voicemail.

"Are you calling your parents?" Kenna asked.

I shook my head. "She wouldn't have gone there. It's too late. And I don't want to worry them. I was trying Hunt."

Crosby's brow furrowed. "He didn't pick up?"

"No." I scowled down at my phone. I'd seen him flirting pretty hard with a blonde. He probably took off to get laid.

"Let's go to my place, make sure Bell isn't there. Then we'll make a plan." I turned to Darlene. "I need you and Hank to hold down the fort here. Be my eyes and ears. Call me if anyone saw anything suspicious."

Darlene opened her mouth to argue but then thought better of it. "Of course we will."

"Thank you." The rest of us headed for the parking lot. This island, this bar, they were supposed to be safe. But nowhere truly was. It was something I'd learned long ago, but it seemed the Universe was just dying to give me another lesson.

Chapter Forty-Three

Bell

I LET OUT A LOW MOAN. MY HEAD WAS KILLING ME. IT SEEMED to be throbbing in time with the beat of my heart. I moaned again, rolling onto my back. I hit something. The back of a couch? Had I had too much to drink with the girls and passed out on Kenna's ridiculously uncomfortable sofa?

My eyes blinked open. It was dark, but there was a low light shining through a window. A car window. I was in a car? No, an SUV. I blinked more rapidly, trying to clear the slightly wobbly tinge to my vision. The side of the vehicle was smashed in.

My breaths came faster, each tripping over the last, and none of them seeming to take hold. Had I been in an accident? My gaze darted around the vehicle. It was familiar. Too familiar. Nausea swept through me as I took in the splatters of blood that dotted the door. I'd been stuck in this SUV for moments that had seemed like hours, holding on to my dead sister's hand, waiting for the EMTs and fire department to arrive.

I scrambled, trying to sit, but something stopped me. Bonds.

Ropes on my hands and feet. A scream gathered in the back of my throat, but I swallowed it down. Whoever had done this might be close. I couldn't let them know I was awake.

I tried to slow my breaths, inhaling deeply. My stomach pitched. *Don't puke. Do not puke, Bell.* I closed my eyes, willing the sensation to pass. When I opened them again, it was a little bit better. I looked around the vehicle's interior, searching for something—anything—that might help.

Slowly, I eased myself up, using my elbow as a hoist. I looked out the front of the car and saw only the cliffside and the ocean below. My gaze swept around until I twisted to look over the backseat. The back and side windows were smashed, but there was no hint of remaining glass.

Movement caught my attention, a figure pacing back and forth in the darkness. I squinted. I couldn't make out who they were. My breathing grew quicker again, and I had to force myself to slow it. I couldn't risk passing out again.

Out. I had to get out. Out of the ropes. Out of this SUV. And far, far away from the person pacing this cliff. I tugged at the bonds around my hands. They were tight, so much so that my fingers were tingling. There was no way I could get them off without a knife. Why wasn't I the kind of person who carried a pocketknife with them wherever they went? From now on, I would. First stop I was making tomorrow was The General Store, and I was getting the best pocketknife they had.

I let out a long, shaky breath. That wasn't going to help me now. I tested the ropes around my ankles. They were just a little looser, not so tight they were cutting off my circulation. I bent down, my head throbbing sharply with the motion, making my stomach pitch. I closed my eyes for a brief moment, trying to still the onslaught of sensations.

When my eyes opened, I tested the ties around my legs with my fingers. I could slip in one digit, maybe two, but the knot tying the ends together was too tight for me to have any hope of undoing it. It was some sort of sailor's knot with what seemed like endless loops and ties. I muttered a curse and tried to come up with a different plan of attack.

I studied the loops of rope, willing it to give me a clue. The material of my jeans bunched beneath the bindings, creating waves of fabric. I tugged on the material of one leg. It moved. My breath hitched, and my fingers started flying, pulling as much as they could with the limited dexterity they had. I grabbed and tugged, working as fast as I could, even after I lost all feeling in my fingers. Finally, one jeans leg came free and bunched above the ropes.

I tested the bonds. There was a little more movement. Maybe with both jeans legs absent, I'd have enough room to make progress on the knot. The second leg was easier with that little extra breathing room, and before long, that side's fabric was bunched above the ropes, too.

My chest heaved, and my head pounded in time with my heartbeat. *Come on, come on, come on.* I tested the knot again. Nothing. I cursed. "You can do this, Bell."

I gave my leg a little tug. Movement. My heart rate picked up its pace. I wiggled my foot in my boot, trying to slide it out while the rope tore at the bare skin of my leg. I didn't care. I would take all the pain if I could just get out of here.

I grunted and pulled, twisting my leg in any way I could think of. With one final yank, my foot escaped my boot and the ropes. I bit back my yell of victory. I quickly used my bound hands as best I could to free my other leg and get my boot back on. I would need shoes when I ran. My fingers felt sticky liquid on my calf as I pulled the boot on. I winced.

It didn't matter. I was getting out of here. The sound of footsteps against gravel infiltrated my senses. Too late. I was too late.

"Good. You're awake."

"E-ethan?" I had to be wrong. He'd always been so kind to me. Protective, even. The pieces were trying to come together in my mind, but I couldn't make sense of it.

He leaned into the smashed-out window, and I quickly shoved my feet under the seat in front of me. "Hey, Bell."

He said it so matter-of-factly, the same way he'd greeted me a million times at the bar. This wasn't real. Couldn't be. "What's going on?"

Ethan grinned, and it was one I'd never seen on him before. It was almost a touch evil, deranged. Or maybe I was just seeing it through the eyes of someone he'd clearly tied up in the back of a car. "I have to admit, your little innocent act had me fooled for a while."

"What innocent act?" My heart hammered in my chest, rattling painfully against my ribs.

Ethan's eyes went cold. "Don't try that bullshit on me. You're done. You're not manipulating anyone else."

"What are you talking about?" None of what he was saying made sense. And the more Ethan spoke, the more my stomach sank.

"I have to make you stop."

"Stop what?"

"Manipulating! I told you!" He shoved off the SUV and began that same erratic pacing I'd seen earlier. "I have to send you over. You have to go."

My fingers dug into the ropes securing my hands, the ragged pieces cutting the skin under my nails. My voice shook. "Over where?"

Ethan's gaze snapped back to me. "Over the cliff. So you can die. Like you should have all along."

Chapter Forty-four

Ford

"FINALLY!" I GLARED AT MY BROTHER AS HE STRODE through the door.

"What did you mean Bell's missing?"

"Exactly what I said, genius. Maybe if you answered your phone instead of worrying about getting laid, you'd be in the loop."

"I was out of pocket for an hour, I didn't think the world would fall apart in that time."

But it had. My world had come apart at the seams in a matter of seconds, just like it had before. Only this time, there wouldn't be any coming back from it, not if something happened to Bell. I squeezed my eyes shut, pinching the bridge of my nose as if that would miraculously change what lay in front of me.

"Okay, okay." Crosby stepped in between Hunter and me. "We're all worried. What we need to do now is come up with a list of places to check and people to talk to."

We'd stopped by Vi's grave and Caelyn's and Kenna's houses

already. No sign of Bell. I couldn't think of anywhere else she'd go. Not willingly, in the middle of the night.

Hunter rubbed a hand over his jaw. "I saw Bell right before I left. She was upset, said all the stares and whispers were getting to her. But I don't think that was the whole story." His gaze cut to me. "You want to tell me why Bell was upset, brother?"

I bristled at Hunter's tone. "None of your damn business."

"Shut up!" Kenna yelled. "Enough of this macho bullshit. You two need to get it together, or I'll come up with a reason for the sheriff to put you both in cuffs. I'll lie if I have to." Both Hunter and I stayed silent. "Hunter, stop goading your brother." She turned to me. "Ford, we need to know everything, and that includes why Bell was upset. I know it's probably personal, but any little thing might help."

Crosby leaned closer to me. "I love it when she cracks the whip like that."

"Not the time, Crosby," Hunter warned.

I laced my fingers behind my head, pressing my hands against my skull, trying to hold back my desire to punch something. "She was doubting how I felt about her." Saying the words out loud sliced at my throat, ravaged my chest. The last thing Bell had felt in regard to me was doubt. And that would stay with me forever. I cleared my throat. "Lacey Hotchkiss showed up at the bar." Kenna let out what sounded like a growl. "She was trying to hit on me. I shut it down. But Bell was still upset."

I inhaled, the air seeming to have jagged edges, the way it felt when temperatures were below freezing. "We fought. She stormed outside. I gave myself a couple of minutes to get it together, and then I followed. I knew she'd be pissed, that she likely wanted to be alone, but I was worried. By the time I got out there…she was gone. I heard a vehicle peeling out of the parking lot." I swallowed back the burning in my throat that was somehow creeping up behind my eyes.

Crosby squeezed my shoulder. "We're going to find her."

Caelyn leaned forward. "Hunt, have you called Ethan? Maybe he saw something and just hasn't put it together because he doesn't know that Bell's missing."

Hunter nodded and hit Ethan's contact. The room was so quiet, I could hear the ringing on the other end. It went on and on, no answer in sight. Garbled words sounded, and Hunter hit end and dialed again. This time, it rang once, and then a muted voice answered. Hunter's brows drew together. "He sent me to voicemail."

I began pacing. "Call him again. Maybe he thinks you're trying to drag him out of bed for a ride."

Hunt nodded and hit Ethan's name again. "Same thing." A flicker of something passed over my brother's features.

I stopped pacing. "What is it?"

"Nothing."

My muscles tensed, and I fought the urge to deck Hunter. "That doesn't sound like nothing."

He let out a frustrated breath. "I swear it's nothing, my mind is just looking for zebras when I should be thinking horses."

"What the hell are you talking about?" I stepped towards him, but Crosby put a hand firmly in my chest.

"It's stupid. I just remembered something from high school."

"What thing from high school?" I gritted out.

Hunter toyed with the cell phone in his hands, spinning it in circles. "Ethan had a massive crush on Violet."

Dread slid through my veins, thick and suffocating, like tar, slowly drowning out my ability to breathe.

"Don't freak, Ford. He'd crushed on her forever, even gave her flowers in middle school, violets, but he never actually made a move. I told you, paranoia is getting to me."

Caelyn pushed to her feet, her body seeming to tremble. "He was around a lot, and for no real reason, especially after Vi died."

Kenna's brow pinched. "He came by the hospital a few times, even offered to drive Bell to physical therapy if her parents couldn't."

"You guys, it's called being a good person," Hunter argued.

Crosby held up a hand. "You had that moment of doubt for a reason. It doesn't cost us anything to check it out. You know where he lives, right?" Hunter nodded slowly. "We'll go knock on his door. No harm, no foul. We need to know if he saw anything regardless."

"No." My vision was going unfocused as that dread sank its claws in deeper. "We have to go somewhere else first." This was about Vi, her death. Whether it was Ethan or someone else, there was only one place they'd take Bell.

"Where?" Kenna asked.

"The cliffs." Where the nightmare began.

Chapter Forty-five

Bell

OVER. ETHAN WANTED TO TOSS ME OFF A CLIFF. LIKE A rock or a piece of trash he'd kick over the side. His eyes seemed to gleam unnaturally in the moonlight. Garbage was exactly what he thought I was. "W-why?" I couldn't help the slight tremble in my voice.

Ethan stopped his pacing and turned to look at me. "Someone has to put Violet first."

"How is sending me over a cliff putting Violet first?" Yes, I was buying time, but I also genuinely wanted to know. Needed to understand how a mind had twisted things to such an extreme.

His face hardened. "You're spitting on her grave. On Violet's dead body. You say you love her, but you're fucking the man who killed her!" Ethan began pacing again, muttering to himself about traitors and other things I couldn't quite make out.

My hands shook as I tested the ropes again. Too tight. They weren't loosening. But my feet were free. That would have to be enough. Ethan was bigger and faster, but I had adrenaline on my side. Adrenaline and a desire to live. I just needed a chance to break away.

Hands slammed down on the side of the SUV as Ethan's face appeared in the smashed-out window. "Why did you do it? Why did you let her killer in?"

I let out a shaky breath. "Because I love him."

Ethan's hand struck out quicker than I could move, and he latched on to my hair with a viciousness that startled a yelp out of me. He yanked on the strands, bringing my face close to his. The pain had tears gathering in my eyes. "You're so damn selfish. You love him more than your sister? Your blood?"

"I love them both." I did, there was no one on this Earth I loved more than Vi and Ford. I could feel it, rooted deep in my chest. It wasn't a competition like I had feared. It was like trying to compare the sun and the moon. They both tugged at me like they pulled the sea, strong and swift, but I needed them each in different ways.

Ethan's face reddened as his grip on my scalp tightened. "You are sickening."

Spittle dotted my face as he cursed, throwing me back against the seat. My head rang with the force of it, a renewed beat thundering through my skull. Nausea swept through me in waves. I let myself close my eyes for just a moment, trying to still the riot of pain and sickness coursing through me.

I took a deep, shuddering breath and forced my eyes back open. Ethan was back to pacing. Cursing. Kicking rocks. The stones went flying over the side of the cliff. In the same way I would if I didn't get out of here. I straightened in my seat, wincing as I awkwardly pushed myself up to a sitting position.

I doubted the doors with the smashed-out windows would even open, but when Ethan had thrown me, he'd scooted me towards the other door. Closer to freedom. I glanced at Ethan. He was still pacing. I eased my hands over to the door, onto the handle. It was difficult, but I could just get my fingers around the latch and—

"Maybe we should call him."

I froze. "Call who?"

Ethan's face appeared in the window opening again. "The killer. Violet's killer. Maybe we can get him out here and then send you both over. That's how it should be."

My heart hammered in my chest, shaking my rib cage. "No. Don't call Ford."

Ethan grinned, the smile sick and twisted, and pulled out his phone. He scowled at the screen. Time. I needed to buy time. To get free. To run. And he couldn't call Ford in that time. My stomach roiled at the thought. "You loved my sister?"

Ethan froze. I'd said the first thing that came to mind. I hadn't had time to put all of the pieces together, but my brain must've been doing the work subconsciously. No one did something like this just for kicks. There had to be a reason. And at the root of this much hate could only be one thing…love.

Ethan's throat worked as he swallowed. "She loved me, too."

I stayed silent, hoping he'd continue. I searched my mind for any memories of Ethan and Violet together. Nothing other than football games and school events came to mind.

Ethan took my silence as disagreement. "She did!"

"Okay," I hurried to assuage him. "I just—I didn't know. She never told me. It's hard to learn things about your sister after she's already gone." Ethan nodded slowly. "Did you get the SUV because you loved her?" My mind had been going in circles on how the vehicle even still existed.

"I get everything of hers I can."

I gripped the armrest as best as I could with my fingers that had lost all feeling. "How'd you get this?"

"Wreck lot. They were going to take it to Shelter Island to crunch it. I bought it for two hundred bucks." Who wouldn't have asked any questions about a sixteen or seventeen-year-old buying a wreck of an SUV that had been part of a deadly accident? Why hadn't his parents asked any questions? "I got it working again, just enough. I was waiting. Waiting for Ford to come back. I was going to kill him in this thing." He blushed. "Got a little impatient, though."

My hands spasmed. Ethan had been impatient when he'd smashed Ford over the head with a piece of driftwood and dragged him into the ocean. "Ethan," I whispered. "The accident wasn't Ford's fault. A deer jumped out into the road. Ford tried to save us."

"It *was* his fault! Don't you dare say different!" Ethan strode away to the back of the SUV. "It's time for you to go. Time for this to end."

Shit, shit, shit. I'd pushed too far. There was no time for distraction or anything else. It was now or never. My fingers pulled on the door latch just as the vehicle began to roll forward towards the cliff. I scrambled out, tripping as I went. My bound hands caught the brunt of my fall, and I lurched to my feet.

Ethan cursed. "No! You don't get away. Not this time."

I ran—as fast as my muscles would allow. My head swam. I kept blinking, trying to clear my vision so I wouldn't trip. Footsteps on gravel sounded behind me. Getting closer and closer. I pushed my muscles harder. I pictured Ford in my mind, running to him, into the safety I felt while in his arms.

A hand snagged the back of my shirt, yanking me back. "I don't think so." I slammed into a hard chest. "You're going over tonight. No more breaks for you."

Tears streamed down my face as I kicked and clawed, trying to get purchase on anything. I had no luck. The steep, rocky incline grew closer, the black sea swirling around the jagged rocks below. *No, no, no.* My life wasn't going to end like this. But Vi hadn't wanted hers to end the way it had either.

My feet scrambled as rocks gave way along the cliff. It was too steep. I'd roll down and land on the rocks below. If the fall didn't kill me, the mixture of injuries and the sea would finish the job. I had nothing, no one, not a single thing that could save me now. But as Ethan forced me over the edge, I wasn't alone. My mind saw only one thing: Ford's face.

Chapter Forty-Six

Ford

I SLAMMED THE DOOR OF MY SUV, AND MY BREATH STUTTERED in my lungs. Memories hit me one after the other. Laughing with Vi and Bell as I drove. Bell yelling out. Me trying to swerve. The sickening crunch. The nothingness that followed.

My SUV, the one from the accident... It was sitting before me. Same license plate. Same...everything. Except the side was completely smashed in. The damage that must've been done in the collision. My gut twisted and roiled.

A scream jerked me out of my daze. I didn't think, I just ran towards the terrified sounds coming from the woman I loved more than life itself. That familiar vise tightened painfully around my ribs again, each step seeming to twist it tighter. Footsteps behind me told me that Crosby and Hunter were close.

I yelled, but it was drowned out by the ocean winds and the sound of the waves below. I pushed my muscles harder as the cliff's edge came into view. Time slowed, seemed almost to stop, as if someone had pressed the Universe's pause button. Bell was being held over a cliff by only a fistful of her shirt, flailing, searching for purchase, for anything that might save her. I was close, but not close enough. She was alone. I'd left her when she needed me most and now…Ethan released his hold.

A guttural cry tore from my chest as Bell slid over the side of the rocky incline. Gone. She was gone. This wasn't happening. The pain tearing through me was like nothing I'd ever experienced before, fire and ice licking through muscle and sinew, ripping me apart.

"Go, Ford! We've got Ethan."

It was Hunter's order that snapped me out of it. Maybe… Maybe the fall hadn't killed her. Maybe Bell was in the water below. I ran towards the edge of the cliff, skidding to a stop just a breath away from going over. Black water swirled below. I strained to see any movement.

"Ford?"

The single word, shaky and uncertain, was the most beautiful thing I'd ever heard. My gaze snapped down. "Bell." I sank to the ground and lay on my stomach so I could lean over the side. The cliffside was made up of a series of steep inclines, and Bell was teetering on one of them, hands bound but hooked around a bunch of roots and rocks. My heart slammed against my ribs as rocks gave way under her feet.

"Ford!"

The panic in Bell's eyes nearly broke something in me. I didn't think, just reached, trying to ground myself with one hand and grab hold of Bell with the other. "I've got you."

Terror flashed in her eyes. "I'm going to fall."

"No. You're not." I gritted my teeth against the strain of gravity and my awkward position. I'd grabbed her with my weak arm, the same one that had been dislocated only weeks before. I willed my shoulder to stay in place. I would not let Bell fall. I would not lose her.

There was a gasp behind me. "Oh, God. What do we do?" Caelyn's panicked voice cut through the night air.

"You and Kenna grab my ankles. I need weight to hold me in place."

They moved in a flash. Their arms and weight grounded me. I reached down with my left hand, grabbing hold of Bell's other wrist. "Okay, Trouble, I need you to listen to me." Bell's eyes were wild, jumping from me to the rocks and swirling ocean below and then back again. "Bell! Eyes on me." She obeyed, but the fear in them cut so deep, I knew it would leave a scar that would last forever.

"Listen to me. On the count of three, you're going to let go of those roots, and I'm going to lift you up." I could've lifted Bell easily with an uninjured arm, she was a lightweight, but I had no idea if my shoulder would give out when I began to pull.

Bell's head shook back and forth frantically. "I-I can't. I'll fall."

"You can, Bell. You're so damn brave. You can do this." It all came down to one thing. Trust. I'd put her through so much. Left her when she needed me most. But I was here now. And I was staying. I locked my gaze with Bell's. "I love you. I'm not going anywhere. You are stuck with me forever. Please…trust me."

Bell let out a shuddering breath. "Okay."

The word was soft, almost lost in the sound of the waves crashing into the rocks below and the wind whipping through the trees. "On the count of three." She nodded. "One, two, three!"

Bell released her hold, and I pulled with everything I had in me. I felt a tearing sensation in my right shoulder like someone had taken a blowtorch to the joint, but I didn't care. She was closer. Almost to safety, nearly in my arms. With one more hard tug, I rolled us both over onto solid ground, Bell landing on top of me.

Her body shook with violent sobs. I wrapped my arms around her and held tight, needing the feel of her against me, alive and breathing. "You're safe, Trouble. You're safe." I said the words over and over as if I were incapable of saying anything else. Sirens sounded in the background.

"I'm sorry, Ford. I'm so sorry." Bell pressed her face into my neck as she wept.

I held her tighter, uncaring that my shoulder was raging in pain. "You have nothing to be sorry about."

"I trust you." She hiccupped the words on a half-sob.

"I love you, Bell. More than anything or anyone. You are it for me."

"Good," she mumbled against my throat. "Because I'm not letting go."

Chapter Forty-Seven

Bell

I BRACED MYSELF AGAINST THE SHOWER WALL, LETTING THE hot water cascade down my body. It stung the cuts and scrapes, but I relished the sting. I would've doused myself with rubbing alcohol if it were possible. I'd scrubbed and scrubbed as if that might erase what had happened.

I jumped at the sound of the shower door opening. Ford stepped inside, the tension running through him, causing his muscles to ripple. "Hi." The word came out with a tremble, and I hated it, the uncertainty in my voice, the weakness.

"Come here." I went without hesitation, Ford wrapping me in his strong arms. "You're safe."

"I know." And I did. Ethan was locked up in jail with a black eye and broken nose courtesy of Crosby and Hunter, and he wouldn't be getting out anytime soon. It wasn't that. It was as if I couldn't feel that my feet were indeed on solid ground.

As if reading my mind, Ford pressed his lips to my wet hair. "It's going to take time. But I'll be with you every step of the way."

I melted into him at those words. I wasn't alone. I never had been, and I never would be. The thing I hadn't realized before was that even when Ford was gone, I still carried him with me, the same way I held Vi inside me now. The things they'd taught me, the encouragement and support they'd given, but most of all, I'd always had their love, and I would forever. No amount of cold could drown out that warmth.

I tipped my head back, meeting Ford's gaze. "I love you."

He closed his eyes as if soaking in every syllable and embedding it within him. When his eyes opened, they blazed with that blue fire I loved so much. "I love you too, Bell. I've always felt it in one way or another. I didn't say it because—"

"You don't have to explain, Ford."

He brushed his lips against mine. "I *want* to explain." He took a deep breath. "The last person I said those words to died. I haven't said them since. Not to my parents, to Hunter, to anyone. I didn't realize it, but I was holding those words back out of fear. As some form of misguided self-protection. And I hurt the people I love most because of it."

My heart broke a little more for the boy who'd lost so much so long ago, whose broken bones hadn't quite healed right, and now he had to reset them to make sure everything worked again. I pressed a kiss to his stubbled jaw. "Thank you for giving me the words."

He grinned. "I'll give them to you as many times as you want."

I bit my bottom lip. "Like now?"

Ford took my mouth in a long, slow kiss. "I love you."

"And now?"

He trailed his tongue down the side of my neck, catching stray droplets of water. "I love you."

I gripped his waist harder. "Show me."

Ford pulled back, his eyes burning a deeper shade of blue. "Trouble, you've been through a lot tonight."

I pulled him tighter against me, his body hardening beneath my hands. "I need this, need you, need to know that I'm alive."

Ford dropped his forehead to mine, breathing deeply. "I can never deny you."

"Good." I took his cock in my hand, guiding us back into the spray. I took my time exploring Ford's body, my fingers testing each dip and curve, discovering what movements drove him crazy.

I swept a thumb over the head of him, and he hissed out a breath. "I need inside you."

My core tightened at his statement. "Please."

It was the only word he needed. With a smooth shift of his position, Ford glided in. His strokes were slow and deliberate, one hand braced on the wall behind my head, the other cupping my face. He never once looked away. He was imprinting himself on me, body and soul. With each stroke and caress, with each brush of his lips and nip of his teeth. And when I came, it was with the bone-deep knowledge that I was his, now and forever.

                                         ✺

Ford wrapped me in one of the massive fluffy towels in his bathroom. "Are you sure you're okay?"

"I'm fine." I studied his movements. "But you look like your shoulder is bothering you."

He winced slightly. "I think I might've tweaked it tonight."

My stomach sank. Of course he'd tweaked it, he'd lifted a human being over the side of a cliff. "We need to get it checked."

"I will, after you get checked out."

I growled at him. "I don't think it's smart for us to wait until tomorrow. Maybe we should catch a boat into Seattle and go to the ER."

Ford rubbed the back of his neck with his uninjured hand.

"Actually, your dad's here. He's in the kitchen with Crosby, Hunter, and the girls."

My face heated. "You had sex with me while my father was in the house?"

Ford pressed his mouth into a hard line, as if he were trying really hard to keep from laughing. "You were the one who was all 'show me, Ford.'"

"I'm going to kill you." It was going to be a slow and painful death, too.

Ford pulled me into his arms. "He's worried about you. Said he wanted to check you over himself, see if you needed to go to a hospital."

"It's just a few bumps and scrapes."

Ford gently lifted my arm to examine my wrist. "This isn't just bumps and scrapes."

I winced at the raw, exposed flesh. "I'll let him examine me if you get your shoulder looked at first."

"Deal."

Ford was dressed in a matter of seconds while I delayed. I wasn't sure I was ready to face my dad. He felt like a stranger now instead of the man who had raised me. I glanced up at Ford. "You go ahead, get that shoulder examined. I'll be out in a minute."

Ford studied me carefully. "Are you sure?"

I nodded. "Go."

He went, and I carefully slipped one of Ford's tees over my head. The worn cotton was perfectly soft, just what I needed in this moment. I pressed a hand to my chest, where I knew the tattoo and mottled skin lay below. "I need you with me for this one, sissy." I couldn't hear her, but I knew she was there.

I took a deep breath and headed out of the bedroom, moving towards the muted voices in the kitchen.

"I'm going to order an MRI and set you up with a specialist

I know in Seattle. I'll call him first thing in the morning and make sure he gets you in this week."

"Thank you, Dr. Kipton."

"Please, call me Bruce."

I hovered at the edge of the kitchen until Caelyn caught sight of me. "Bells! How are you feeling?"

I wrapped her in the thirtieth hug I'd given her tonight. "I'm fine, I promise."

"Let's let your dad be the judge of that, Trouble."

I glared at Ford, who just chuckled.

"Please," my dad said. "I'd like to check you over to make sure there's nothing the EMTs missed."

I nodded, slowly heading towards the kitchen bar, where my father had set his medical bag. He looked different, older, and a little harried. I was surprised that my mother had let him out of the house in his track pants and a rumpled sweatshirt. I eased up on one of the stools and Ford was instantly at my back.

My father's gloved hands were gentle, reassuring. The feel of them heartbreakingly familiar. How many times had he lifted me up onto the kitchen counter to tend to a skinned knee or twisted ankle? Tears burned the backs of my eyes, but I refused to let them fall.

"I'm so sorry this happened to you, Bell."

I jolted at the sound of my nickname coming out of his mouth. Not once had he ever used it before, not even when we were alone. I swallowed against the emotion gathering in my throat. "I really am okay."

"I'm just going to get these wrists and ankles cleaned and bandaged. You should keep them covered for the next few days, at least."

"Okay. Thank you."

We stayed silent as he worked, Ford rubbing a hand up and down my back and occasionally dropping a kiss to my head.

My dad snapped off his gloves, throwing them into the trash. "All done." He glanced around the room and then back to Ford and me. "I was wondering if I could have a private word with you and Ford?"

I stiffened, but Ford squeezed my shoulder. "Of course."

"We should be going anyway," Kenna offered.

Hunter pressed a quick kiss to my cheek. "Call me if you need anything."

"Me, too," Caelyn said. "I'll bring you guys dinner tomorrow night."

"Thank you." I smiled at her.

"I can't bring dinner, but I can bring beer," Crosby said with a grin.

Kenna muttered something under her breath and gave Crosby a hard shove towards the door. When the sound of the front door closing reached us, I looked at my dad. "What is it?"

He sighed, easing himself onto one of the stools. "I tried to be a good father, but I can see now that I made a lot of mistakes along the way."

He rubbed a hand over his face and looked deeply tired. I couldn't help the way my heart squeezed in sympathy. I swallowed, my throat having gone dry. A part of me wanted to reassure him that he had been a good dad, but there was so much pain and hurt standing in the way of those words. Instead, I opted for silence. Ford pressed in at my back, and I grabbed hold of his hand, twining our fingers.

My dad let out a breath. "Violet was always the easy child. She just went along. Didn't ask why. Seemed happy to do whatever your mother and I asked. But you..." He chuckled. "You *always* wanted to know why, always went against the grain. I should've seen that quality in you for the strength it is, but instead, your mother and I got easily frustrated. I'm sorry for that."

The threat of tears reemerged, but I forced them back and nodded for Dad to go on.

"Your mom and Violet had cheerleading and their charity work to bond over. Violet and I would always talk about medicine. It was effortless. I should have found things to do with you, Bell. I should've taken up drawing or painting or…something."

My breath hitched. "It's not that we didn't enjoy the same things that hurt. It's that you wanted me to be someone else. You wanted me to be *Violet*. Especially after she was gone."

My dad's Adam's apple bobbed as he swallowed. "You're right. I never should've pushed you like that. Let your mom push you. I'm so sorry if you ever felt alone in our home or somehow unworthy."

"I wasn't alone. I had Ford." As much as I loved my sister, she didn't understand me either. It was Ford who had always been there, gently encouraging me to follow my own path.

Dad gave me a gentle smile. "I'm so glad you did. Thank you, Ford, for loving both my daughters and treating them so well."

Ford's hand spasmed in mine. "You're welcome, sir."

My dad sighed. "I'm not sure if sharing what I have to tell you is the right thing or not, but I've shared it with Sheriff Raines, so I feel it's only right to give it to you, as well."

My stomach pitched, and I gripped Ford's hand tighter. "Okay…"

"A few weeks before the accident, I was up late catching up on chart notes for the month. Violet came home past her curfew, which was so unlike her. When I stopped her in the hallway, she dissolved into tears. I brought her into the kitchen and made her a cup of tea, told her that whatever it was, we could talk it out, the way we always did."

Dad was lost in the memory as if he were back there at the kitchen table with Vi. "She said she'd made the worst mistake of her life. I told her that everything was fixable, we just needed to talk it through. That's when it all came tumbling out. She'd had too much to drink at a party and slept with someone that wasn't Ford. She slept with Ethan."

Ford froze. The only movement I could feel in his body was the beat of his heart. No one said a word. With a whoosh of breath, something in Ford eased. He wrapped his other arm around me, even though I knew the pain in his shoulder had to be killing him. "We were so young. Babies, really. We were bound to make mistakes. It would've hurt something fierce back then, but now...I just hate that she lived with all that guilt."

I let out a breath I hadn't realized I'd been holding. Tipping my head down, I pressed my lips to Ford's arm. He pulled it tighter around me. "I guess we know what made Ethan fixate on her even more."

Dad gave his head a small shake. "I guess so. The sheriff should be able to put all of the pieces together. But what's important for you two is the why."

"Why what?" I asked.

My dad met my gaze head-on. "Violet saw something before any of the rest of us. She was beginning to realize that she and Ford might not be a forever match, but that *you* and Ford might be."

"What?" That was ridiculous. Vi loved Ford like crazy. Sure, she'd messed up, but...my thoughts trailed off as Dad interrupted.

"Violet always saw the bond between you two. Knew you shared something special. Something she thought might turn into more than friendship when the time came." He looked from Ford to me. "She was trying to gather her courage to step out of your way."

A faint shudder ran through Ford's body. "She told me there was something important we needed to talk about that weekend. We were going to hike out to our spot and talk. I thought it was about our college plans."

My dad gave Ford a sad smile. "She was trying to let you go."

Epilogue

Bell
TWO MONTHS LATER

"S O, WHAT DO YOU THINK?" I NIBBLED ON MY BOTTOM lip as I watched Caelyn take in the space around us. I tried to picture it through her eyes. It was small, but my wallet needed that when I was starting out. And the location couldn't be beat. Right on Main Street, prime for all the tourist traffic.

The shop itself was long and narrow, but I was already visualizing how I could best fit my furniture pieces into the space. I'd started picking up little bits and bobs that could be used as decoration and later sold to shoppers. But the best part of all was that there was an old storage space behind the row of stores that was currently going unused. The landlord was giving me access for just a couple hundred dollars more each month. It would be my workshop and storage unit for overflow pieces. If a customer was looking for something specific that I didn't have up front, I could take them to the workshop.

Caelyn beamed. "It's absolutely perfect. When are you going to open?"

My belly did a series of what felt like cartwheels and backflips, a mixture of excitement and nerves. "I'm hoping to be up and running in two months. There's still a lot of work to be done. I want to refinish the floors, change the paint—"

Caelyn reached out and grabbed my hands. "You'll get it there. Have you settled on a name?"

"Second Chances." It was perfect in every way, for the furniture and for me.

Caelyn sniffed. "I love it."

"Don't you cry on me, Caelyn. If you cry, I'm going to cry, and then when Kenna gets here, she'll make fun of both of us."

Caelyn laughed and pulled me into a hug. "Okay, okay. So dang proud of you, Bell."

I soaked up the warmth of her love and support, simply taking a moment to think about just how fortunate I was. "Thanks for being here every step of the way."

Caelyn and Kenna had stuck close to my side ever since that night two months ago, lending their shoulders, ears, and whatever else I might need. Ford had joked that he was going to need a bigger house, or at least a bigger couch, if Caelyn and Kenna were moving in.

My whole family had been amazing. Hunter, Crosby, the girls, the Hardys, and Ford had been with me every day of Ethan's trial. Making me laugh when I thought it would be impossible, holding me when I needed to cry it out. They were the family I'd built for myself, and I couldn't love them more.

The biggest surprise of all had been my father. He'd started showing up. It began with a couple of coffee dates, but now he was learning to restore furniture right alongside me. He'd said that he'd need a hobby when he retired from his island practice in a few months. We were getting to know each other for what felt like the first time.

My mom had not come around. In fact, the growing closeness between Dad and me had turned her venom up a notch. But it didn't bother me the way it used to. Instead of feeling hurt, I just felt sad for her. My dad did not share my sentiments. After years of trying to talk her around, he'd finally served her with divorce papers a month ago and was living in my apartment above the bar while he looked for a house.

"Does the store meet Ford's approval?"

I groaned. "Barely." Ford's overprotectiveness had not lessened all that much and spanned every aspect of my life. That included wanting me to have the best storefront money could buy. *His* money. It took many long conversations to make him understand that I needed to do this on my own. Or mostly on my own anyway. I fully intended to use his muscles to help me lift furniture and rehab the space.

Caelyn chuckled. "Have you two made the move-in official?"

"Not yet." A week after Ethan's attack, Ford had made it clear that I was staying with him. It had been hard for him to even let me out of his sight for a time. And I gave that to him, slowly easing distance back in for a girls' night or a trip to another island to hunt estate sales. But I'd never left his house. Hadn't wanted to.

And now, Ford was officially making Anchor Island his permanent home. He'd placed his bars in the capable hands of his manager, Luke. He just flew down every other month or so to check on things, meet with the staff, and the like. I'd even flown down with him last time, and LA wasn't as bad as I'd thought it would be. But Anchor would always be our home.

"I bet he'll ask when he gets the keys to the new place."

My stomach flipped. I wanted him to. Ford had gotten better at giving me the words along with his actions. He told me he loved me every single day, and I never tired of hearing it. But he still didn't always realize that certain things needed to be discussed. Things like officially asking your girlfriend to move in with you. He probably just assumed I'd come along for the ride. It was only a little frustrating. Mostly, it was adorable.

I grinned at Caelyn. "I'm meeting him over there after this."

Caelyn gave a little squeal and jump as she clapped. "And then you'll show me and Kenna tomorrow, right?"

I laughed. "I don't even know if I'll be living there."

She rolled her eyes. "Like that man is going to let you sleep without him." She had a point.

The antique bell over the door jingled. I turned and gasped. "What in the world?" Kenna stood in the doorway, not stepping inside, drenched from head to toe. "What happened?"

Color rose in her cheeks. "Crosby." She said his name in a growl.

I had to press my lips together to keep from laughing. "He threw you in the dunk tank?"

"No—I—I can't even talk about it. I am going to take sweet, sweet revenge on that man, though. I don't know what it's going to be, but it's going to be epic. Like pink dye in his shampoo bottle."

Caelyn laughed. "But don't you have a date in like two hours?"

"I did. Obviously, I had to cancel." She blew out a breath. "Can one of you give me a ride home?"

"I will," Caelyn offered. "Bell has to go check out her new digs."

Kenna's eyes widened. "Did he ask?"

"No, he did not ask me to move in." I whirled on Caelyn, giving her a mock glare. "Stop getting my hopes up."

Caelyn smacked a kiss on my cheek. "Your hopes should always be up."

✎

My car eased around the curve of the private lane that led to Ford's new house. The warm breeze cut through my open window, the faint scent of the sea and the blissful quiet easing something in me. This truly was the perfect property. It wasn't that I didn't like Ford's rental, but it was so sterile, almost overly modern. I'd always been afraid I would break something worth thousands of dollars.

I smiled as my car crested the hill and the old farmhouse came into view. This place fit us. Lush grass and brightly colored blooms filled a large yard that was surrounded by forest. While the property didn't have beach access, it had a gorgeous view of the ocean. I couldn't help the image of little blond-haired children running around the yard while Ford and I sat on the front porch sipping lemonade.

I gave my head a little shake. Not the time. I pulled my car in next to Ford's on the gravel drive. Climbing out, I took a minute to soak in the house. It needed work, sure, but the bones were wonderful, and it was a project Ford and I could take on together. If he wanted me.

I climbed the stairs, pulling open the screen door. "Ford?"

"Back here."

My breath caught as I stepped into the foyer. All around and leading the way down the hallway were pots full of the most brightly colored flowers of every shape and size. A smile slowly stretched across my face. "What did you do, Cupcake?"

"Why don't you come in and find out, Trouble?" Ford's voice came from what sounded like the sun porch—a room enclosed by paned windows that would be perfect during the winter months, when it became too cold to sit outside.

I let my fingers trail lightly over the leaves and petals of each plant as I passed, their heavenly scents filling the air. As I stepped through to the sun porch, I gasped. There were flowers everywhere, filling every corner and crevice of the space. I'd never seen so many outside a nursery.

When my gaze caught on Ford, I stopped breathing altogether. The blue of his button-down shirt seemed to make his eyes glow, but it was the love in them that seared me, simultaneously freezing me to the spot.

His lips twitched. "Bell, come here."

My legs seemed to obey without my brain even reasoning through the command, taking me right to the man. I inhaled deeply as Ford wrapped his arms around me, his unique, woodsy scent cutting through the floral-scented air around us. I pressed my face to his pec, lifting my lips to kiss his throat.

"I missed you."

"Me, too." It was all I seemed to be able to return.

Ford chuckled, pulling me tighter against him. "You like this place?"

I nodded.

"You want to make it a home with me?"

I nodded again, my heart picking up its pace. "Yes."

"You want to make a life with me?"

My heart seized in a rapid, stuttering beat. "Give me the words," I whispered.

Ford pulled back, slipping a hand into his jeans pocket and pulling out a ring box. "Marry me."

There was no hesitation, I launched myself at him. Luckily, Ford caught me with one hand under my butt and the other around my back as my legs wrapped around him, and my lips crashed into his. I took his mouth in a hungry kiss, one that said everything that words couldn't.

When I pulled away, Ford laughed. "Does that mean yes?"

I grinned. "I didn't think it was a question."

Ford squeezed my ass. "It wasn't. But I thought you might want to see the ring before you agreed."

I gave my head a little shake. "The ring doesn't matter. Only you and this life we're going to build. That's what matters."

Ford eased me down his body and then cupped my face. "I love you, Bell."

"More than breath," I whispered.

He pulled the ring out of the box and slowly slid it onto my finger. It was perfect. The band a rosy gold, the ring itself almost looking like a flower with its intricate setting surrounding a round diamond. I sucked in air. "Okay, maybe the ring matters a little."

Ford laughed, pressing a kiss to the ring now firmly planted on my finger and then pulled me back into his arms. "I'm going to make you happy, Bell."

I looked up into Ford's face, my eyes brimming with unshed tears. "You already have, happier than I ever thought possible."

THE END

Bonus Scene

Want to know what happens when Bell and Ford tell their families and friends that they're engaged? Find out in this adorable bonus scene. Sign up by going to the link below.

www.subscribepage.com/recklessmemoriesbonus

Enjoy This Book?

You can make a huge difference in *Reckless Memories'* book life!

Reviews encourage other readers to try out a book. They are critically important to getting the word out about a novel and mean the world to every author.

I'd love your help in sharing *Reckless Memories* with the world. If you could take a quick moment to leave a review on your favorite book site, I would be forever grateful. It can be as short as you like. You can do that on your preferred retailer, Goodreads, or BookBub. Even better? All three! Just copy and paste that baby!

Email me a link to your review at catherine@catherinecowles. com so I can be sure to thank you. You're the best!

Acknowledgments

If you've read a few of my books, you might have guessed that I have a thing for gratitude. I love shouting out to the Universe just how much I have to be thankful for. And with each book, there are a whole lot of people to appreciate. Here we go…

The first thank you always goes to my mom. She gave me my insatiable love for books and is my biggest supporter. Thank you for everything, Mom!

Writing can be lonely at times, but the internet can be a beautiful place. If you're lucky, you'll meet some of the most amazing women you can imagine. Those who encourage, share wisdom, and generally keep you from rocking in a corner when things get tough. Thank you to all the wonderful authors who have been supportive in every way possible. An extra special thank you to Emma, Grahame, and Meghan…I'm so grateful to have you in my life!

To my fearless beta readers: Angela, Ryan, and Trisha, thank you for reading this book in its roughest form and helping me to make it the best it could possibly be!

The crew that helps bring my words to life and gets them out into the world is pretty darn epic. Susan and Chelle, thank you for your editing wisdom and helping to guide my path. Janice, Julie, and Steph, for catching all my errors, both big and small. Hang, thank you for creating the perfect cover for this story. Stacey, for making my paperbacks sparkle. Becca, for creating trailers that give me chills. Jenn, Sarah, and the rest of my team at Social Butterfly: thank you for believing in me and working so hard to get my books into as many hands as possible.

To all the bloggers who have taken a chance on my words… THANK YOU! Your championing of my stories means more than I can say. And to my launch and ARC teams, thank you for your kindness, support, and sharing my books with the world.

Ladies of Catherine Cowles Reader Group, you're my favorite place to hang out on the internet! Thank you for your support, encouragement, and willingness to always dish about your latest book boyfriends. You're the freaking best!

Lastly, thank YOU! Yes, YOU. I'm so grateful you're reading this book and making my author dreams come true. I love you for that. A whole lot!

Also Available from

CATHERINE COWLES

Further To Fall

Beautifully Broken Pieces

Beautifully Broken Life

Beautifully Broken Spirit

Beautifully Broken Control

About

CATHERINE COWLES

Writer of words. Drinker of Diet Cokes. Lover of all things cute and furry, especially her dog. Catherine has had her nose in a book since the time she could read and finally decided to write down some of her own stories. When she's not writing, she can be found exploring her home state of Oregon, listening to true crime podcasts, or searching for her next book boyfriend.

Stay Connected

You can find Catherine in all the usual bookish places…

Website: catherinecowles.com

Facebook: www.facebook.com/catherinecowlesauthor

Catherine Cowles Facebook Reader Group: www.facebook.com/groups/CatherineCowlesReaderGroup

Instagram: instagram.com/catherinecowlesauthor

Goodreads: goodreads.com/catherinecowlesauthor

BookBub: bookbub.com/profile/catherine-cowles

Amazon: www.amazon.com/author/catherinecowles

Twitter: twitter.com/catherinecowles

Pinterest: pinterest.com/catherinecowlesauthor

Made in United States
Orlando, FL
18 May 2023

33258998R00198